LOW HANGING FRUIT

Susan Johnson

Low Hanging Fruit

Ron,
I hope
you like the
book!
-Susan Johnson
6/10/11

A Tigress Publishing Book

TIGRESS

ISBN: 978-1-59404-041-2
1-59404-041-9
Library of Congress Control Number: 2011921269
Printed in the United States of America

Book Design : Steve Montiglio
Editor: Amelia Boldaji

10 9 8 7 6 5 4 3 2 1

Requests for such permission should be submitted to:
Tigress Publishing
4831 Fauntleroy Way SW # 103
Seattle, Washington 98116

FOR STEVE

1

June 19th, 1980 was Erica's very last day at High Point Junior High. She had managed to survive the eruption of Mt. Saint Helens a month prior and she'd made it through her final and seemingly endless days at that wretched school. Being that she lived nowhere near the impact zone, the latter was the greater achievement. Fourth period had just let out and most of the students were either forming a lunch line in the cafeteria or sitting outside in the sun, opening something their mother had packed. Erica, by contrast, was sprinting across the east lawn, books in hand, hair flapping. She raced towards the blessed hedges that surrounded the school. Not that anyone was likely to really give a damn if they found that she had elected to ditch the second half of an arguably pointless school day. After all, is there any reason why the last day of school is full length? Grades are in, papers submitted. There's nothing to do but celebrate with the nice teachers who bring cake or suffer through the nasty classes where students are held like hostages, watching the clock, awaiting the bell, suppressing screams. But, while she may have thought the last day to be superfluous and needlessly tedious, people of far greater import and position than Erica felt otherwise. So there she was, running as if her life depended on it.

Reaching the hedges, she tumbled and rolled like an overzealous stunt woman hoping to be discovered by a talent agent. After righting herself, she began walking away from the school with an arrogant gait. And then… at last: the school bell. Even from the mini-mart a block and a half away Erica heard it toll the end of lunch and signal the beginning of fifth period, (Algebra. Ugh!!). But not for her, she was free. Besides, it was too late to go back now. Better to enjoy truancy than to defend tardiness. Erica felt the warmth of the late spring sun on her face and she delighted in her new found freedom, never to return to that school again, Thank God! Why they had named it High Point Junior High she never knew. It was located in a valley and if attending there was anyone's high point it could only be because their life went terribly downhill thereafter. Walking alone that day somewhat aimlessly, she felt more liberated than she'd ever felt, prior or since.

Erica Elizabeth Tambo didn't know where Tambo came from any more than she knew where her ancestors had lived and died. She knew that Erica Elisabeth came from the fact that her mother loved e.e.cummings. She was known by most of the ninth grade and a goodly part of the eighth as Erica Tampon, which was lovely. Learning about her family history had never been a big priority for her. Actually, she preferred to distance herself from her family as best she could. Erica lived with her mother and younger sister in Bellevue, Washington which, at the time, was just a small suburb east of Seattle. Her mother had convinced Erica's father to move there from bitterly cold Wisconsin for a job he'd been offered. By this time, however, they'd since divorced but had managed to both stick around the area. So her parents had agreed on one thing after all.

Erica liked Bellevue. It's well maintained and expensive, not unlike many of the wives residing there. The Northwest weather, although damp, is mild and beautiful when clear. There are mountains all around and tall green trees everywhere. Quite livable, she always thought—at least once she was old enough to think in terms of cities being livable.

After leaving school and meandering for a while, Erica finally made it home (in about twice the time it usually took, having first stopped at the Mini-Mart for a Hostess Apple Pie and a Slushie which rivaled a small hot water heater in sheer volume). Needless to say, she was running for the bathroom by the time she finally arrived at the old homestead.

Walking in her front door Erica thought sarcastically, 'Ah, home, our home! What can one say? What a disaster!' The house was nothing like its upscale neighbors. It was too small for its inhabitants and too old to warrant any improvements. It possessed no charm, which seemed fitting since neither did its owner, the landlord. He was a sixty-ish man with a stomach that hung so low over his belt and down his one and only pair of trousers that he appeared, from the front, to have no thighs at all. His two bloated calves closely mimicked hams smacking when he walked (or waddled) and his shoes were so old they could start a compost pile. Speaking of piles... her damp, musty house was in such ill-repair that it was actually lopsided. When her mother conjured the nerve to point this out to the equally shabby landlord, Mr. John Grace (such an unfittingly elegant name), he proceeded to point out that, as they had no credit history and no references, they were lucky he had accepted their application at all. He went so far as to suggest that he had rescued them from a life on the streets. Touché.

Erica, fifteen and counting, had one sibling, Ellie who was five years younger. Erica did not care for Ellie in the least. And, based on the overall treatment she received from Ellie, the ill feeling was mutual. They each treated each other pretty horribly, rarely referring to each other by their given names in favor of using names such as Loser or Butthead. They were only nice to each other when someone was looking.

Their mother, Jean, had been diagnosed with breast cancer when Erica was just thirteen. Now, two plus years later, after going through all of the agony, pain and indignities of that awful scourge, her mother was thankfully in remission. It had all been too much for her husband, Erica's father, to endure (or so he'd claimed) and he'd left them when Erica was still thirteen and Ellie eight. Erica watched her mother's life go steadily downhill, financially and otherwise. Her mother had been forced to find a job in a market that had no place for an ailing mother of two, with only two years of college. She had studied nursing just long enough to find out that she couldn't stand the sight of blood. Jean was forced to accept menial jobs such as housecleaning and waiting tables to support her family. As a consequence, there was never enough money. More than anything else, lack of money was the most significant aspect of Erica's adolescence. There was rarely enough money for clothes or food or even electricity. At times, candles were all that lit their way to bed at night. Erica often unfairly blamed her mother for this. Only later did she come to understand that her family's predicament was not the fault of her mother.

Their's was not a close family, by any means, (except literally, of course). Nor was it particularly friendly. The only glue holding them together at all had been Erica's maternal grandmother, who had died the previous fall, leaving virtual anarchy and her daughter (Erica's mother) lost and distraught with no one to turn to for help or advice or sympathy. Her already broken family quickly disintegrated into nothing but a few miserable people forced to live together like cellmates, counting the days until their release.

School for Erica wasn't any better. She was unfairly singled out for being poor as well as a loner. Kids would tease her mercilessly, taunting her about their ramshackle house, their crappy old car and her shabby clothing. They often reminded Erica that her head was too big for her body and her teeth too big. And there was the ubiquitous 'Bongo Lips' zinger. Erica would usually just stand there and take it for a minute or two because experience had taught her that running would incur the wrath of a disrespected superior, and the punishment could be anything from additional chastising to shower banishment. Needless to say, she spent a great deal of time alone, avoiding the lot of them.

Probably in response to her utter powerlessness, Erica chose to torture her little sister, here and there, whenever she deemed it necessary, to keep the chain unbroken.

And so it was on this day, as she flew in through the front door of the dilapidated old shack that was home, that Erica found herself actually being happy for two very good reasons:

1: She was alone and that is what dreams are made of when you share a tiny house.

2: The knowledge that she was in her house, about to watch whatever she wanted on TV and eat whatever she chose to eat while everyone was sitting in a stuffy classroom watching the clock caused almost more euphoria than she could stand. Not that there would be anything to eat in the house besides a giant brick of government issued cheese and moldy bread but, if that was the price of freedom, she was willing to dine like a serf.

Erica went in to the bedroom she shared with Ellie. She looked at her pathetic self in the long mirror she had stupidly hung on her door. That was a big mistake! She hated how she looked and always felt a little down at the reminder of it. At fifteen she looked about twelve thanks in part to her screamingly blonde hair and in large part to the fact that puberty seemed to be eluding her. She'd just started her period, which came to her much later than most girls. Her legs could pass for eighteen but her boobs were decidedly pre-pubescent. In fact, they hardly existed at all. She looked a little like Tatem O'Neal had at thirteen, kind of cute but in a snarling, dirty face, tom-boy sort of way. Boys liked her to play baseball with them, (the actual game, not the childish sex scoring system), but nothing else. Let's just say she wasn't being asked to "go steady." What with no boobs and no car, what would there be to do? As she peered into the mirror at herself, Erica thought about how stupid she must look when she ran or played tennis, with her dumb blonde ponytail and flat, braless chest. She couldn't wait to grow up, drive a car, live on her own and have breasts.

Erica spent most of her spare time playing sports. You name it, she played it. Usually well (except soccer). She loved tennis, softball, and basketball, but it was track that she really took to. Having always been rather a loner, the singularity and solitude of long distance running really drew her to the sport. She felt very free and very autonomous when she ran.

All that time to herself, unfettered by family or school. She was passionate about running. Nevertheless, it wasn't helping her social life.

She left the mirror and her bedroom behind in search of the kitchen, seeking food like a missile seeks heat. She had just started to concoct something from almost nothing when her little sister Ellie came running through the house, crying. Erica stepped out into the hall just in time to see her sister throw herself headlong onto the bed, wailing. She was screaming something unintelligible, something about her friends, and how their mother just wanted her to be miserable. (Hey! That's my line! Erica thought). Erica instantly began to pray that Ellie was being shipped off, perhaps to live with relatives (in Wisconsin? That was too much to ask for). Then it hit her. Does this include me? Erica wondered. Was this a "we" situation, as in her mother, Ellie and Erica? Where? Seattle? It couldn't be to a lesser home? A lesser home couldn't possibly exist, (or so she mistakenly thought at the time).

Erica's mother came through the front door, sighing as if to say, "How to handle this now?" She put her things down by the front door. Jean always carried armloads of stuff: a mammoth purse in which she'd lose car keys for days, books, paperwork, and even clothing. It was as if she knew she was destined to be a bag lady and was just practicing. Her mother walked past her with a look that all at once said 'I need to talk to you. First let me deal with Ellie.' Erica made her way into the living room with her biscuits and cheese and plopped herself down on the sofa. A spring popped up to greet her. She reached for the remote and turned on the TV before her ass even hit the cushion. They only had one television and it wasn't too great either. Although it was born a color TV, it was nearly black and white due to a worn out picture tube. It only showed color in places. Even so, Erica was drawn to the thing like a bee to a flower. Escapism, she figured.

Erica could hear her mother trying to calm Ellie down with her soothing voice. She knew that soothing voice would soon give way to cracking and then yelling due to the fact that Ellie was a tenacious, relentless little shit when she wanted to be. Ellie kept yelling "What about my friends? I don't know anyone there! How far is it? I wanna live with Daddy" That final plea would normally be enough to push her mother over the edge to the yelling stage, but not today. Today, Little Sister would have to work a lot harder to get her mother to completely lose it. Ellie moved in for the kill and there it was, in her wee little voice "You're stupid and you're dumb and you don't even have a job!" That of course provoked a response and a great deal of yelling and door slamming. Erica tuned it out. Eventually her mother managed to calm herself down and make her way out to where her eldest child was sitting which, to be honest, wasn't a very long trek.

Jean, it must be said, had always been and was still quite beautiful. Even after battling breast cancer, she maintained a serene beauty. This fact, however, seemed lost on her. She was like a gorgeous cat that is oblivious to its outward splendor. She had dark auburn hair, some of which she'd lost during chemotherapy. It had come back to its original fullness over time. She inexplicably kept her hair short and permed, even before she'd gotten sick. Erica couldn't understand because she had seen pictures and knew her mother's hair to be very pretty when she'd worn it long several years back. Jean also had a terrific figure. Curvy but slender. A perfect size four with huge breasts, (how unfair life could be). But she chose to cover it all up with layer upon layer of loose, unflattering clothing. She wore no makeup. She really didn't need any but she looked better with a little (which she would apply once in a blue moon). She was average height and olive skinned but never went near the sun so people mistook her for being a fair-skinned person who would burn with the slightest exposure. She had huge, beautiful sage colored eyes, framed by long, dark lashes. She walked like someone meant for something better, like she was just walking through this room or that but not staying. Overriding all of these qualities, there was on feature that was unmistakable. It was the sadness she carried with her. Even when she laughed it was right there, just below the surface as if to chastise anyone for thinking she just might be having a good time.

Jean stood in front of the TV, trying to get her daughter's attention. Erica sat up asking "What's up with her?" feigning disinterest but actually nervous about what her mother's answer might be.

"She'll be okay. She's just upset about leaving her friends."

"She moving?" Erica asked hopefully.

"We all are. At least I think so."

"Where?" Erica asked, thinking perhaps it would be just a few miles away.

"Leavenworth."

"The prison?"

"No, the town. It's in eastern Washington, not far from Wenatchee. It's beautiful and pristine and much more affordable than here." She sounded resolute and defensive at the same time.

"I don't wanna move to Leavenworth." Erica spat out the last word contemptuously. "Who do we even know there?"

"Jillian," said her mother. "She lives there with her two daughters, your cousins."

"You mean your freak of a sister? The glassmaking hippie with all the beads and shit? Is that supposed to reassure me?"

"Listen. All I do is work to pay for you kids. Your sports and your piano."

"I don't play piano."

"That's right," Jean shot back. "I pay for your clarinet lessons, which you don't appreciate at all."

"I'm supposed to appreciate a man who smells like old gym socks? He makes me nauseous, literally sick. Really! I almost threw up the other day when he tried to teach me something, waving his arms around the room. God! The guy is disgusting. He never takes a shower or brushes his teeth. Is he homeless?" Erica asked. She sometimes had trouble staying on point.

"You see! It's just that kind of attitude that I'm talking about. Do you know how much those lessons cost me?"

"No, but whatever it is, you're overpaying."

"You ungrateful..." Her mother said, turning all red and lifting her open hand as if ready to smack her eldest child.

"I never asked for 'em."

"Yeah, you'd rather play baseball or watch TV. Where do you think that'll get you in life? Nowhere, that's where!"

"Why Leavenworth? Why not Seattle or Redmond? We could move out a ways from the city and pay less. Why do we have to go so far away?"

"Because I like it there and, for once, I'm gonna do what I wanna do."

"You always get to do what you wanna do. I'm not moving to Leavenworth! Forget it!"

"In what way do you think I always get to do what I want to do? Do you think I like waitressing? Cleaning other people's houses? Driving you bratty kids all over town and back? Is this the way you think I planned my life?"

"It's not my fault you and Dad divorced. You should have stayed married."

"He left me, remember?"

"Well maybe you should have tried harder to stop him." Erica knew she was getting into dangerous territory but she just couldn't seem to stop herself. "If you had, we would be a normal family instead of starving in this dive!"

"The reason we are starving is because your father is too busy running around with a woman half his age and can't be bothered with the burden of his family."

"He pays you!"

"Ha! That's a laugh! Do you know how much he pays? $150 a month! Not even enough to pay the utilities."

"What about the house money? Where'd that go?"

"You make it sound as if I received some huge sum of money. I had to sell the house to your father because I couldn't afford the repairs and all the medical bills. No one else would buy that old house as it was, so I agreed to sell it for what we paid but only after deducting the cost of the repairs and the balance of the mortgage. To top that, I didn't get a lump sum. He makes payments monthly, which don't even cover our rent. We cannot afford to live here anymore. You don't understand, I know that, but that's the way it is. In Leavenworth, we would have our own place on our own land"

"Our own house?" Erica asked.

"No, not at first. We'll build later, as we can afford it. At first we'll be living in a mobile home"

11

"Mobile home? Like hillbillies?!!"

"Damn you kids! It's only for a while. You never appreciate anything I do for you or how hard I work. I need a break once in a while, too, damn it!" She was becoming hysterical.

"I'm not going to live in a mobile home in Leavenworth! Forget it!"

"You don't have a choice, Missy!"

"I could go live with Dad!"

"Erica. Erica, Dear. You know full well you cannot go live with your father. There is no way he's going to let you cramp his style. After we separated he became a regular Hugh Hefner and now he's about to marry a woman who doesn't like kids."

"I could ask."

"Don't."

"He has plenty of room. He wouldn't even know I was there."

"Four bedrooms does not a family make."

"What?"

"Never mind, just trust me on this one."

Erica's mother left the room to deal with Ellie, leaving Erica to her thoughts. Erica had several questions but she didn't dare ask them out loud because that might imply she was actually considering moving to Leavenworth. And she wasn't. Why did her mother pick Leavenworth? Because of Jillian? Erica hadn't seen Jillian since her grandmother's funeral the previous fall. Before that, she hadn't seen her for a couple years. Erica didn't much care for Jillian. She looked scary with her long, Medusa hair that she was forever raking from forehead back with her long talon nails. She had wild eyes and rotten teeth. She was arrogant without cause, had a sharp tongue and lacked intelligence. Instead of being witty,

Jillian was just mean. Erica didn't really know her two cousins because they lived so far away and they rarely accompanied Jillian when she would come to visit Jean during her illness and treatment. The only thing Erica remembered about her cousins was the older one was blond and the younger one had dark hair.

Erica recalled that her father disliked Jillian enormously so maybe that had colored her view of her aunt. On the other hand, Erica had listened in on enough conversations to know that her aunt was not a very nice person.

Erica had no intention of moving to Leavenworth but she also had no intention of calling her father to ask if she could live with him. Later that afternoon, her little sister tried it. Ellie had hung up in tears, confirmation that Erica had made the right decision in not calling first. He actually told Ellie that he didn't have the space. Erica took that excuse more figuratively than literally. She knew he had room in his home but not in his life for full time parenting. She kind of understood her father's feelings. She herself longed for her own space and she could understand why he might regret having children. She could see being frustrated with the situation and even why he would have left since they, her mother and father, had nothing in common. What she could not understand was in his inability to take responsibility for his children. After all, they did exist, did they not? Why not accept it? There had to be some benefit to having children, hadn't there? Other parents seemed so involved. She had watched them at her various meets and matches and recitals. Where was her father? What good did it do for him to virtually deny their existence? Had they failed him as children? Had she? She didn't know. Anyway, even if she could have won her father over, Karen, his bride to be, would never have stood for it. Karen made it abundantly clear from day one that she disliked children and did not want them around. That worked out pretty conveniently for Erica's father since his two children chose to vilify Karen rather than him. Holding their father accountable would have been too painful.

Erica walked back to Ellie's bedroom, ignoring the slammed door, which was universal language for 'I'm pissed and I don't know what the hell else to do.' Erica felt a little sorry for her young sister, despite her normal aversion towards her. Ellie, unlike Erica, was well-liked at school. She had cultivated a lot of friends and she seemed to cherish them more than anything else. Upon moving, Ellie could only feel a great loss and Erica did see that. Also, juxtaposed to Erica, Ellie was adorable. She was blond with big blue eyes and a tiny little voice. She appeared to be seven or eight, not the ten years she actually was.

"Hey, what are you cry'in about? It's not for sure, ya know."

"Yes it is," she yelled back "She already told the landlord we're moving."

"Oh, well that doesn't mean anything." Of course it did.

"You're so dumb. Oh, I forgot, you don't have any friends. It doesn't matter where you live. You'll be a loser there, too."

"I have friends, you little shit. I just don't sell out to have everybody love me like you do. My friends care about more than just what they wear." Erica spit back.

"Correction, you said friends. You mean friend since you've only got one. And everybody hates her. What's her name? Marcy?"

"Everybody does not hate Marcy. You and your dopey friends hate Marcy 'cuz you're so dumb and she's so smart!"

"If she's so smart then why did she get caught shoplifting, and cheating and get kicked out of school?"

"She was only suspended, you idiot!"

"Still."

"Why are you so afraid to move and make new friends anyway? It wouldn't be that tough. Maybe you'd like it there. All of your friends here are bitches anyway." Christ, Erica thought. Have I already resigned myself to moving there? Have I given in that easily? Or was it just the reality? Do I really have no choice but to move there?

"Shut up and get outta my room!" Ellie screeched. Her voice faltered as if she were about to have a nervous breakdown.

As requested, Erica left, feeling bewildered by the exchange. Was Ellie right to be so upset? Why wasn't *she* more upset about their impending move to the sticks? Despite such harsh words to her mother, Erica actually was not completely opposed to moving. Why not? She was unhappy where she was so maybe a move to anywhere else seemed like an improvement? Or was she just open for adventure? She took those and other questions with her, back to her room.

Erica's bedroom was a menagerie of every kind of animal you could think of: giraffes, lions, tigers, horses, dogs, oh my! All pictured or stuffed or molded out of clay or plastic. The only living breathing one was her dog, Alias. Alias was a Husky Shepherd mix. He was smart and loyal and fun to play with. Erica loved him more than could possibly be healthy.

She plopped down on the tiny twin bed nestled between all the shelves of animals and her single, rotting window, which looked out at the street. She began to ponder her life and all of its perplexities while petting Alias and half

15

listening to her mother trying again to reason with Ellie. As she listened, Erica couldn't quite shake the feeling that she had too quickly accepted this new development. She had fought harder when her mother tried to rearrange the living room to suit the plants, which were overtaking the house. Why the complacency? She didn't know that either.

She sat in her room for hours, unaware of the time that had passed. It had grown dark, which put the time well after nine pm. She glanced at her Mickey Mouse watch: 9:10. Alias needed a walk so she put on her tennis shoes, grabbed his leash, and headed out. Walking in the dark was probably not the safest thing to do but it was something she often did. She usually loved to walk and dream and fantasize about her future as an adult but on this June evening she did none of those things. She only thought about moving away, leaving Bellevue and starting new.

2

Moving day finally came and it was a fiasco. Their car, a forest green Ford Pinto was packed to the ceiling. Alias ran away (dogs are known for having a sixth sense about impending disasters). Erica eventually got him back thanks to a neighbor's call. The car wouldn't start because the dome light had been left on overnight. The same neighbor that called about Alias gave them a jump start, apparently anxious to rid his neighborhood of the Tambos. The U-Haul trailer they rented was much smaller than anticipated which meant that many of their belongings would have to remain behind until they could make another trip back for them. When they finally got the car and trailer loaded, Jean discovered that Ellie had taken off to see her friends "one last time." They couldn't find her for almost two hours, by which time it was already six pm which meant they'd have to arrive and unload in the dark. Erica's mother was frantic. She was certain Ellie had run away. When Ellie finally did return home, Erica pinned her up against the wall of their soon to be ex-living room and calmly but through gritted teeth told her what a stupid brat she was.

They were finally on their way. When Jean pulled out on to the highway heading east, all the things they'd loaded on top of the car slid off onto the highway. Cars dodged bags and boxes going sixty miles per hour, while their mother desperately tried pulling their possessions to the side of the road. Erica and Ellie just watched because their mother had screamed at them to get back when they had tried to help. It was quite a sight and all Erica could think was that this mayhem could only bode poorly for their new adventure. Quite an omen! What else could go wrong? What else was beyond belief, worse than she could ever have imagined.

The rest of the two hour trip, after they had retied the bags and boxes to the top of the car, was relatively uneventful. They drove in silence most of the way, save for the sound of the radio fading in and out. Erica thought the drive was pretty with all the mountains and trees and she let her mind wander. She could never remember which mountain range was which. Were they in the Cascades or the Olympics? She decided they were the Cascades. Then she wondered which range Mt. St. Hellens was in. Erica remembered when Mt. St. Hellens had exploded the previous May and how the skies over Seattle suddenly got hazy.

"Mom?" she asked. "Which way is Mt. St. Hellens?"

"South."

As they drove, Erica thought about home and her only friend, Marcy. She wondered what Marcy would do the rest of the summer. She'll probably knock over the mini-mart, Erica thought.

Less than a month had passed since her mother had dropped the Leavenworth bomb. Erica spent those final days deep in thought, taking a lot of walks, running and pondering the past as well as the future. She even wondered why she'd ever been born in the first place. She wondered about that a lot anyway, but with the big move looming, it became an ever-present thought to which she had no answer. She thought about how her mother had danced around the fact that she was determined to move to Leavenworth, even though she pretended to be on the fence about it. This actually made accepting the move harder for the girls. Especially forEllie, because they never knew until about a week before that they were moving for sure. Also, Ellie used the alleged indecision to bawl anew each time any hint of it came up. Jean would say "In Leavenworth, there's a lake nearby to swim." And Ellie would say "What?! You mean we really are moving? I don't wanna move!"Then she'd go throw herself on her bed and start wailing. Again.

Driving along this hot July evening, they passed over the mountains and down into eastern Washington. The landscape changed as soon as they'd crossed over the mountain pass. There were different types of trees and it didn't seem as lush as Seattle. The road followed a fast moving river for a while and then it turned off towards the town of Plain. Erica thought it was an odd name for a town. As it turned out, it was a rather fitting name. There was nothing there besides a few old homes, farmland and a dusty old diner with a giant clown cutout on top. The clown looked a lot like the serial killer John Wayne Gacy. The diner was called The Happy Clown but Erica thought The Psycho, Homicidal Clown would have better described it. They pulled into the diner and Jean used the gas pumps in front of the diner while. Ellie and Erica hit the restrooms. After finishing pumping gas, Jean joined the girls and they all ventured into the grocery/restaurant/bar/fly fishing store. It smelled of old leather, spilled beer and flapjacks. The floor was an old, dark wood and the walls, once white, were dirty gray with years of grease and dirt built up. The walls were covered with pictures of men posing with fish and beer ads featuring women in bikinis. Smoke wafted from the bar like it was on fire and the sound of a baseball game resonated throughout the entire building. The girls looked over the cheap souvenirs in the store, finding only old dolls and trinkets covered in dust. They gave up looking for treasures in the store and headed out, anxious to be on their way. As they left, the old attendant who appeared to have a marble where his right eye should have been, asked, "Where ya moving to?" Jean answered "The Ponderosa" and the man responded "Oh, then we'll be seeing you around" in such a suggestive manner as to make one hope never to see him again.

"The Ponderosa, like on Bonanza?" Erica asked her mother.

"It's just the name of the development. Has nothing at all to do with the TV show." Actually, if it had, it would have been more appealing, Erica thought.

They drove on and eventually came to a valley where the road came to a T. They turned right and followed that road across the valley. They passed several horse acres and their accompanying little houses with fences and barns. Most looked okay. Clean. They passed a tiny restaurant called Ginny's Café and then the road turned and began twisting its way up a steep hill. Just as they were reaching the crest, Jean turned off onto a dirt road so narrow and steep that it would challenge a tractor, let alone their little Pinto with trailer in tow. The Pinto and trailer made it up the hill, and Jean pulled up next to a dirty, off white trailer with what once must have been apple green trim but now more closely resembled rust.

Both Ellie and Erica drew the same wrong conclusion

and almost in unison asked why they were stopping.

"This is it!" their mother announced as if introducing the next contestant on a game show. She turned off the engine. This ugly piece of tin? Erica thought. She had thought it couldn't get any worse than their previous house. How wrong she'd been!

The girls got out of the car and slowly walked up to what passed as a front door. Their mother was already inside, fussing with the drapes and talking really fast and upbeat as if to keep her two daughters from mentioning that the Emperor had no clothes.

"What the hell is this? Where's the mobile home? This is a goddamned trailer!" Erica screamed (she was known to swear when riled). Her mother just looked at her and shook her head saying "Such language! And I am not in the mood to argue with you right now."

"Not in the mood? Not in the mood? You said we were gonna live in a mobile home! What else are you lying to us about? This is not a mobile home. This is a trailer! A crappy, old, smelly trailer!"

"Just let's fix it up. It'll be nice when we're done."

"It'll never be nice. It's awful and you know it."

Ellie was standing in the doorway with tears streaming down her little pudgy face, saying nothing. Erica suddenly felt protective of her little sister. She didn't know why but she just didn't want to see her so upset. Then she started to cry. Then their mom started crying. The three of them began walking in and out, to and from the car, unloading and saying nothing, crying all the while, like something out of a Jane Austen novel. Erica's only thoughts were of how terrible their lives had become over the years. She was pretty sure her mother and Ellie were thinking the same thing.

The place really was awful. Erica wondered what swindler had sold her mother such a piece of shit, and for how much. She later found out that her mother had paid a thousand dollars. In Erica's opinion, that was about $990 more than it was worth. Once you entered the narrow front door, to your right was the "living room" which was actually a tiny, beat up couch under a window with torn, yellowing, flowered drapes and a metal and plastic table held up by a single metal pole. The kitchen was less than tiny. It was a kitchenette with a mini bar refrigerator and an Easy Bake Oven. The sink was the size of a soup bowl and the counter top was scarcely large enough to hold a single plate-which seemed reasonable since the place was never intended to hold more than a single person, maybe two and, even then, only for a road trip, not for permanent housing in the harsh climate of eastern Washington.

Walking further towards the back, there was a small door leading to the bathroom. The bathroom had a tiny pink sink, a pink potty training toilet and a small mirror, which doubled as a rusty medicine cabinet. There also was a baby tub, pink with a baby blue flowered shower curtain that was all frayed and torn at the bottom. The tub was also full of mold. The walls were papered with faint pink flowers on a cream background. Beyond the bath was a room purported to be the bedroom, although it more nearly resembled a small closet, especially because there was a clothing rod above the bed. A small window was perched at the head of the bed and a tiny door to a tiny storage closet sat at its foot. The room was about 6x8 feet, the entire trailer about 8 x 25. Their Bellevue house seemed palatial by comparison.

Erica walked back into the living room where her mother had begun to unpack the boxes marked 'kitchen.' How she thought she'd fit a normal size kitchen worth of stuff into a dollhouse kitchen was a mystery. They ended up tossing a good deal of it out. Erica decided to start with her clothes and personal items as she wanted first dibs on the clothing rod and figured that possession was nine tenths of the law. Ellie eventually joined her and began to unpack her own clothes. She didn't even fight Erica on her bearishness so she knew Ellie was really distressed. They worked in silence for a couple of hours and then took turns brushing their teeth. They finally fell into bed, sleeves dusting their noses. Their mother slept on the couch that night and every night thereafter. Alias slept on the floor next to their tiny bed, oblivious to the fact that they had just taken another very definite step down towards utter deprivation.

3

Erica awoke the next morning sore from travel and moving boxes. Feeling kind of dazed, she stepped outside the trailer to see what she could see. Alias tagged along as he always did. In the light of day she could see that there were lots of tall fir trees. Where the trailer was meant to hook to a car, it had been put up on a cinder block and there were big pieces of angled wood wedged under the tires on both sides. There was an old, beat up picnic table with chipped yellow paint just up the hill from the trailer. It's like a permanent camping trip, Erica thought.

Her mother poked her head out the front door and asked "Isn't it beautiful up here?" Erica sneered at her and turned away.

"We'll go down to the café for breakfast, okay?" her mother asked.

Erica was famished so she nodded her head in agreement. It was as close as she could come to acknowledging her mother at that time. Twenty minutes later, they piled into the car and began to back out when they remembered that the U-Haul trailer was still hooked up. The trailer was already empty so they decided to leave it hitched to the car and return it after they had eaten breakfast. This seemed like a good plan and an opportunity to check out the town, maybe even drive by the schools.

School! Erica thought. She didn't even want to think about school. She felt as though she'd just escaped it and now she had to think about starting again.

"When does school start here?" she asked, the first words she had spoken since arising.

Ellie's head whipped around to look at her mother in anticipation, forgetting her resolve to appear disinterested.

"Nine am, I think" their mother replied.

"No, I mean when in the year?"

"Oh. Late August."

"August?!" both girls cried in unison. "We have to start next month?"

"Yes, but you get out sooner."

"Yippee" Erica said sarcastically.

God! We just got out of school! Now we have to go back so soon? Erica thought. She figured that, since her mother had said late August, that probably meant school really started August 5th!

They managed to maneuver their little car and the trailer down the driveway and onto the main road. They arrived at the café in just a few minutes. Pulling in, Erica saw several people turn to look at them through the windows. She felt very self-conscious as they got out of the car and walked inside. They left Alias in the car with the windows down a little for him because it was already threatening to get hot, despite the fact that it was only 9:30 in the morning.

As they entered the front door of the café Erica was struck by how good it smelled and how warm and inviting it felt. There were blue and white gingham drapes and tablecloths. Each table had a little glass vase with a fresh flower. The walls were covered with flowered wallpaper and pictures of barns, geese and cows. It smelled of pancakes and maple syrup. The people already eating stared at them from their booths but they also were smiling. There were approximately 18-20 people in the place, quite a few for such a tiny town. Of course, it was the weekend, she thought. The hostess took them to a booth near the rear of the cafe. She seemed pleasant and brought their mother coffee and hot chocolate for her and Ellie, almost before they'd ordered it.

"You the new folks that just moved in up the hill? the hostess asked smiling.

"Yes," their mother said.

Erica wondered how the hostess had known that. The three newcomers looked around and smiled at the other patrons who smiled back at them. They turned to their menus because they were starving and had enough of the socializing.

They ordered breakfast and it came quickly. They wolfed it all down, sacrificing etiquette for much needed sustenance. The townspeople must think us scavengers, Erica thought. Their mother asked for the bill and paid it, leaving too small a tip. They thanked their waitress and the hostess, taking parting gifts of mints and toothpicks on their way out. As they were approaching the exit a man with reddish hair and a cowboy hat walked in with a buxom blond girl of about sixteen or seventeen. Erica's mother said hello, of course.

"Howdy," said the man. "Name's Moon. Jack Moon. This here is Jenna," he said in a strong southern accent. He put his arm around the girl. The girl said nothing.

"I'm Jean and these are my daughters Ellie and Erica," their mother said rather formally.

27

"Gladta meetchya," he said as if he meant it.

The three smiled and nodded as they walked past Mr. Moon and Jenna to the door and out to their car. They got in and were on their way again.

As they pulled out of the parking lot, Erica glanced up to see that every person in the café was looking out the window at them. Are we that interesting? Or were they just that bored? She wondered.

They drove up a very steep hill on a very windy road and then started back down the other side of the hill towards the town of Leavenworth. One could see the little hamlet from the hill and it did look charming. As they descended into the town, Erica noticed that all of the buildings were of a particular theme. Before she could ask why, her mother began to explain.

"Leavenworth is modeled after a town in Bavaria. Germany. That's why it has the chalet style everywhere. There are bands that play and different festivities. There's a Christmas Tree lighting ceremony in December and Oktoberfest in October. It'll be fun."

"Sounds thrilling," Erica said sarcastically.

"Can't you two just try? Just try to make the most of the situation? Who knows, you may like it here."

"Fat chance," Ellie said.

Despite her outward attitude, Erica was actually a little excited about checking out the town and starting at a new school. She had liked Bellevue but hadn't been at all happy at her old school. Why not start anew? The good news was that, since they'd be living so far out in the sticks, no one at this new school ever had to see their horrible, little trailer. The bad news was her wardrobe, or lack thereof. Erica knew she needed to do something about her lack of clothing, but what?

Ellie never seemed to suffer from a lack of attire. She was always wearing something new. In fact, Erica had often seen Ellie pulling tags off clothing just before putting them on. Erica had initially believed Ellie when she said that she had bought the new clothes with money from chores but, seeing as she rarely lifted a finger, it was doubtful that she could afford a stick of gum, let alone nice clothing from department stores. Erica herself had never even been in a department store but she knew that her dad had taken Ellie a number of times. Erica finally realized that her Dad was secretly buying these things for Ellie because she was his favorite. Ellie was everyone's favorite because she was so cute. Erica didn't really resent it so much but she did internalize it and blame herself for not being adorable, like Ellie.

As their little car approached the town, Erica's mother spotted the U-Haul store and they turned in there. A greasy guy with tattoos on his face (ugh!) came out and removed the pin from the hitch that Erica had never noticed before but was grateful for in case they decided to move their present home. Jean returned from the ramshackle office and got back into the car, mumbling something about being charged for an extra day. Erica elected not to indulge her and Ellie didn't care.

The trio made their way into the heart of Leavenworth, parked their little piece of shit, and got out. It was a beautiful day, one which made the town seem enchanting. There were cute little shops all along the main drive and pretty plants and flowers in flowerboxes and just about anywhere else they could fit them. There was a modest park with a small pond and a large gazebo in the center of town. In the gazebo was a Bavarian band comprised of men in lederhosen playing the most annoying music ever. The three of them walked around and took it all in, letting the fact that this would now be home sink in.

After taking in the sights, they walked by an old brick elementary school where Ellie would be attending school. It was small and looked as if it had been around for a while. Compared to the sprawling schools they were accustomed to in Bellevue, this seemed more like a large house. Ellie cried, of course, convinced that there couldn't be anyone cool attending such a school. Erica thought she had a point. They then strolled over to what would be Erica's new school, Leavenworth High. It was considerably larger than the elementary school, and more modern looking. It looked a lot like the high school she would have attended had they stayed in Bellevue. It had a nice track (very important) and decent tennis courts. Peering inside the classrooms, she saw that they looked large and sterile like any other high school. She found herself getting kind of anxious to start, partly because she'd be at a new school and partly because she was finally starting high school. She only had about one month of waiting before she'd find out.

After walking the entire length of the town and checking out the schools, they stocked up on groceries at the Bavarian style Safeway grocery store. It was exactly like a regular Safeway store only with a Bavarian façade. Erica realized she was hungry and suggested they get something to eat. They decided on sweet little Bavarian restaurant named 'Katzenjammers'. It was crowded and they had to wait twenty minutes for a table. While they were waiting, their mother struck up a conversation with a woman next to her who actually lived in town. Jean was always striking up conversations with people she didn't know, usually weird people. This particular woman was there because her daughter worked as a waitress for the restaurant. As with most towns, there are tourist traps, and then there are local hangouts. This place was decidedly the former. Erica's mother mentioned that she played tennis and asked where she might find a game. The woman brightened and said, 'Oh, yes! Funny you should mention it. They're having a tennis tournament next week at the High school." The woman wrote down the name of the person to talk to and even had the number. Just then, the hostess came up and called, "Tambo, table of three?"

"My name is Jean and these are my daughters Erica and Ellie," their mother said graciously.

"Nice to meet you" the woman said with a cheerful smile.

"Thanks for the information."

"You're welcome. Bye."

"Goodbye."

They followed the hostess to a cute little dark wooden table nestled in the corner. It had steins for flower vases and plastic coated menus which also featured a map of Leavenworth. Their window overlooked another park.

They watched the tourists in the park, some picnicking, others strolling. When the waitress came Erica wondered if she might be the woman's daughter but Erica didn't ask. A heartbeat later, Jean did ask and the girl, who was pretty with blonde curly hair and a tiny nose, confirmed that she was indeed the woman's daughter. Her name was Maggie and she pointed at her name tag in case they were deaf.

"Hello Maggie. I'm Jean and this is Erica and Ellie. We

just moved here. You look to be about Erica's age. What grade are you in?"

"I'm going into the tenth grade," she said.

"Oh, that's great! Erica is too," Her mother said excitedly.

The girl looked at Erica and her expression changed from sweet to slightly arrogant and dismissive, as if to say 'you'll never fit in here,' Erica thought.

"What can I get for you?" Maggie asked. She took their orders and then turned and headed towards the kitchen. Erica had already decided she disliked her.

They lingered over lunch for a while, eventually paying the bill and heading back to their new home in the hills. They took a different route this time, opting to go around Icicle Canyon which encircled the hills where they now lived. The route followed the Wenatchee River along an especially rough stretch. Ellie and Erica stuck their heads out the window and watched the dancing white water. Their mother insisted on stopping at another little tourist trap called the Icicle Canyon Inn. The Icicle Canyon Inn was not just an Inn. It was also a souvenir shop and a café. Walking in, they saw large picture windows at the other end of a vast room filled with tables and chairs overlooking the fast-moving river. They continued around the corner and into a room with an arched doorway and a stenciled sign above it which read 'GIFT SHOP.' The three of them looked around a little, bought nothing, and stayed only briefly. It seemed silly to buy souvenirs from a town in which you lived, even if you had only lived there for less than a day.

When they finally got back to the trailer, they got out of the hot car and Alias bolted down the hill. It concerned Erica a little but she was certain he'd come back soon enough. He always came back. She went into her little shared room and began organizing her few possessions. Ellie came in briefly, told her not to hog the whole closet and left to sit outside with her mother. Erica could hear them talking but couldn't make out much of what they were saying. Ellie seemed a little more at peace now that she'd seen the town. Erica thought it might be the fact that, despite the way they were living, at least there seemed to be some normalcy and prosperity there in Leavenworth. Or perhaps Ellie was just tired of crying about it and wanted to move on. At a certain point, when you're a kid, you realize how little power you really have and then you adjust to situations pretty quickly.

Erica finished color-coding, folding and hanging her clothing. She fished out her stereo from the back of the car and brought it in and hooked it up. She put in her favorite tape, Fleetwood Mac's *Rumors*, turning the volume way up because she figured no one lived close enough to complain. And surprisingly, her mother didn't yell at her to turn it down like she usually did. Erica suspected this was because her mother was tired of fighting but perhaps it was because Jean wanted her girls to feel at home.

Erica loved to listen to music really load, probably because she was a musician and was used to loud music. Not that she got to play with very many bands. She didn't. But she did play in the school Jazz Ensemble and she occasionally played with some of the kids from school. Erica knew she was a so-so musician but she loved playing to the stereo really loud.

She glanced at the clock. Almost 2:30 pm. She felt a sudden panic and her throat tightened as she realized Alias had been gone for nearly half an hour at this point. She turned off the stereo and went outside to where her mother and Ellie sat.

"You seen Alias?" she asked expectantly.

"No" her mom said. Ellie said nothing. Ellie wasn't a dog person. She was a social butterfly and clothes-horse kind of person. Sometimes Erica hated her.

With growing alarm, Erica set out looking for Alias. She possessed no knowledge of the area whatsoever. She remembered that he had headed downhill, back towards where they'd come from the day before so she started off in that direction. It occurred to her that he may have tried to go back home, to Bellevue. The thought scared her and she tried to think positively. "Alias is smart. He'd know to stick around with her- his bread and butter. Wouldn't he?" she thought.

Erica walked down the hill towards the café, peering through the shrubs and trees that lined the curving road. She kept calling Alias. There was a different smell in the air. It was a smell she wasn't familiar with, like dryness and wildflowers. It was hot out and she could hear the humming of the electrical wires that paralleled the road and the snapping of some insect she'd never seen before. By the time she made it to the bottom of the hill she nearly screaming. "Alias! Alias!" Where had he gone? She started to panic. Why had we moved? She thought. Everything has gone wrong. Everything! And now my dog is gone! My only friend in the world and now even he's gone!" She started weeping, the tears mixing with all the dirt and dust on her face. She was sure she looked a fright but she didn't care.

Just then a Jeep came up the hill. The driver stopped, noting her obvious distress.

"Whatsa matter? You lost?" he asked. He was about thirtyish and very tan with sparkling blue eyes and medium brown hair under a dusty red baseball cap. His hand was gripping the door where the window was rolled down and the other loosely gripping the wheel.

"I lost my dog," she said, choking back fresh tears.

"Well, hop in and I'll help you find 'im. What kind of dog?"

"He's a Husky/ Shepherd mix. We just moved here and he doesn't know the area. I'm afraid he tried to go back home."

"Where's home?" he asked.

"Bellevue," she replied.

"Oh, you're the new people, huh?"

"Yeah, how'd you know that?"

"Everybody knows when somebody new moves here. Small town" He smiled, displaying perfect teeth, like large white Chicklets, Erica thought.

"Hop in. I'll help you find him," he repeated. Erica climbed in, the door creaking as she opened and closed it, the smell of fish assaulting her olfactory. She tried to hide her revulsion but he saw her grimace. "Yea, I'm sorry. Just got back from Fish Lake," he said sheepishly.

"He was headed down this way when I last saw him. He was running," Erica said holding back more tears.

"Probably went to the creek," He said softly. He has a nice voice, Erica thought.

"Where's that?" she asked.

"It's just around the next bend. It shoots off of the river. I'll show you."

Erica began to feel a little nervous about this man. She realized that she didn't know him and had gotten into a 'Stranger's' car. At this point, she began to worry more about her own safety than that of her hapless dog. They turned in at the bend he'd mentioned and he stopped his car. She got the hell out and began walking quickly up hill, towards home.

"Hey! It's this way!" he called after her.

"I gotta go home. My mom's waiting," she said and started running, fear pushing her harder. She got a little ways up the hill when the man in his Jeep pulled up slowly beside her, nearly scaring her to death. He was telling her not to be worried, that her dog would come back soon and, son of a bitch, before he could even get the words out, there he was. Alias! He came running up to her from just where the man said he would be. She hugged and kissed him (the dog) and thanked the man. Then she raced the rest of the way home with Alias leading the way. The man hollered after her, "Hey! What's your name?"

"Erica," she yelled back over her shoulder as she continued to run.

"I'm Rick Peters," he called after her.

She began to feel foolish for having feared him so much. He was probably harmless. He must have thought she was terribly rude.

Returning home with Alias, Erica saw that her mom and sister were still sitting in the same spot and realized they had no idea of what she'd just gone through. Her mother would have killed her if she knew Erica had climbed into some stranger's car so Erica didn't tell her. Jean looked up and smiled and said stupidly "You found him?" No shit, Ma! Erica thought to herself. By way of answering she got down on her knees in front of Alias and hugged him. Alias wagged his tail and panted. She got him some fresh water and he lapped it right up. It's awfully hot to be wearing a fur coat, Erica thought. She got the hose and sprayed him with it. He hated it but she knew it would make him feel better. Then she went inside and glanced at the clock. 3:10 pm. She had only been gone half an hour! It had felt like an eternity. All the fear and running had made her hungry again so she called out to her mother.

"What's for dinner?"

"How about that stew?" Her mother suggested.

Stew! In July? Yuck! Erica thought. Jean couldn't cook a decent meal to save her life. A typical offering in their house was raisin wheat English muffins topped unevenly with cheddar cheese and then cooked in the oven on low heat. Sometimes they had this meal for two or three days in a row. Erica knew her mother had suggested stew because it easy. The stew was canned, so all you had to do was heat it up. No preparation involved. Erica looked in the refrigerator, noting that someone had put the groceries away, probably her mother. She grabbed an apple and a glass of water and took both back to the bedroom.

It was hot in the trailer so she chose to lie on her bed, flat on her back. She tried to expend as little energy as possible and hoped for a breeze to come through the tiny window. A breeze did come in but it was scarcely detectable and didn't afford her any real relief. She lay there for quite some time, awaiting the cooling effect of dusk and eating her apple. She kept thinking about her day. She rather liked the town. It was quaint, if a bit contrived. Most of the people seemed nice enough, except that superior, tiny-nosed bitch Maggie at the restaurant. She wondered if her mother had called the man about the tennis tournament. Earlier Erica had checked the single phone just adjacent to the couch in the living room and she had been surprised to find it was in working order. She wondered about the cute guy she'd met, Rick and whether he'd tell people what a brat she was. She thought about Alias and how much she'd have missed him if he hadn't come back. She thought about Marcy, wondered whether they'd actually write to each other, and vowed to write Marcy a letter soon. Erica thought about her dad and how little their moving away seemed to affect him. Perhaps because they rarely saw him, even when they had all lived in the same town. And finally Erica dozed off.

She woke up a few hours later to find Ellie pulling on a t-shirt and telling her that dinner was ready.

"If I were you, I wouldn't eat any cuz you're already fat enough," Ellie taunted. Erica ignored her. She had been dreaming about floating down a stream on a really dirty boat with a filthy red flag at its bow. In the dream, the boat hit rough water and she fell into the turbulent waters. She was drowning and swallowing too much water when Alias came out of nowhere. He dog paddled to Erica, bit down on her shirt, and pulled her to shore. That's when Ellie awakened her for dinner.

They ate the stew despite the odd timing for it and Erica proceeded to spend the rest of the evening trying to get a few channels on the twelve year old television Jean had inherited from her mother. The small ancient television was kept on a small shelf under a tiny window next to the front door. She finally managed to get NBC just in time to watch Little House on the Prairie. Erica and Ellie watched TV while Jean knit hats on a contraption she'd purchased as a means of income while starting out in the woods. (like Laura Ingles' family except at least they had a house). How her mother had thought that she could make enough sweaters and ski hats to support herself, as well as two young girls, Erica would never know. She knew her mother set unrealistic goals

38

and, when they inevitably failed, she would internalize that failure and take it as a confirmation of her ineptitude. Jean was a pessimistic dreamer. It only sounds like an oxymoron.

Erica spent the next few weeks waiting for school to start and working on her tan. She ran a little and walked a lot through the neighborhoods. Why was the neighborhood named The Ponderosa? It was another mystery to her. Instead of a beautiful ranch, there were some nice homes, some run down houses and a few trailers. Most of the houses were summer homes but there were a few houses that were lived in full time, mostly log cabins. She would occasionally see a girl who looked about her age, but Erica never spoke to her. When she wasn't wondering the neighborhood she was reading. Reading everything she could get her hands on. She loved to read and would often get lost in a book, losing track of time. She read Jacqueline Suzanne's 'Valley of the Dolls', which she liked and Margaret Mitchell's 'Gone with the Wind', which she loved, (despite the fact that about one hundred pages were mysteriously missing from dead center of the beat up old copy she'd found amongst her mother's things). She read several Nancy Drew books that she had checked out from the Bellevue school library. She had never returned them knowing the old bird who threatened certain death for late returns couldn't catch her in Leavenworth.

Her mom had managed to get her into the tennis tournament they'd heard about on their first day in town. Erica had competed in it and had easily won. She also met a few kids her age at the tournament. One in particular seemed really nice and Erica hoped they could become friends. Her name was Nancy and she was the same age as Erica. Nancy had lost in the very first round but didn't seem to mind losing.

She was pretty and had a winning smile. Erica hoped Nancy might become one of her friends but worried that Nancy already had all the friends she needed because she'd lived in Leavenworth all of her life. Erica decided she'd wait and see what happened when school started.

4

One day, about a week before school was to start, Jean took Ellie and Erica to go see Aunt Jillian and her two daughters, Katie and Chloe. Katie was almost three years older than Erica and would be a senior at the high school in the fall. To Erica, those three years difference in age seemed more like ten years. Chloe was seven and had a different father than Katie. Jillian had never been married and was still, not surprisingly, single.

They pulled in to Jillian's driveway, having foolishly driven when they could have walked the short distance and been there in less time than driving took. The road leading to Jillian's house was a long, narrow, dusty, one and their little Pinto had kicked up a tremendous amount of dust heralding their arrival. A tiny, dark haired girl with huge black eyes and olive skin came out of the dilapidated old house. She walked right up to their car window and said, very precociously, "Hello Jean" to their mother and then to the girls, "Hello. My name is Chloe. My mom says we met before but that I was too little to remember. You're Erica and you're Ellie." She said, pointing at the girls respectively.

"Hello, Chloe." Jean said.

The tiny girl smiled impishly with a slight tilt to her head.

41

She then turned on her heal and walked back into her house before Ellie or Erica had a chance to say anything. Chloe reappeared in the doorway with a taller, dark-skinned woman sporting a rat's nest hairdo and gypsy clothing. It was Aunt Jillian. She smiled smugly and disappeared back inside. Erica had forgotten how much she disliked her.

Their mother turned off the car (always risky) and the three of them rolled out very slowly because they were all wearing shorts, it was hot and the car seats were vinyl. The heat hit Erica like an open furnace. Electrical wires ran directly overhead and they could hear snaps and a low pitch buzzing as soon as the engine was silenced. They walked up to the front door. It was obvious that Jillian expected her guests to just come into the house, but Erica's mom knocked on the beaten screen door nonetheless, forever playing the naïve waif and applying etiquette where it was neither called for nor appreciated.

The house smelled of baked bread, hair spray and an underlying unfamiliar fragrance. The unfamiliar scent was musty, masculine and strong. Erica wondered if it was cologne or a natural body odor. It wasn't really a bad odor, it was just overwhelming. Upon entering, one was immediately in the small kitchen. It had cobalt blue countertops with little specks of gold and snow white inlay, like a fifties diner. There were thin, black rods holding up short fabric curtains on the shelves below the counter. The kitchen was L-shaped and contained a chipped porcelain sink and a hundred year-old white range with chrome fixtures. The cupboards above were painted a teal green but the paint was peeling and revealed a brownish wood underneath. The kitchen bled into the living room where there was a ripped, floral fabric chair, a couch and a lopsided wooden table. The table piled high with paperback books and an ashtray containing a spent joint. There were fabric pieces haphazardly hung over the two dirty windows on the far end of the room, below which was a young blonde woman in cutoffs and a homemade halter top, lying on the worn velvet Victorian style couch. She was reading a Sidney Sheldon book and pretending not to notice her guests.

Jillian stepped out of what Erica assumed was the bathroom, flashing brown teeth and contorting her face into something approaching a smile. Her face was over-tan and leathery with heavy lines criss-crossing like a relief map of Idaho. She motioned for her guests to sit and she pulled out a pitcher from the refrigerator "Would you like some lemonade?" she asked.

"Oh, yes please. That would be great! It's so hot out! Would you girls like some?" their mother asked sweetly.

"Sure," Erica said. "Thanks," Ellie nodded.

Jillian noticed Erica looking at her other daughter on the couch. She bobbed her head towards the blonde and said "You remember Katie, don't you? Say hello Katie." Katie finally lifted her head to look at the intruders and said "Hi." She smiled slightly and nodded her head. It was obvious she had already heard that her aunt and two cousins had moved nearby but she wanted them to know her book was more interesting. She resumed reading *The Naked Face*.

Jillian asked how Jean had been feeling now that she was in remission. Erica's mother nodded her head and said she was feeling pretty good. Jillian began chattering on about everything from the tennis tournament, to the town, the schools starting and what to expect come winter time. Ellie and Erica just sat there, eyes glazing over until Erica finally got up and walked outside to check out the surroundings. Maybe she could find Chloe who seemed more likely to talk to her. Ellie followed as she always did.

Once outside, Erica noticed a broken down school bus that had once been painted deep purple. It must have once looked really outrageous but now it was faded to an ash grey. It was parked on the side of the house, next to an embankment. There were weeds growing up through the grill and bumpers. It resembled something Abby Hoffman might have toured in fifteen years ago. Erica stepped inside and smelled pot, (Marcy's sister was a total pothead). There was a large piece of plywood serving as a workstation covered with dried flowers and pieces of glass in various colors. There was also a soldering iron and another full ashtray. Bunches of dried flowers hung upside down from the ceiling and a worn-out wooden chair with a tapestry pillow sat just to the side of the worktable. The windows were so dirty that you couldn't see out. The driver's seat was still in its original position but, having endured some twenty odd years of wear and tear, it was now shredded beyond repair. A few springs coiled up, long free of captivity. Ellie stepped in behind Erica and the look on her face confirmed that she thought it just as disgusting as Erica did.

"She makes those flower hanging things, between glass. Remember?" Erica said.

"Yeah, they're dumb."

Descending the steps, they saw Chloe walking towards them with some sort of doll in her hands. She squinted in the sunlight and said "Yer not s'posed to go in there, ya know."

"We were just checking it out. We didn't touch anything," Erica replied.

"Yer not s'posed to go in there. Ever."

"What grade are you in, Chloe?" asked Erica trying to get Chloe off the topic of the damn bus.

"I'm s'posed to be go'in into second grade but I'm go'in into third grade 'cuz I'm too smart for all the other kids," she said arrogantly. 'Geesh, what a brat,' thought Erica.

"How old are you?" Ellie asked.

"I'm gonna be eight in twenty-three days. I already know how old you are. Yer fifteen," she said, pointing at Erica "And yer ten," pointing at Ellie.

"That doesn't mean you're smart. Your mom told you our ages and I'm almost eleven," Ellie said, mimicking Chloe's pose and voice. Ellie never did take too kindly to snobbery. At least, not when directed at her. She could dish out plenty.

"Where's the river from here?" Erica asked, trying to defuse the fight that was brewing between Chloe and Ellie.

"Its right over there," Chloe responded, pointing downhill, "Behind those houses. There's a pool and a club there, too."

Ellie's eyes lit up instantly. "There's a pool? We could use it?" she asked, her voice shrill with excitement. Ellie loved to swim, a real fish.

"Yeah, dummy. Everybody knows that. It's public," Chloe said.

"Can we go now?" Ellie asked. Chloe didn't even bother to respond, she just rolled her eyes and motioned for her cousins to follow her with a wave of her tiny brown arm. Ellie and Erica looked at each other for a split second and then chased after the girl, who was already halfway down the hill.

They walked down the hill and into a neighborhood, which Erica realized she must have missed on her many walks around the area. There were far nicer homes in this neighborhood. Not grand by any means, but nice and inviting. None were on wheels, either. There were several mobile homes but they were quaint and looked permanent. Many of them even had picket fences and television aerials.

"Do these people live here year round?" Erica asked.

"Some do, some don't," Chloe said. "That's Agnes' house. She's really old," Chloe said, pointing at what looked to be an exact replica of the gingerbread house from Hansel and Gretel. They walked three or four blocks, passing cute houses and mobile homes that Erica found herself envying.

"There," Chloe said, pointing at a large, log building that was clearly not a house. From a distance, the building looked massive. It loomed at the end of the street, resting on a cliff and overhanging the river, which ran directly behind it. As they approached, Erica could see that this was a well-kept lodge, flanked by tall fir trees and pretty flower beds. The entry consisted of two huge pine doors with iron handles and Native American art burned into the wood. Above the entry were several mammoth log beams jutting out and running the length of the building. There was a small parking lot adjacent to the building with one lone car parked in it.

Chloe stepped up to the doors and struggled to open one of them. They were heavy and Erica had to help her with it. They stepped inside the large entry, which was dark and somewhat unfriendly. The wooden ceiling was a mile high with the huge log beams they'd seen outside holding it up. The floor was solid rock and at the far end of the room was a colossal rock fireplace. "That fireplace is bigger than our entire trailer," Erica thought. There were two large, overstuffed chairs in front of the fireplace and a brownish couch between them. There was also a pool table (which looked like it had seen better days) placed smack in the middle of the room. Chloe kept walking through the room towards the deck on its far end. They could hear voices coming from down below so they followed her out onto the deck, which overlooked the river. Peering over the log rail, Erica saw a pool with three kids swimming in it. Ellie came up behind Erica and peered over.

"It's solar heated," Chloe said. "But it's never warm."

Ellie asked if she could swim and Chloe nodded so they followed her down the steps and into the pool area. They hadn't brought swim suits, but Chloe said no one cared if they swam in their shorts and t-shirts.

As promised, the pool was cold but it felt good to get wet and free of dust for a while. Erica was amazed at how quickly and noticeably she reverted back to a child when she hit the water. She was keenly aware that this was one of those instances when she was fifteen and straddling the fence between childhood and adulthood.

They splashed around for a while until somebody mentioned that their mothers may be getting worried. They got out of the pool and headed back. With no towels, they would have to drip-dry, but fortunately, it was so hot outside, that by the time they got back, they were nearly dry.

Inside the small house, Jillian and Jean were still chattering away. They had no idea the girls had gone anywhere until the girls came back and told them. Jillian mentioned that she had to get to work on her glass shit so she could pay for her ungrateful kids. And Jean, taking this as a cue to leave, gathered up Erica and Ellie and they all headed home, kicking up another dust storm.

A few days later a strange thing happened. Erica had

decided to take a walk with Alias to Ginnie's Café at the bottom of the hill. She wanted a chance to get away from the family for a while and read. There was shade for Alias under the eve of the building and a big bowl full of water nearby so Erica knew Alias wouldn't get overheated or too thirsty.

Stepping inside, it was nice and cool due to an air conditioning system. Erica had brought Ethan Fromm with her to read. Leave it to a weird kid like her to opt for a depressing, nineteenth century novel about a devastating sledding accident as summer reading. As she walked in, she noticed a small chatty group of teenage girls at the far end of the tiny establishment. The hostess sat Erica at a tiny table in the other end of the room. Suddenly a loud burst of laughter from the teenagers drew Erica's attention. She glanced up and saw that it was her cousin Katie sitting with three other girls. Katie was motioning for Erica to come to their table. She hesitated for a moment but, realizing she had no choice, she stood, very self-consciously, and slowly walked over, unsure of what to expect. Would Katie be rude again? Would she make fun of Erica? Would she make fun of the way Erica lived which she'd surely heard about and perhaps even seen? As she approached their table Erica could see that we were smiling.

Katie said "This is my cousin Erica. She just moved here with her mom and sister. Erica, this is Lisa, Jill and Marie."

Erica said hello and Katie asked if she wanted to join them. Caught off guard, she stammered for what felt like about a minute or two. Katie scooted over to make room for Erica. She was obligated so she sat. The girls seemed so grown-up and sophisticated. Erica felt herself turning a little crimson from the shame and embarrassment of being only fifteen and probably covered in dust from the long, dry hike down the hill.

"Whatchya read'in?" one of the girls asked, looking at her book.

Erica looked at her book still in her hand as if she'd forgotten it.

"Ethan Fromm" she responded. She had no reason to believe that these girls read much of anything that didn't come out monthly and discuss how to rate your mate or apply eye liner so she offered nothing else on the matter, not wanting them to know so quickly what a geek she truly was.

At this point, another of the girls asked about whom they each had for English Lit. Erica became invisible for about twenty minutes. She felt ridiculous and out of place on the one hand but happy to be included on the other. They weren't talking to her, not including her in the slightest, and yet they were letting her stay so she chose to see her glass as half full on this one.

Finally, Katie asked if she had received her list of classes yet. Erica told her she had not and Katie suggested they go into town someday and "check it out." Erica was shocked. Katie seemed too cool to want to be hang-out with a pre-pubescent, fifteen year old malcontent like herself. She couldn't fathom why Katie would opt to spend any time with her at all, other than possibly out of familial obligation. Perhaps that was it, she felt obligated. Erica nodded in the affirmative, too nervous to speak. They decided that the following day would work and Katie promised to call. Erica took that as her cue to leave, (that along with two of the girls standing up and collecting their handbags,) so she said her goodbyes and nice to have met yous and walked back over to the table at which she had originally been seated.

Erica ordered lemonade instead of soda because that's what the girls were drinking and now that seemed more sophisticated. She also ordered a very unsophisticated cheeseburger, but what the hell? She sat there for over an hour, consuming Wharton and the greasy fare. She found it hard to concentrate on Wharton, because her mind kept going to the plans for tomorrow and the girls she'd just met. She tried to imagine the girls place in the high school hierarchy. She thought they were probably considered cool but not particularly popular. Definitely not the cheerleader types she had despised back in Bellevue. She wondered how many of Katie's friends had their own cars? She knew Katie had one, a beat up Buick. In fact, she'd just seen them all drive away in somebody's car when they'd left so at least one other girl must have a car. Erica figured the driver must also have a job to afford her the car. Or it could have been her parent's car. It looked like a real heap, though, so Erica concluded that it was more than likely her own car and all she could afford. Erica wondered why Katie had been so nice to her with her friends and so distant and rude in her own house. Maybe she was nicer when her mother wasn't around.

Erica paid the bill with the money she'd taken from her mother's purse. Then she went out to collect her dog and head back home. As she was making the long hike back up the hill, Alias suddenly took off running, cutting in where that man Rick had indicated there was a creek. Alias seemed to know where he was going so Erica followed him. There was a faint path overgrown with weeds. After a short walk, she could hear the sound of water moving over stone and then there it was; a little offshoot from the river, about six feet across, moving relatively fast. Alias was already in the water, cooling off and lapping it up before she'd even gotten to its edge. In the clearing where she stood, she could see several beer bottles strewn about.

Erica threw a stick for Alias several times. After a few minutes, she opted to head home and called for Alias to follow. He reluctantly left the coolness of the creek and obediently walked at her heels.

Once home, she found her mother on the tiny couch with a hideous gold blanket strewn over it. She was crying. "What's wrong?" Erica asked as she walked in.

"Oh, I'm just sad. I miss grandma. I feel so alone up here. I know I have you kids but I miss her," she said weakly.

"Yeah," Erica replied wondering what the hell else she could say.

"Katie called for you. She said to call her back if you wanted to go into town tomorrow. Where did you run into her?"

"I saw her at the café." Erica was surprised she'd called so soon. Her mother gave her the number and Erica picked up the phone to dial.

"Hello?"

"Katie?" Erica asked.

"Yeah?"

"Hi Katie, it's Erica."

"Oh, hi. Is tomorrow around eleven or so ok? I can pick you up."

"That sounds great. Thanks."

"Ok. See ya then."

"Okay. Bye."

She thought about protesting because she didn't want her to see where they lived but, realizing she'd probably already seen it, she let it go. She seemed pleasant enough so Erica concluded that Medusa/Jillian must not have been within earshot.

Erica went directly in to her room. What was she going to wear? She wanted to look nice but she also didn't want to look like she was trying too hard. She went on a frantic search for the perfect check-out-the-new-school-look-good-in-town-but-still-casual outfit. She decided to wear her best jeans with a brown leather belt, a white t-shirt and sandals that matched the belt. She couldn't ever remember caring so much about what she wore before. She usually put no thought into it at all except for the sake of comfort. Why was she suddenly so concerned about how she looked?

After she'd chosen her all-important ensemble for the following day, Erica went back into the front room and sat near where her mom still sat crying. She asked her mother if she wanted anything to drink and Jean shook her head no. She told Erica she was sorry to cry in front of them and that it would pass. She said that she knew they couldn't understand and she didn't expect them to. Erica asked if someone had said something to upset her. Her mother said nothing, she just stood up and walked over to where Erica was sitting and hugged her, her cold cheek touching her daughter's. Erica could smell her perfume, lilac something. Her mother's tears wet her face a little. After a few seconds she pulled back and walked to the sink for some water. Erica felt helpless and guilty for not knowing what to say or do. She wanted to help her mother but had no idea how.

Ellie came in a few minutes later. She'd been at the pool again. Her hair was still wet from swimming. Erica told her she'd better wash her hair right away if she didn't want it to turn green from the chlorine. Ellie looked at her like she was insane. "I don't care!" she said. How could she not care if her hair turned green?

Jean turned on the radio. There was only one radio station that came in with any decent reception. It was KLLY. They had one a.m. and one f.m. station. The AM station was mostly news and talk, with an occasional oldie thrown in for the elderly. The FM. station was pretty lame, nothing like the stations in Seattle, but they did play some top forty and some rock here and there. Erica actually liked the AM. station better. They had Paul Harvey on every day. "And that's.... the rest of the story. Good day!" She liked his long stories. They'd sit and listen, hovering around the radio like something out of the pre-television thirties. Paul Harvey had a soothing, pleasant voice. He sounded to her like he was well into his eighties but her mom said he was much younger.

"Did you see any kids you knew at the pool?" Mom asked Ellie. "Just visitors," Ellie replied.

"So you just swam by yourself? How boring" Erica said haughtily.

"No! We played Marco Polo and Sharks and Minnows and stuff."

"How dumb."

"You're dumb!" Ellie said, getting angry. And so on it went, as it always did between Erica and Ellie.

The next day Erica woke up in a good mood, excited to see the town with Katie. She took Alias for a walk, thinking about what school would be like.

Katie came around eleven, as promised, her crappy car laboring up the steep drive. She pulled up just next to the trailer hitch and turned off the engine.

Erica came out and waved to Katie as she walked down

the three steps from the trailer door. Just as she was opening the passenger door to get in, her mother poked her head out and asked what time they'd be back.

"Around noon or one, I guess," Katie said.

"Hey, I have a thought," her mother said. Oh God! Erica thought. "I need to go in to town today. Why don't we meet in town and I'll take Erica back with me. We can have lunch or something."

"We have plans," Erica said dismissively."

"How about after your plans then?" her mother pressed.

"Then I'd be stuck with you," Erica snorted.

"That sounds okay to me, Erica," Katie said, making Erica feel immature.

"All right," Erica said begrudgingly. She kind of hated her mom for ruining this for her.

"Ok, so let's say we'll meet at the Inn at one. Is that okay?" her mother asked.

Katie nodded her head. "See you then," she said brightly.

"Okay Erica?" Erica said nothing as she got in to the car.

"Okay," her mother yelled to her again.

"Okay! I heard you!" she screamed.

Katie gave Erica a strange look and then turned her car around and headed down the driveway.

Erica struggled with the seat belt for a while, finally getting the thing to click. Katie's car was messy with papers, pop cans and leftover fast-food boxes. Her radio was blasting so Erica had to yell to be heard.

"So when's the first day of school?"

"August 7th," Katie yelled back over the song on the car stereo. It was The Cars, Candy O.

"What time?"

"Starts at eight fifteen."

"So you leave around seven forty-five or so?"

"Yeah, I'm always running late, though. I take the bus some days 'cuz of gas prices. This old thing is a real gas guzzler,"

"Oh," Erica said, disappointed Katie hadn't offered to take her to school.

"Bus comes around seven fifteen."

"So early!" Erica said with dismay.

"Yeah. Welcome to the sticks!" Katie said wryly.

They arrived at the school and Katie pulled in to the closest space.

"This parking lot is packed on school days. Hard to get a spot," Katie said.

Katie and Erica walked up to the main building. Erica had already seen most of the school but Katie didn't know that. Besides, she hadn't had a tour guide the last time. They walked around the buildings and peered in the windows, Katie pointing out which classes were which. There were other, smaller buildings surrounding the main building, which housed classrooms, the gymnasium and the administration office.

Once Katie had finished showing Erica around the school the two walked the short distance into town, leaving Katie's car parked in the school lot. The hotel they went to was Bavarian cutesy, like the rest of the town, with dark wood furniture and bucolic landscapes on the walls. The lobby was dark and cozy. There was a large mosaic tiled fireplace at the far end of the room with little figurines depicting Bavarian maids and wood folk on the mantle. They walked past the main desk into the café, which was through an arched, wood-trimmed passageway with stenciled flowers painted around it. The restaurant was a little lighter and airier than the lobby. The tables were covered in blue and white gingham and a single, narrow candle stuffed into wicker based wine jugs sat on each of them. The waitresses wore colorful, unflattering blue and white dresses with billowing skirts and white aprons. On each of their heads was a white lacy bonnet. Erica decided she could never work there. Katie had said it was dorky but that she knew a girl who worked there who would not charge them for stuff.

Katie nodded to a blonde waitress across the room. The girl waved back smiling, then held up her index finger as if to say "One minute, okay?" Katie and Erica sat at a little table near the window. Katie got up and grabbed two menus, handing one to Erica. Glancing at the prices, Erica wondered if she had enough money. She had about two dollars and fifty cents on her, stolen from her mother's purse. The cheapest sandwich was more than that so she opted for some soup, a dollar fifty, and water, usually free.

The blonde waitress was heading for their little table and, as she approached, Erica began to recognize her. She walked deliberately, tossing her hair behind her shoulder. Where had Erica seen her? The girl reached their table and she was kind of smiling and smirking at the same time. That's it, Erica thought. It's that girl from the diner with her father. What was her name again?

"Hey, Jenna. I thought we'd stop by, see you and get a bite. This is Erica. She's a sophomore."

"Hey, how's it go'in? Hey, I think we've met before at Ginnie's. Remember?"

"Yes, I remember. Hi," Erica said smiling, being polite.

"What are you having?"

"I'd like the soup, please," Erica said.

"And to drink?"

"Just water."

"Katie?"

"Is it on the house today?"

"Of course." Damn, Erica thought, why hadn't she ordered a hamburger or sandwich or something? What a putz!

"Okay, in that case, I'll have a Monte Cristo."

"Anything to drink with that?" Jenna asked with a sly wink.

"You know what I like," Katie said in a low, devious voice.

"I'll see what I can do. Coke okay if not?"

"Diet."

Jenna turned and walked back towards the kitchen.

Erica told Katie about the waitress Maggie they'd met their first day in town and how she'd seemed stuck-up.

"Oh, she's alright."

"Then why was she so rude to me?" Erica asked.

"'Cuz you're new to town and you're pretty. Maggie doesn't want any competition." Come again? Had she just referred to her as pretty? No one had ever referred to Erica as being pretty in her entire life. If she were referred to at all it was usually as 'The blonde kid.' Embarrassed, Erica changed the subject, never one to graciously accept a compliment.

"Is Jenna your age?"

"Yeah. She's a senior. She dates lots of guys. She went out with Rob Jamison for a while." Erica looked puzzled. "The Jamisons practically own this town. You'll see. Brad's about your age. I think he's a junior, though. That's Rob's younger brother. They're all arrogant but good-looking and pretty fun to hang out with. Their dad owned most of the property this town is built on. Town nearly went bust a long time ago 'til someone came up with the brilliant idea of making it Bavarian tourist attraction. Actually, it saved it from dying but now we're stuck with all the tourists. You'll come to hate the tourists" Katie said, rolling her eyes.

"Why?"

"'Cuz they're annoying! Taking pictures all the time, asking questions, ugh!"

"Oh."

"You might like Brad. He's cute. I'm sure he'll like you."

"No one ever likes me. Not boys, I mean," Erica said, shaking her head.

"Oh please," Katie rolled her eyes again.

"It's true," Erica protested.

"Uh huh," she said, unconvinced.

Jenna delivered their order and left them to eat in peace. They talked about Katie's friends and foes. She seemed to have lots of both. Turns out she hated this one girl who'd stolen her boyfriend the previous spring, a skanky girl with a reputation for promiscuity. Katie said she thought that was what had lured him away.

"Actually, Jenna, our waitress? She's the real slut. She's easier to get in to than a community college," Katie said.

Erica laughed. "Did you just make that up? I mean about the community college?"

"No. I heard it in a movie once," Katie admitted. They both laughed.

"Seriously, a different guy every week!" she said with one eyebrow lifted.

"Wow," was all Erica said amazed.

Katie told Erica about another one of her friends whom, as it would happen, had had an affair with a married man in town. Someone Katie wouldn't name. Erica suspected there was much more to the story but didn't dare push it. Katie's other friends were less interesting in that they had normal boyfriends their own age.

Jenna made her way back over to say she couldn't talk anymore as her manager had returned. She left the bill for a small coke and lemonade. Erica insisted on paying and Katie let her. Erica had never paid a bill before that day. It made her feel very grown-up and she liked the feeling.

It was getting close to the time Erica was expected to meet her mother at the Inn, so they walked back to the school parking lot and said goodbye to each other. Erica watched her new friend get back into her car before she turned and headed towards the Inn, worrying, as all teenagers do, of what further embarrassment her mother would bring her.

5

August came quickly and school was due to start the following Monday. Only five days of summer remaining. Ellie spent her final days baking bread and writing letters to her friends back home. Erica read a lot and took long walks. Twice she went over to see Katie. The first time with Ellie, because her mom made her take her along. That time was pretty dull. The second time she went alone, which was much nicer because she could be herself and didn't have to edit what she said. That time, Katie and Erica had talked about hair and makeup while flipping though fashion magazines and commenting on the models. Katie told her about the various guys at the high school, some of whom she'd dated, some of whom she'd like to date, and some she said she'd never go anywhere near. Erica didn't have much to add to the conversation because she didn't have any dating experience and she didn't know any of the people Katie was talking about. Erica marveled at how fascinated she'd suddenly become with subjects she had previously, until now, found to be so pointless and dull.

That day, she and Katie talked well into the early evening. It was past dark by the time Erica began walking back home. As she walked through the neighborhood, she looked at the nicer homes she had first noticed when she and Ellie walked to the Clubhouse with Chloe earlier in the summer. Erica had taken this more populated, albeit longer route back home because it had street lights and she was afraid of bears.

Erica eventually made it home, where her mother yelled at her for being so late and not calling. Erica mumbled something in response and her mother let it go, like she always did. She took a shower, which was mildly amusing because Ellie needed to use the bathroom and couldn't because Erica had locked the door. Ellie yelled and pleaded for a while, and then had finally given up. Later, when Erica opened the door to the bedroom she pretended not to have heard her sister yelling at her. She wasn't above indulging in some petty little cruelties.

Crawling into bed she thought to herself, 'two more days.' She wondered what it would be like at her new school. She was glad Ellie wouldn't be going to her school. One tired of always having a little sister around.

Erica woke up later that night to Ellie's screams. She was yelling something about a rat. She'd seen a rat. Oh my god! "Look, there it is!" Ellie cried. She was pointing. Their mom came running in. "What is it?" she yelled, a raccoon's mask of smeared mascara around her eyes.

"A rat!" Ellie squealed.

They looked towards where Ellie had pointed and saw only a tiny tail poking out from beneath a shirt Ellie had left on the floor. Erica got up and lifted the shirt. A tiny field mouse scurried across the bare linoleum floor. Their mother let out a little shriek and Ellie screamed anew. Erica opened the door wider and the little thing ran through the bathroom into the living room and under the couch. Erica followed and opened the front door, grabbed a broom from the kitchen closet, and swiped it under the couch until the little thing darted out the front door. The poor thing was far more scared than her two wimpy roommates combined.

Erica sauntered back into the bedroom with a look of both superiority and disgust on her face. "Is it gone?" her mom asked.

"Yeah, you wimps. It was just a mouse. God!"

"It looked like a rat," Ellie protested.

"You look like a rat. He looked like a field mouse, which he was, you idiot!"

"Well, the important thing is that he's gone. Now let's all go back to bed," their mother said.

"I can't sleep now!" Ellie wailed.

"Ellie, you can sleep. It was just a mouse. He can't hurt you. Besides, he's gone," her mother wearily replied.

"Maybe we could get some mouse traps tomorrow?" Erica asked, deciding not to go into a tirade about how horribly they were living. She was too tired.

"Uh huh," Her mom agreed weakly as she headed back to her bed.

Erica crawled back into bed where Ellie lay complaining. Erica told her to shut up and go to sleep, which she eventually did, as did Erica.

That next morning, they piled all of their dirty clothes into the car and headed for the Happy Clown, the café and laundromat in town, for breakfast and a chance to do the wash. Erica planned to look for some mouse traps at the market across the street, as well.

The Happy Clown was about five miles from their trailer on the hill. They'd gone about three miles when they ran out of gas. The car sputtered along for a block or two and finally gave out. Their mother pulled the car to the side of the road.

"If you'd put more than thirty cents worth in at a time, maybe this wouldn't happen," Erica said coldly.

"Maybe I didn't have more than thirty cents at the time," her mother said defensively.

"Well then that's pathetic."

"Didn't you know it was low?" Ellie asked with disgust.

"Yes, but I thought we'd make it to the gas station."

Erica got out of the car and yelled "Fuck!" as loud as she could. Katie swore all the time and it was beginning to rub off on her. I know how this will go, thought Erica. Her mom would take forever to walk to the gas station, Ellie would get lost and complain the whole time so that left Erica. She would have to walk for the gas. "Damn it!"

"Don't you swear, young lady!" Her mother always sounded unconvincing when she scolded her for such things. It was almost as though she knew she couldn't both be her mother and expect her to keep saving her ass all the time.

"Don't you check the gas gauge?" That shut her up. "I'll be back in a while," Erica said irritably.

She started off. It was getting hot already and it was only around 8:30 am. She was wearing a light sweatshirt and jeans with a t-shirt underneath. It wasn't long before she was taking the sweatshirt off and wrapping it around her waist. She really didn't mind the walk so much. After all, she walked all the time. It was more the principle of the matter. She was beginning to feel like she wore the pants in what was left of their family. Neither her mother nor Ellie had any kind of strength or common sense. They treated Erica like the matriarch and she was letting them.

It made her feel both proud and cheated at the same time. She thought of Katie and how strong and independent she seemed to be. Katie made her own decisions and handled her own problems. Katie's mother never leaned on her, she merely tolerated her presence. Erica supposed that was what had made Katie so strong and independent. Perhaps Katie resented her mother for her indifference like Erica resented hers for her dependence. She didn't know which was worse. That is to say that Erica had more of a burden at a younger age but at least she knew her mother loved her. She wasn't so certain about her Aunt Jillian. Did Jillian love her children? Probably, Erica thought. She just didn't often show it, at least not that Erica had seen.

Erica eventually reached the gas station at the Happy Clown. The gross, greasy, marble-eyed guy was there, asking her if she needed anything. She told him that they'd run out of gas and he expressed sympathy and disgust. He asked if she might like a ride back to their car.

"How far away are ya?"

"Bout a mile or so," she said, shielding her eyes from the sun that was really going to work on the day.

"Well, I'll get Brad ta take ya back. You can borrow the can, long as ya promise ta bring it back and fill 'er up here." He laughed because his was the only gas station around for miles.

"Of course," she said and smiled.

"Allrighty then, I'll git ya yer gas and fetch Brad." He spoke like a southerner with a drawl. He came out a moment later with Brad, a very cute guy with dark hair and tanned skin.

"Hi, I'm Brad. Ran out of gas, huh?" At least he didn't look repulsed by the idea. If he was, he hid it pretty well, Erica thought.

"Hi Brad. Yeah, my mom forgets to check sometimes," she lied.

"Well. All git yer gas can filled for ya" said the greasy man. Erica noticed for the first time that the name Tom was embroidered on his coveralls.

"Thanks Tom," she said.

"I'll get the truck," Brad said. Erica noticed that he was wearing shorts and a t-shirt instead of coveralls.

"Thanks," was all Erica could say. She hoped she didn't look too awful. Brad came around with an old beater truck. Tom put the can spilling over with gas onto the truck bed. She climbed in and nodded to Tom and they headed off to find the Pinto and its wretched passengers.

"There they are, right up there, on the left," Erica pointed unnecessarily as he couldn't help but see them stranded there on the side of the road, sitting in the car, waiting for aide, as usual. Her mother got out of the car and started talking really fast. She thanked Brad for the gas and for driving Erica back and for being so quick, blah, blah, blah. She went on and on about how tough it was without a gas station nearby and how finances were tight, telling the poor guy her whole life's story.

"Mom, I'm sure he doesn't care about our problems. Besides, you coulda gotten more gas when you had the chance," she said, embarrassed by her mother's rambling excuses.

Brad emptied the can into the tank and waited for it to start up which, surprisingly, it did. Erica was always surprised when their car started up. That was the difference between Erica and her mother. Her mother was always surprised when her car wouldn't start and Erica was always surprised when it did.

Brad pulled away waving so they all three waved and thanked him and said they'd be right behind him. They followed him back to the gas station where Erica insisted on filling the tank. Her mother always said she didn't like to fill it because that's just when they break down, which was, of course, ridiculous. Erica knew the real reason was because, in her mother's mind, she'd rather have more cash on hand longer. Erica vowed to always fill her tank once old enough to drive. Erica decided that the only excuse for running out of gas is if you're trying to get gas but the gas station blows up just when you pull in due to an earthquake caused be Lex Luthor, like with Lois Lane in Superman, Erica's favorite movie.

Erica finished filling up the tank and Jean paid for the gas-half of it in quarters. The next stop was the laundromat. They went in with their arms full of clothes. Inside the laundromat, it was humid and the paint was peeling off the cement walls. There were several other people there, loading, unloading, folding or reading. They found a couple of washers and loaded them both up to capacity. Erica looked around the room for someone close to her age but saw only moms. They wandered towards the café, the smell of bacon grease and pancakes wafting out and reaching their noses like long fingered ghosts well before they'd reached the door. Stepping in, Erica saw that this place, too, was filled to capacity, mostly couples with small children crawling over the booths and middle-aged men digging into huge piles of food.

"How many?" said a fiftyish blonde woman with too-bright pink lipstick and nails to match. She was not smiling, in fact, she looked pretty pissed off. Her painted patina contorting into a smug, forced smile.

"Three," her mom said, holding up three fingers as if the lady were not only tacky but illiterate as well.

They were seated off in a corner booth and Erica looked

around the room, sizing up the customers. She noticed a dark-skinned girl sitting with an older, white-haired man at a table just across the way. The man had such white hair against such dark skin that it reminded Erica of some the trashy books she'd been reading and how they would have referred to his hair as a "shock of white hair." What was even more shocking was the sight of 'ethnic' people dining in a decidedly white café in an overtly red-necked town. Erica couldn't place their ethnicity. They looked more Polynesian than black but that wouldn't matter out here in the sticks, Erica thought. They were both pretty striking and Erica wondered what the hell they were doing in Plain but decided not to ask.

"Aren't they attractive?" her mom volunteered. Ellie and Erica said nothing. "I wonder what brings them here?" she continued. "Do you think they're just passing through?" Ellie and Erica looked at their mother like she was the dumbest person they'd ever known, opting to respond to her query with the facial expression it so richly deserved rather than with words that could never express how stupid they thought she was at that particular moment.

"Oh, you two. Honestly!" She was smiling. One thing about Mom, Erica thought, she could take a little ribbing.

"Well, I'm going over to say hello." Oh God! Their mother walked over to the unsuspecting table and started chatting with them, reaching her hand out to the old man to shake it. They smiled sweetly at her. Erica could hear nothing of their conversation but she had a pretty good idea of what her mother would be saying. She could see that her mom was doing most of the talking.

After about a minute or two their mother came back to where Erica and Ellie were sitting mortified.

"They're very nice. They just moved here, too. He buys and fixes up houses and that's his daughter. I didn't ask about her mother and they didn't mention her. The girl is your age, Erica and she'll be starting the tenth grade with you. They're half Polynesian. They're from Hawaii originally, he said. They live right near us in the Ponderosa, near the clubhouse."

"Did she seem nice?" Erica asked.

"Lacy? Yes, very nice. She asked about you too."

"What did she ask?"

"She asked if you were anxious to start school."

"Oh."

"And I told her that, yes, you were."

"Great. She'll think I'm a dork now," Erica said, irritably.

"She will not. She's nervous, too."

"You told her I was nervous?" Erica sounded shrill.

The waitress brought the food they'd ordered and that ended the conversation. When the plates had been cleared and the bill had been paid, the older man and his daughter came over, smiling and showing huge, white teeth.

"Hello," he said.

"Hi," Erica and Ellie said back, smiling sweetly.

"Your delightful mother told us that you'll be attending school here, as well," said the old man.

"This is Lacy. She'll be starting the tenth grade with you," he said, looking at Erica and smiling. They sure smiled a lot Erica thought.

Ellie and Erica just smiled back and nodded their heads. "And you'll be starting the fourth grade at the elementary school, is that right?" he asked Ellie. She nodded and smiled some more.

"Very attractive girls you have there, Mrs. Tambo."

69

"Oh, call me Jean, please."

"Jean."

"And your name is Michel, isn't that right?'

"Yes, that is correct," The man said formally. He sounded like he was running for office, either that or applying to be a butler, Erica thought.

"Girls, this is Mr. Edwin," their mother said very formally.

"Well, I guess I'll see you on the bus Monday," Lacy said, her smile having completely overtaken her face, her teeth gleaming white.

"Okay. Bye..." More smiles.

Lacy was pretty and seemed sweet, Erica thought. She wondered if they'd end up being friends or not.

After folding their laundry, they came out to load up the car Erica looked around for Brad but didn't see him anywhere. They thanked Tom for the twelve thousandth time then stopped at the Tumwater grocery, directly across the street, where they again saw Lacy and her father. The three waved to them, embarrassed at having seen them again so soon after having said goodbye. Erica went to find some mouse traps, thinking to herself that she'd be the one to have to set them, of course. She ran into Lacy on the same aisle. "Hi again," Erica said.

"Hi," she said smiling broadly. "Are you excited for school?"

"I guess," she said, nonchalantly. "Where are you from?" Erica asked.

"Well, the last place we lived was in California, near Sacramento, but we've lived all over."

"Oh." Erica said brilliantly.

"Your mom says you're from Seattle."

"Bellevue, actually, it's near Seattle."

"How long have you lived here then?"

"About a month or so."

"How do you like it?"

"It's okay. How 'bout you?"

"I miss California but it's okay. It's pretty here." She said.

"Yeah," was all Erica could think to say.

"Do you want to get together tomorrow? Maybe we could go for a walk?" Lacy asked

"Sure," Erica said, trying not to sound too anxious.

"How do I get a hold of you?"

"Um, are you listed?"

"Yes, I think so."

"Okay, then I'll call you in the morning, okay?" And she intended to.

"Okay. Bye," Lacy called out as she walked away.

"Okay. See ya tomorrow. Bye."

Erica found the traps and grabbed four of them, figuring that would be plenty for such a small area. Driving home she realized that she was actually looking forward to getting together with Lacy the following day. It was clear to her that she missed the company of a good friend her own age. Perhaps she'd find one in Lacy.

Her mother practically threw a party when Erica casually mentioned that she had made plans with Lacy. "A new friend" as she put it. It made her mother feel better to know that her daughter was perhaps making friends and fitting in, Erica assumed.

Once they were back at the trailer, Erica almost felt bad for Ellie. She'd become so accustomed to having so many

71

friends around all the time and now she hadn't a one. But that didn't keep Erica from rubbing her nose in it.

"I'm meeting Katie tonight to look at clothes for Monday, then I'm meeting Lacy tomorrow morning. What are you doing? Oh yeah, you don't have any friends here." Pretty mean and petty but she kind of had it coming after all these years, Erica thought. Ellie went in to where her mother sat knitting and started to complain about there being no one around for her to hang out with. Oh God, Erica thought, she'd better not try to tag along!

"Erica, come in here a minute" her mother called out. She walked in to where they were sitting. "I want you to take Ellie with you tomorrow, when you go to see Lacy."

"No way!"

"Yes, she wants to go along."

"Too bad! We don't want her there!" What had she done? She knew she never should have rubbed it in like that. Ellie probably didn't even want to go. She just wanted to get even with her, the little shit!

"Either she goes with you today or she goes tomorrow. What'll it be?"

"Neither!"

"Pick one."

"God! Why can't she go find her own friends? School starts in two days, can't she wait two days?"

Her mom got a puzzled expression on her face and looked at Ellie solemnly. "She has a point, Ellie. You are going to be meeting a whole new crop of kids your age in just two days, less than two days." Thank god she was being reasonable, Erica thought.

"Ellie started crying as Erica walked away, victorious. She

overheard her mother reassuring Ellie of her great ability to make friends and how well-liked she'd be, blah, blah, blah. She was off the hook but Erica was also realizing that sometimes cruelty, however justified, just isn't worth it.

She went over to Katie's as planned and they talked about clothes and hair and boys. It wasn't as much fun as the last time because Aunt Jillian was hovering which seemed to cast a spell of indifference on Katie. Erica left earlier than she'd planned, making something up about needing to get back home.

When she got home, she went straight to her closet in search of the perfect first day outfit. My God! When did I become such a girl? She wondered.

The following day she called Lacy as promised and they met at the clubhouse. They hung out there for a while, talking about the new school, their old schools, and siblings. Lacy was very nice and Erica liked her. She wasn't athletic at all, preferring to take long walks and read rather than play sports. That was okay with Erica. She liked to read and walk, too. Plus it gave them books in common which was great for her since no one else she knew, aside from her mother, really liked to read. She noticed how pretty Lacy was while they talked. She had beautiful dark skin and a pretty smile, unlike Erica's dorky grin.

They walked the short distance to her house. It was nice. Not huge but nice and clean. It had a cozy feel in the way log cabins always do. Her father Michel was there, working outside in the garden. She saw no sign of a mother.

"Good morning," Lacy's father said cheerfully. "What are you two up to this morning?"

"Nothin," Lacy said. "Let's go to my room," she said

and Erica just smiled weakly and followed her new friend down the dark hallway into her small but cute room. There were pictures of Lacy and her father in Hawaii along with pictures of Lacy with various friends. One of the pictures looked pretty old. It was of Lacy, her father and a pretty lady with dark hair and dark skin. Erica thought better of asking Lacy if it was her mother. Her room was immaculate. The bed made tightly with a floral bedspread tucked neatly under the mattress. Erica didn't dare to sit on the bed at first but Lacy did so she went ahead and sat down next to her.

Hours passed as they sat on her bed talking and looking at pictures of her old town and their old house. She seemed to miss it a little but she also seemed okay with being in Leavenworth. Maybe she'd just gotten used to moving around a lot, Erica thought. Erica found herself being very jealous of Lacy's nice house and the fact that they had a kitchen full of food, something she noted when she followed her out there to get a drink. She had her own room with a real bed. Their house didn't have anything in miniature like Erica's had. Their toilets and refrigerator were regular size, as were their other appliances. Erica hated for Lacy to see the way they lived but she knew it was inevitable if they were to be friends.

Eventually Erica decided she had to go. She said her goodbyes and walked back home past all the nice log homes on Lacy's street. She began to feel sorry for herself as she sometimes did when confronted with the financial disparity between her family and everyone else she'd ever known. She started crying, wallowing in her feelings of injustice. She was tired of being poor and it felt like they were getting poorer all the time. She decided that when she grew up, she would always have plenty of food around, a new car and a nice house.

Erica didn't crave wealth but merely comfort. She just wanted to not have to be worried about money or embarrassed about where she lived. She promised herself that she would have a better life. She had no idea how she was going to pull that off, however. Being a kid, that thought didn't really occur to her.

When she walked in the front door, Erica was told to get in the car because they were late meeting her Aunt Jillian and Cousin Chloe at the Cougar Inn on Lake Wenatchee. What? Apparently they were meeting them for lunch at some Inn. It took about ten or fifteen minutes to get there, during which time their mother filled them in on what the place was like. Her mother had been to this Inn before when she had come out from Bellevue to see the area at Jillian's behest. This one visit out was what had convinced her (along with her sister Jillian) to make the move. As she was describing the Inn to them Erica noticed that her mother's face looked a bit drawn and tired, as if she hadn't slept.

They turned down a steep road leading to a big log building perched on a slight incline, overlooking a pretty lake. There was a well-kept lawn running the length of the property and a line of trees which stood tall and dense on either side. The lake seemed large and there were hills all around it. There were several cars in the lot and Erica saw some tents off in the distance amongst the trees, near the water. Stepping inside the rather grand entrance, one looked past the hall and through windows and out to the lake. There was a reception area and a cocktail lounge. The restaurant was next to the lounge and that's where they headed. It was kind of casual and woodsy with big tables and another commanding view. Looking around, they saw Chloe and her mother already seated near a window. They said hello and sat down, getting a nod back in response. Erica wished Katie were there.

Aunt Jillian began talking to Jean about the guy that she'd been seeing. Chloe was coloring in her coloring book. Ellie and Erica just sat and stared out the window, watching the people walk by, saying nothing until, finally, sensing her daughters' boredom, Erica's mother asked if they would like to go walk around. Erica and Ellie jumped up and bolted out, saying they'd be back in a little while.

As they left the building and headed for the lake, they saw two boys sitting on the front stoop, eating sandwiches. They were tall, but kind of chubby with buzz cuts. Looking closer, Erica realized that they were identical twins. Erica thought they looked to be about her age but it was difficult to tell because they also resembled old men. The girls ran off down to the end of the dock which darted out from behind the building they'd just departed. There were some speedboats tied up to the sides of the dock and they could see a few more boats towing skiers out on the water. It was nice here and Erica wondered why they hadn't come sooner. She dared Ellie to go swimming so Ellie stripped down to her ever-present swim suit, (which she wore as underwear all summer long), and dove right in. Erica hesitated, worried she'd be sorry if she got her hair wet. She was well aware that a few months earlier, she would never have worried about wet hair and yet, there she was, on that fence between child and adult again. Was she woman or child? She took her sandals off and sat at the edge of the dock with her legs dangling and her toes skimming the cool water. The sun was high and blinding so she kept her head down and looked at the water.

"C'mon, get in," Ellie yelled to her from the water about twenty feet out.

"Nah, I don't have my suit on."

"So? You can swim in your underwear and shirt."

"No. I don't wanna."

"God! yer such a priss!"

"Shut up!"

Ellie shook her head and dove under. Erica looked around at the rest of the lake. It was really big and beautiful. There were some homes in the distance but it was mostly unspoiled. She heard someone behind her. Turning to look she saw it was the twins they'd seen on the landing.

"You got ta drive last time. It's my turn, you Shithead!"

"Dad told me I could take it out. Not you. I don't even have to take you with me."

"He meant both of us."

"Go ask him."

"Oh, so you can take off with it? Fuck you!"

Both of the boys scrambled into one of the boats on the side of the dock. Erica watched with feigned disinterest as one boy untied the lines while the other one started the engine. It roared up loudly and they began to pull away from the dock, looking at her as they passed by. Erica glanced away, as if bored by them and their boat. They sped off. She'd rather liked to have gone along but she hadn't exactly encouraged an invitation. Oh well, her mother would be upset if she had gone. Besides, she was hungry.

"Ellie! Ellie! Let's go!"

"No!"

"C.mon. we gotta go back!"

Ellie said nothing. "Fine," Erica said "Suit yourself."

She stood up and took one last look around, trying to see if she could make out the twin boys. Blinded by the sun, she turned and headed back inside.

Erica walked back in the restaurant and sat down next her mother. She and Jillian were still talking about something boring. Chloe was still coloring, obviously possessing no artistic talent as she was all over the page.

"Where's your sister?"

"Swimming," Erica said irritably. She got cranky when she was hungry.

"That girl! She should have been a fish." Erica silently wished Ellie had been a fish.

"Here she comes, nice and wet," Jillian said, shaking her head and smiling.

Ellie had traipsed in dripping wet and carrying her sandals. "Where are towels?" she asked, aware that she was making a mess but not knowing what to do about it.

"Go ask at the front desk," her mom suggested. Ellie turned and walked back out, a stream of water falling from her suit to the hardwood floor. Erica was glad she'd thought better of joining her. She really looked childish walking in all wet like that.

Jillian was drinking beer while Erica's mom sipped on lemonade. They had already eaten and their plates had been cleared. There was a hamburger split in half and divided onto two plates along with French fries for Erica and Ellie. Erica began to eat hers and soon Ellie came back, wrapped in a huge yellow towel, she plopped herself down and began devouring her food. She didn't seem to care at all what people thought.

They left a short while later after splitting the bill with Jillian. Out in the parking lot as they were making their way to their crappy little car, Erica's mother called out to Jillian,

"I'll call you tomorrow." Jillian nodded and got in to her own crappy car, some tiny foreign job.

On the drive back home Erica's mother drove like an eighty year old woman down the narrow, two lane highway. A few miles from the Inn, they noticed a commotion about a quarter of a mile in front of them. They slowed down and, as they got closer, Erica could see a small car on the right hand side of the road, a group of maybe eight people hovered together on the left side of the road and a few cars lined up ahead of them, completely stopped. People were milling around near their cars, shaking their heads. Suddenly, a dark haired woman broke through the crowd and ran towards what looked like a blanket on top of a small log. The woman began to moan loudly, falling to her knees, her head and torso moving up and down like a giant fan.

"Oh God!" Their mother said.

"What?" Erica asked, but she was beginning to understand.

"That poor woman! Oh my God! She must be the mother."

"Who's mother?" Erica asked anxiously.

"Don't you see it?' she asked in a shrill voice. "The blanket, under the blanket. That's a little boy or girl. Must have been hit by a car."

It was then that Erica saw another woman, maybe thirty or so, with short blonde hair, also on her knees on the opposite side of the road near what must have been her car, her arms wrapped tightly around her middle. She was rocking back and forth, tears streaking her face. Their mother spotted her, too.

"She must be the driver." She said in almost a whisper,

nodding her head towards the woman.

Someone appeared at her mother's window. It was a tall bearded man about fifty or so. Another driver, perhaps? Their mother rolled down her window quickly.

"What's happened?'

"That lady there," he was pointing at the blonde woman near the car. "She hit a little girl. Three years old. She's dead. That's the mom over there." He said like he was giving directions or something, nodding his head in the other woman's direction. The mother was now kneeling over the girl's lifeless body, her arms wrapped around her with her head resting near the top of the blanket. Erica looked at Ellie whose mouth was agape, her blonde hair curling up around her pudgy face as it dried. Erica mouthed "Oh my God" to her sister and Ellie just stared. Erica felt her chest tightening up. She'd never seen a dead person before, not even covered up and she knew Ellie hadn't either. The three of them sat there for what seemed like hours, waiting. Finally, their mother got out of the car and walked over to the crowd of people. She could see that the blonde woman was still on her knees on the side of the road, all by herself, rocking away.

Their mother talked to some of the people in the small crowd and her girls, still in the car, could see her shaking her head over and over again as they peered through the car window. Their mother kept wiping her face with tips of her fingers. She then walked over to where the blonde women sat rocking and knelt down with her, putting her arm around her for a while. Erica was a little embarrassed by the display but moved at the same time. It was as if she was glad someone was comforting this poor woman but uncomfortable with it being her own mother. However, she did feel a tinge of pride that her mother had taken it upon herself to try to console the lone woman.

Eventually, their mother made her way back to their car and got in, her face ashen. She said nothing. They began to hear the wail of an ambulance coming towards them. Soon the flashing lights became visible as it approached quickly. As it pulled up three men got out. A police car also pulled up behind the ambulance and two policemen got out. The driver of the police car went over to the crowd and appeared to ask questions. Several in the crowd pointed at the blonde woman, prompting him to head over to where she was kneeling. The other policeman got out and walked towards the cars lining up. He walked up to the driver's side of the first car, saying something to the driver who then began to pull away with the policeman standing between the car and where the paramedics were trying in vain to pry mother from daughter. Because theirs was only the third car back, the policemen soon had Erica's mother pulling away from the scene as well. They drove very slowly past everything. Ellie and Erica looking at the woman hunched over the blanket as they passed. They began to pick up speed but never got above thirty.

Finally reaching home, their mother eased the car into the parking spot near the hitch of the trailer. She got out of the car and walked inside, saying nothing. No one said a word. Alias ran out as soon as Erica opened the front door, happy to see people and blissfully ignorant of what they'd just witnessed. She went inside to put on her tennis shoes then she headed out on a walk with Alias. She couldn't get the accident scene out of her head. How had it happened? Had the little girl run out in front of the car? Had the blonde woman been speeding?

When she returned Erica noticed it was past six. She'd been out walking for over an hour.

She spent most of that night lying on her bed, thinking about the accident (which she realized they must have missed by mere seconds). She felt sorry for the mother who'd lost her little girl but also for the driver of the car. She wondered what would become of them both.

Eventually Erica walked out to where Ellie and her mother were sitting. "Mom, what'll happen to the lady who hit that little girl?"

"I don't know. Depends what happened. I don't know if she was speeding or if she veered off the road or if the little girl just darted out onto the street. It'll probably be in the paper."

"Yeah," Erica said glumly.

She made herself a sandwich using the bread which Ellie had added far too much baking soda, rendering it nearly inedible, which she of course pointed out to her younger sister. The three of them sat in silence for a little while until Erica finally went to work on the television and its foil wrapped rabbit ears, trying to get in some station, any station. She finally found a movie of the week to watch, something about child beating. Just the uplift they'd sought.

The following morning her mother turned the radio on to listen to Paul Harvey and, during the local newsbreak, the newscaster mentioned an accident which had killed a little girl. They said that the driver of the car was a woman of thirty-two who lived in a nearby town. She'd been visiting a friend in Plain and was returning home on that stretch of highway when the three year old girl came darting out into the street after a ball. No charges were filed, nor did the authorities anticipate filing any as the woman didn't seem to have been at fault in any way. It was just a tragic accident.

The three listened motionless as the commentator spoke, stirring again only when he'd moved on to the next story. So that was that. Just an accident. No one to blame but fate. Erica wondered again how both mother and driver would fare.

Erica took her dog for a long walk down the hill towards the café. She followed him as he pulled her in towards the creek, letting him drink for a while from the cool water. Erica couldn't get the image of the little girl under the blanket out of her head, no matter how much she tried to think of other things. Why had she gone into the road? Where had her mother been?

She left the creek and she walked Alias a little ways further down the hill, following the windy road, then turned around and walked back home.

Since tomorrow was the first day of school, Erica decided to lay her clothes out on her bed so she could be sure they were really what she wanted to wear. The weather was still pretty hot so she couldn't yet opt for her nicer fall wear (you only make that mistake once). She couldn't decide between her flair leg jeans paired with a white, oversized, short-sleeved blouse or the more conservative white slacks and light blue top with a loose tie at the collar. Both outfits lay sprawled on the bed like two passed out teenagers. She finally decided on the latter as it seemed safer. She put out a bra (the only one she owned and scarcely needed) under the slacks. She had a habit of hiding her under things from the rest of the world.

Ellie walked in just then. She pointed at the pile on the bed Erica had just spent so much time deciding on and asked if that was what she was planning to wear. Erica told her it was and Ellie asked if she'd help her with her ensemble. Surprised at being asked, Erica obliged, first sizing her up and down like she was a fashion designer and Ellie a model. She started flipping through her messy side of the closet, pulling various items out, seeing many in full view that she'd only known previously as sleeves.

"What are you going to wear to Dad's wedding?" she asked brightly.

"What?" A bemused Erica asked.

"We're invited. Mom talked to him and he said we should come."

"Dad's getting married? To Karen? When?"

"Saturday!" Ellie said, looking at Erica like she was crazy.

Erica walked out to where her mother sat on her couch.

"Dad's getting married? When? Why?" she stammered.

"Saturday. He just called. Wanted to invite you kids. I can't believe it." her mother said.

"He's *marrying* her?"

"Appears so." Her mother looked like she'd been sucker punched.

"I gotta lie down," her mother said weakly as she pulled her legs up to her chest and pulled the tattered yellow blanket down from the back of the couch, draping it over her shoulders. She looks so sad, Erica thought. She'd noticed her mother's face looking kind of drawn and colorless of late but now she looked positively ashen.

"How come we're just now finding out about it?"

"He said he didn't want to upset me." her mother said bitterly.

"Until today, apparently," Erica said.

"Until today," her mother repeated, her eyes closed.

"Well, I'm not going. No way," Erica said, shaking her head.

"You have to go," her mother said. "He's your father."

"Are you sure? I don't look anything like him."

"I'm sure, Erica."

"Well I don't want to go."

Her mother said nothing. Erica walked back to talk to Ellie.

"They planned on no kids for a while but everyone thought it was weird that his kids weren't invited so now we're invited." Ellie said matter-of-factly.

"Yippee!" Erica said. "I don't even wanna go. Do you?"

"Kind of. Lots of people will be there."

"Oh goody! That really makes me wanna go!"

"Well you have to. What are you gonna wear?"

"I don't know. I haven't exactly thought about it, you know."

"Well, I'm gonna wear this." She pulled out a pretty floral dress with a long skirt and a bow at the waist. Erica had never seen it before."

"When did you get that?' she asked. "I don't remember you having that. Did Dad buy that for you?"

"Yeah but I'm not supposed to tell you."

"Why not?" Erica knew why not.

"I don't know, he just told me not to tell you."

"Oh." Erica said, suddenly feeling dejected.

"You should wear that dress you wore to Grandma's funeral."

"Oh, I see, so you get a new dress and I get to wear a hand-me-down that I wore to a funeral. That's fair."

Ellie didn't say anything else after that about the wedding.

Perhaps feeling a little guilty about being so obviously favored. The dichotomy between the way Ellie and Erica were treated by their dad was glaring. Erica knew that her dad and Karen, his bride-to-be, would prefer that they didn't attend the wedding. If they had been given the choice between Ellie and Erica attending, they'd choose Ellie attending over her. Ellie was cute and adults loved her, always had. Erica cast no such spell.

"I think you should wear something more summery for your first day of school," Erica suggested.

After an exhaustive search of Ellie's side of the closet (during which Erica saw that she had obtained *several* new outfits) they finally arrived at a mid-length, floral skirt with blues and purples on a cream background with a matching plum top. She would look cute in it and she knew Ellie cared more than she pretended to about that.

Ellie thanked her for helping and left the room. Erica felt tears welling up in her eyes and her throat began to tighten, making breathing difficult. She tried to change the subject in her head from that of her father to anything else. Unsuccessful, she went to watch television, hoping for a distraction.

That night, Erica thought about the wedding. She really wasn't all that opposed to going. She didn't want them to get married but Erica was kind of excited at the prospect of going home and seeing familiar people. But she dreaded hearing her father's friends tell her how different she looked which is what everyone said whenever they saw Erica next to her father. She knew her father would be distant and cold and his fiancé would insult her hair or her dress, but Erica was used to that. She thought about how she might avoid ending up where she usually ended up, which was in a bathroom stall, crying. Erica decided that she would be very sweet and quiet. She would be helpful but non-intrusive. She began to feel that this wedding might be an opportunity for her to impress the people back home with how grown-up and mature she'd become over the summer. Feeling a little better, she concentrated on the television.

Erica watched 'Charlie's Angels' for a while but it was a re-run so she switched to 'Barbara Mandrell and the Mandrell Sisters' which was totally lame so then she tried to get 'One Day at a Time' but she couldn't quite get it to come in. So finally, she gave up and went to bed with her latest book, Sidney Sheldon's 'The Other Side of Midnight". Getting in to bed she shoved the already sleeping Ellie towards the wall. "Bed Hog." she said, pulling the covers over herself.

6

The sun shone brightly through the dusty window of the small school bus and Erica squinted as she watched the landscape moving by outside. Somehow she'd ended up in an emergency row and her shoulder kept hitting the emergency arm as the little bus bounced around on the untended roads. She sat there because Katie had told her to sit there. Erica had followed Katie onto the bus, having met her at the bus stop, where she had been sitting among a few other younger kids Erica didn't know. Ellie was aboard, as well, but she was on her own as far as Erica was concerned. Ellie had sat in the front row, behind the bus driver, staring out the window, her little legs dangling several inches above the floor.

The morning started out very chaotic for several reasons. First, they hadn't anticipated the lack of hot water after mere minutes of showering, nor the lack of room for two girls attempting to ready themselves for the all-important first day of school. By the time the two of them were ready to go, they only had five minutes to get to the bus stop. Their mom, realizing that she'd either have to drive them to the bus stop or all the way into town if they missed the bus, had already started up the car and was waiting for them when Ellie and Erica ran out. They scrambled into the little car and raced to the bus stop on top of the second hill where they were to wait for a tiny bus, which would rendezvous with another, larger bus, which would finally take them in to town. The process would be reversed on the trip home, forty-five minutes each way for a total of one hour and thirty minutes aboard a bus every school day.

Mortification set in as they approached the crest of the hill and could see several kids standing around, waiting. Erica thought about the ugly, stupid car they were riding in and about how ridiculous she was going to feel pulling up with her mother driving it. She'd probably open her window and yell something embarrassing, or worse yet, get out of the car to hug her two girls, clad in her bathrobe. Erica could feel her whole face getting hot and turning red. She saw Katie sitting on a rock near the side of the road, putting makeup on. What's she doing here, Erica wondered. Why wasn't she driving to school? The other kids were all younger, between eight and twelve. She saw no sign of Lacy. Had they driven in on the first day? As their mother began to slow the car down to a stop Erica said, "Please don't yell anything out the window. Can't we say goodbye here in the car? Please?"

"Afraid I'll embarrass you?" her mother asked with mock irritation.

"I know you will."

"Yeah, just say goodbye to us now, okay?" Ellie pleaded.

"I wasn't going to embarrass you."

"Sure."

"Well, goodbye then. Have a good first day. It'll be fine. I love you, both of you."

"Bye," was said in unison. Their mother turned the car back around and headed back the way they'd come.

Ellie and Erica walked gingerly up to where the other kids were standing. Katie looked up, kind of smirking. Was she laughing at her? At what she was wearing? Erica looked at what Katie had chosen to wear that first day: fitted jeans with a white blouse and wedge-style shoes. Almost exactly what Erica was going to wear but talked herself out of in favor of her dumb blue top and white slacks, which now seemed too dressy and conservative. God! Why hadn't she worn the other outfit? She wanted to go back home and change in the worst way. Too late for that.

Katie greeted them with a "Hey."

"Hey. What are you doing here?" Erica asked. Ellie smiled and said "Hi Katie. I'm so nervous to start school here." What a dork, Erica thought.

"You'll be okay," Katie said reassuringly. She turned to look at Erica, "I told you I usually take the bus to save on gas."

"Yeah but you also said that you were gonna drive the first day or so."

"Car wouldn't start this morning..."

"Bummer," Erica said with a sympathetic frown.

"Do ya wanna little blush?" Katie asked her. She was holding her compact mirror up to her face and applying blush to her pudgy cheeks, too young to have any real facial definition yet.

"Okay," Erica said timidly.

"C'mere." She said, smiling impishly.

Erica walked over and stood directly in front of her. Katie began to apply blush to Erica's cheeks, re-supplying the brush several times. "There, looks good."

Erica smiled at her, "Really?" she asked, squinting in the sun.

"You look dumb," Ellie said, sneering at her.

Before she could punch her little sister, one of the younger kids yelled "There it is," while pointing demonstrably like it was Superman coming to save everyone. They all watched the tiny bus as it crested the nearest hill. Everyone lined up, anxious to get on board. Katie just sat on her rock and waited so Erica waited with her. The bus stopped and the driver, a dark-haired woman with giant purple glasses and red lipstick, opened the door with the rotating chrome handle and the kids all fell over each other trying to get in and nab the best seats. Ellie kept looking back at Katie, not sure whether to scramble on with the rest of them or wait for the dust to settle before climbing aboard. Katie finally stood and got on board. Assuming Erica would sit with her, Ellie sat behind the driver and slid over, making room for her sister. Erica briefly glanced at Ellie as she passed by her, seeing her mouth agape in astonished disbelief. So she wasn't going to sit next to her. Big deal! Erica thought.

Erica sat down and slid over for Katie who was blocking the aisle, rummaging through her purse. She eventually sat down, instantly pulled out her mirror and proceeded to finish applying her makeup. She was pretty adept at anticipating the many bumps and jolts as they went along.

"What's your first class?" Katie asked while putting on mascara.

"I don't know. I have a letter here telling me where to go for orientation. I don't think I have any classes yet," she said, franticly looking through her knapsack for the form she'd received through the mail from the high school. She was suddenly terrified that she had been remiss somehow. Had she missed the class sign-up deadline? "They never mentioned signing up for classes in advance," Erica said anxiously.

"Yeah, first day you'll get a homeroom and then they help you pick out your classes. I forgot this was your first day of high school." So she hadn't screwed up already. Thank God!!

"Okay," she said, now wishing to appear indifferent. She glanced out the window. They were turning down the hill that led to the clubhouse. Maybe Lacy's bus stop was different. Sure enough, as they began to slow down she looked out to see Lacy along with another six or seven kids standing together, waiting to get on. The other kids, all blonde and of various ages, got on first, one older girl taking a seat next to Ellie in the front. Finally Lacy came on. Erica smiled at her and indicated by pointing her index finger that she would sit in the seat behind them if she could. Lacy smiled, her teeth like dice being rolled, "Good morning," she said. She was wearing a taupe blouse with matching slacks. She looks nice, Erica thought. It was obvious that Lacy had put a great deal of thought into what she'd wear that first day. Of course, so had Erica.

Lacy took the seat just behind Erica and Katie. She sat very primly, her back perfectly straight, her hands resting on her notebook atop her lap. "Hello," she said sweetly, smiling brightly.

"Hi," Erica said back. Katie put her compact down and looked at her oddly. "Oh! Katie, this is Lacy. Lacy, this is Katie. Sorry." Erica said, realizing her faux pas.

"Hi Lacy." Katie said with mock disdain directed at Erica.

"Hello Katie. Nice to meet you."

"Likewise, I'm sure." Erica wondered where Katie had gotten that line, some old movie, maybe, or one of her trashy novels.

"Do you have your orientation form with you?" Erica asked, turning to look at Lacy.

"Uh huh. Do you?"

"Yeah, where do you go?"

"Room A110, how 'bout you?"

Erica looked. "Room C220" she replied, her face registering disappointed that they wouldn't be in the same homeroom. Erica would have to go it alone.

The bus made a tight three hundred and sixty degree turn and headed back up the hill, hitting every pothole along the way. They then turned back on to the main road and headed down towards the café, passing her driveway on the way. Erica deliberately didn't look at it so no one would suspect they lived there. She looked over at Ellie and saw she her pointing at their narrow drive and then up the hill as they passed it. That stupid little shit!! Now everyone would know where they lived! Her mood darkened briefly at the thought of it.

"You two may still have classes together, you know." Katie said.

"Yeah. That's true Erica. I have a class schedule. We could pick out our classes now and try to get some together."

"Okay. Let's see." The two girls looked through all of the classes as well as the list indicating which were required versus elective. Katie told them which teachers were good and which were to be avoided. One in particular she strenuously warned against as being a pervert, Mr. Simpson. Both Lacy and Erica wrote the name down. They had gotten about a third of the way through the list when the bus came to a complete stop and the driver cut the ignition. She picked up the p.a. and announced that there would be a change of buses that day and everyday thereafter. With that she put the p.a. back in its cradle, opened the door and began sifting through her handbag as everyone filed off and crossed the short distance from the bus they'd taken thus far to the much larger bus waiting about twenty-five feet away. Erica looked around and noticed that they were in a deserted lot, no cars or buildings or houses or trees, just vacant land in the middle of nowhere, making a bolt for freedom difficult if not impossible.

Once on the new bus, the girls were again able to tender two seats together near the middle of the bus, despite the fact that this bus was already more than half-full with kids from the other end of town. Katie took the seat furthest back and then motioned for the two girls to sit together in front of her. Looking around Erica recognized no one. Erica and Lacy nodded and smiled at the passengers in general as they sat. They resumed their task with Katie interjecting as she saw fit. Erica occasionally looked out the window to see where they were, having once again found herself in a window seat (albeit not an emergency exit). As Lacy read off the various class options she studied the new bus driver, a fat, old, balding man with a reddish face and a matching plaid shirt who grunted on sharp turns. The road zigzagged a lot as it meandered up the steep hill and then back down the other side, the giant bus taking up both the oncoming and the right hand lanes. There were several times when she felt they just weren't going to make it all the way up. It felt a little like The Grinch's attempt to scale Mount Crumpet and, like The Grinch, they somehow made it to the top and down the other side unscathed, pulling in to the school parking lot with ten minutes to spare.

Katie stood up and looked at Lacy and Erica with a

knowing amused smirk. She wished them luck, half laughing and then disappeared, leaving Lacy and Erica alone to fend for themselves. Erica stopped to talk to Ellie who was still in her seat, waiting with the other younger kids for the driver to take them to the elementary school. "See ya after," she said to her little sister. Ellie looked away and out the window. "You can sit with us on the way home if you want," Erica told her. She said nothing. Erica stepped off the bus and, as they were unsure where to go, Lacy suggested they just follow the crowd so they did. Eventually they found their respective homerooms and, promising to find each other at lunch, they went their separate ways, at least for the time being.

Entering the homeroom filled with tenth graders, all of whom seemed to look at the door the moment she entered, Erica felt her entire face flush with embarrassment. She looked around the room, desperate for an empty, inconspicuous desk at which to sit and hide. Finally spotting one near the back, she ducked her head into her knapsack, which she held close to her chest and shuffled back to the desk, slipped in and tucked her legs under in one quick, smooth motion. Once seated she felt a little less conspicuous and she was able to look around a little. There were half a dozen or so boys and maybe ten girls in the room, most were milling around, talking to their friends and paying no attention to Erica whatsoever. There was a gal with reddish blonde hair and fair skin who she thought looked remarkably like one of Katie's friends. She wondered if she could be her younger sister. There were a group of boys standing near the back on the other side of the room from where she sat. They were laughing loudly. She noticed that two of them were identical twins, tall and skinny with curly hair. She noticed a couple of blonde girls towards the front of the classroom. Erica was looking at them when they happened to look over at her. One girl whispered something to the other girl and they both burst out laughing.

Feeling foolish, Erica began to take note of the room. There were several different maps papering all four walls, one of the world, another of just the U.S., one was of Europe and Asia, still another of Africa. There was a large globe on a pedestal up near where the teacher's desk sat free of clutter.

The door opened and a tall, skinny man in khaki pants and rumpled blue shirt walked in. He had sandy and gray scraggly hair that reached his shoulders and intermingled with his matching beard. His nose jutted out from the middle of his face about an inch or so then suddenly dove down like a divining rod above an underground spring. His eyes were watery blue with lids at half-mast, his shoulders, decidedly weak and narrow, appeared burdened by life. Had the weather been cooler Erica was certain he'd be wearing a tweed jacket with patches at the elbows. The man was utterly devoid of charisma. She wondered if he were married and, if so, to whom? This is what she was thinking about when the bell rang and everyone took their respective seats, suddenly dutiful children.

"Good Morning, class. For those of you who don't know me, my name is Mr. Simpson." He attempted a weak smile to go with his weak jaw and his weak arms and his weak voice that sounded even older than he appeared. This guy is Mr. Simpson? Erica thought. The pervert?

"This will be your homeroom class for the rest of the year so be sure and remember where it is. I will be helping you to ascertain which classes you will need to take this semester and next in order to fulfill the school's requirements. Does everyone have their list of available classes?"

A few kids raised their hands to indicate that they had either not received it or had neglected to bring it along. Mr. Simpson pointed at a pile of papers near the door and they got up, walked over, peeled off a copy and returned to their seats. Mr. Simpson walked to the back of the room where he placed several note boards in a row on the back table. He then returned to the front of the class and addressed the class anew.

"All right then, let's all turn to page two, the top of the page. Do you all see where it reads required classes?" Nobody said anything so he pressed on. "Okay, these are the classes that you must take this year. If you are unable to get into one of the classes for this semester, we will be sure to get you in next semester. Bear in mind, however, that you must take three of these courses this semester so as not to put too much off to the next. So, why don't you take a look at the classes on the list and when you've decided which ones you'd like to take this semester, why, you can go up to the desk in the back of the room and print your full name on the lists for those classes."

Suddenly everyone jumped up and ran to the back of the room and began pushing and shoving each other to get to the lists first. A mouse of a girl on the far end of the room stayed seated and so did Erica. They were the only ones still sitting, too shocked to move. Erica instantly began to worry that the other kids would take all of the good classes and teachers and that Lacy and she would share no classes and she would get only the leftovers. She was certain she was going to end up taking the worst classes from the hardest teachers with the least popular students. She'd probably get Simpson's class! Wasn't it bad enough that he was her Homeroom teacher?

Looking to the front of the class Erica saw Mr. Simpson stiffen a bit and then quickly walk back to where the crowd had converged. "This is not what I had in mind! Back to your seats! Back to your seats!" He yelled, sounding very much like a woman.

The crowd slowly disbursed and returned to their respective seats. Mr. Simpson then called attention to himself standing at the back of the room near the sign-up table.

"You! What's your name?" He was pointing at Erica.

"Erica," she said quietly, her mouth filling with cotton.

"What about you. Who are you?" he asked the mousy girl. She said her name slowly and almost inaudibly, "Betsy."

"Okay, you two can come back here and sign up now. The rest of you can wait for them to finish up. Once they're done, we'll go row by row." With this the whole room groaned. Erica and the mouse got up tentatively and walked back to the table and began signing up for the classes they wanted as they'd been told to do. Erica felt elated, conspicuous and guilty all at the same time. She was able to get into all of the classes Lacy and she had agreed upon. She hoped Lacy would be as lucky. Erica had brought her list with her so she was able to get signed up and back into her seat quickly. Betsy fussed over the classes for a while, finally shuffling back to her seat with her head down and her straggly, dishwater hair hiding her face.

Erica spent the rest of that hour listening to Mr. Simpson call off the various rows, watching them empty out and then slowly fill back up again. She doodled in her notebook a little. Then she broke into full-fledged drawing, using entire sheets of paper, creating scenes with horses and dogs and birds and trees, all with her trusty #2 pencil and endless imagination. Finally the bell rang. Once most of the class had filed out, she stepped out into the fresh air and sunlight, relieved to be out of the horrible fluorescent glare of the class.

Erica pulled out her new schedule, which she had thought to transfer to a page in her book. Her first class would be Math with Mr. Simpson. She assumed he was the same Mr. Simpson as her Homeroom teacher. She looked at the room number for this class and it was the same classroom she had just left. Mr. Simpson, the pervert, was both her homeroom and math teacher! He was the only math teacher.

English, her next class, in room number B030 and it started in five minutes according to the clock she saw in a classroom she'd passed. She asked some kid walking by and he gave her directions. She found the room, walked in and sat down with three minutes to spare. She took a seat near but not quite in the front row and close to the door to ensure a quick escape. Soon the room filled with chatting teenagers, male and female, short and tall, big and small. She watched the door but saw no Lacy. Erica had attempted to save a seat next to her own with her book bag but, when the bell rang and all were seated, Lacy had still not appeared. Erica reached over and put the bag under her own seat. Obviously, Lacy had not been able to get into this class. Erica hoped she'd have better luck with the other classes they'd agreed upon.

A handsome, youngish man with dark hair and a nice smile walked in. Erica felt a glimmer of recognition but from where? Then she inhaled quickly, making the connection. This was the guy who'd helped her find Alias. The one who she'd met near her home when she'd lost her dog in July. He was tall and dressed in dark blue slacks and a light blue shirt that looked as though he'd tried to match it with his eyes. He had dimples on both cheeks and he was very tan, tanner than she remembered him being. He looked as though he'd been out water-skiing all summer. Best of all, he was her teacher.

"Good morning, class. I'm Rick Peters and this is 10th grade English. I just recently moved here from a little town outside Bozeman, Montana where I have spent the last two years teaching English and fly fishing. Anyone in here who can tie a fly better than me gets an automatic 'A'". He smiled and looked around the room for the slightest hint of laughter. Failing that, he pressed on. "We'll be reading mostly classic works in here, so sorry to disappoint those of you who were hoping for Sidney Sheldon or Jacquie Collins." Erica laughed even though it wasn't all that funny. The joke was lost on the other kids since Judy Blume and V.C. Andrews were authors they knew. They had no idea who Sidney Sheldon or Jacquie Collins was. Erica had read quite a bit of Sidney Sheldon.

Rick Peters passed around and then proceeded to go over a class syllabus, describing the reading and the writing that would be expected of them. She had heard of most of the books, seven in all. One was Harper Lee's *To Kill a Mockingbird,* which she'd seen on TV and had really wanted to read. They were asked to line up in the back to collect their books. The bell rang and everyone headed out. Erica took her time, pretending to be having trouble getting all the books into her knapsack. "You'll be assigned a locker so that you won't have to carry all that around all day." She looked up and it was Mr. Peters, standing in front of her desk, smiling, his arms folded across his broad chest.

"Yeah, they told us to go to the front office for that. I

haven't had a chance yet."

"Don't wait too long or you'll end up in Siberia." He smiled.

Erica smiled back. "Okay. See you tomorrow."

"How's your dog?" he asked, smiling at her.

"Oh, he's fine. Thanks again."

"No problem whatsoever. We must be neighbors then, huh?"

"I guess so," Erica said tongue-tied.

She walked out feeling flustered. 'He must think me a complete idiot', she thought. She headed for her next class, which was ceramics. She loved ceramics, only she didn't go in for the wheel too much. She liked to free throw. Make sculptures. Create things (other than bowls and vases, which are pretty much what you're limited to on the wheel).

Her ceramics class was great, only about twelve kids and an instructor who smelled of smoke and basically just pointed at the clay and said to come find him at his desk if they had any questions. She put on an apron and went to work, making a shoe and a hand with a pen in it. Paperweights, she decided, or bookends.

After ceramics she went to Gym class. Gym had always seemed a silly exercise in futility to her, because by the time you got to class, changed into your gym clothes, lined up for roll call, got instructions on how to play whatever it was you'd be playing that day, the class was over and you had to go in, shower, and dress again. Besides, being naturally athletic, nothing ever truly challenged her in gym class. However, because it was the first day, no one had brought their gym clothes and they merely sat on the benches in the locker room and listened as the instructor who looked about as physical as Betty Ford. Lacy was not in this class either.

When they finished learning how to shower, the bell rang

and she bolted out of the smelly locker room as fast as she could. Erica headed for the office to get her locker number, combination and lunch money. At their old school, Ellie and Erica were on the free lunch program, which meant that each day before school she would go to the office and the secretary would give her lunch money for that day. To qualify you only had to be willing to admit that you were miserably poor and she'd been more than qualified. Unfortunately, this was not the way they did it at this school. Instead, she was told by the rude lady at the front desk, who became even more rude when she realized that Erica was inquiring about free lunches, that Erica needed to get in line with everyone else, get lunch, then tell the lady at the register who she was and she would be allowed to go on by without paying. This was terrible because it meant that all the other kids would see that she didn't have to pay which of course meant she received free lunches. It was public admission of being dirt poor, white trash, destined for welfare and multiple children with multiple fathers.

Erica walked to her new locker trying to decide how she could earn enough money to pay for lunch every day. She thought about packing a lunch but, if this school was anything like her old school, only the dorks would be doing that, and besides, there was never anything to eat at home anyway. She reached into her bag to see how much money she had, about thirty cents. Not enough, she was sure. She thought of Ellie. Ellie wouldn't care. She'd just get her lunch and sit, no big deal.

Erica walked into the lunchroom, suddenly famished. There were dozens of kids milling around, some talking, others walking with trays or eating at one of the ten or so long tables with attached benches set out. She saw the tail end of a line on the other end of the room. There was a large window into the kitchen area with a long bar for trays running in front of it. Two rotund women with hairnets and white smocks were standing in the kitchen, facing out towards the cafeteria and serving the food. On the far end of the tray bar was another woman, also in white, sitting on a stool in front of a cash register.

Erica walked up to the end of the short line and stood behind the last person, a greasy kid with pimples and a striped shirt. He looked at her briefly then turned back to what he was doing, which was staring at his shoes. She thought that if she could just find the board with the list of options and prices she could find something small to tide her over until she got home. Of course, it would also have to cost less than thirty cents. Seeing no such list, she asked the woman at the window if there were a list of prices. The woman looked at her with an expression that conveyed both boredom and irritation and informed her that it was not al la carte but rather an all you can eat buffet with one set price, Seventy-five cents. Forty-five more than Erica had. She knew she could just order and then give the cashier her name and it would all be free but she just couldn't do it.

"Do ya want lunch or don't ya?" Erica shook her head no and said thanks anyway and walked away. She knew she could make it through the rest of the day without food. She'd done it many times before. But she started feeling sorry for herself again, which felt both good and pathetic at the same time. She knew it was unproductive but she couldn't seem to help it, so she indulged in self pity for a minute or two and then, just as quickly as she'd immersed herself in it, she began to climb out of it, telling herself that life wasn't so bad. She had a couple of nice friends and there had to be a way around this problem. One thing Erica knew about herself, she wasn't one to dwell on the bad for too long. She would indulge her need for self-pity, quickly become disgusted with it, and then get over it. Usually in short order.

She left the lunchroom and headed out to the courtyard, which was just outside, between buildings. "Hey, where ya been?" a voice asked. Erica looked around and at first saw no one. "Over here!" She squinted in the noon sun, and once her eyes had adjusted, saw Lacy sitting on a bench by herself. Erica had completely forgotten about meeting her for lunch. She walked over.

"I looked for you in the lunchroom but I couldn't find you," Lacy said, smiling.

"Yeah sorry, I went to go get a locker before the good ones were gone. Did you already eat?"

"Yeah. Hey, did you get lunch yet?" Lacy asked her.

"Yeah but I wasn't very hungry." Not compared to say a concentration camp victim, anyway.

"Sit," Lacy said, moving down and making room for her. Erica sat and they talked about their classes and teachers. Lacy said that she had tried to get into the agreed upon classes but had had to take what she could get, having ended up at the end of the line. Erica explained what had happened in her homeroom during the class sign- up and they both thought what Mr. Simpson had done was good and fair, especially with Erica being so new and all. Lacy felt she should have been given such an opportunity, as well.

The bell rang and they were off to their respective classes, none of which were the same except sixth period Science. It was decided that they would see each other in sixth period and then walk to the bus together.

Erica walked to her fifth period class, Jazz Ensemble. Entering the room, she noticed that most of the students looked to be seniors and juniors. She walked in sheepishly and took an inconspicuous seat near the back. She had no clarinet so she hoped there wouldn't be any playing that day. Some of the people sitting nearby looked at her curiously then turned back to their conversations. The instructor walked in and the room fell quiet. He was kind of diminutive for a man. He had a moustache and his hair was getting gray. His beige suit was two sizes too big and he wore wire-rimmed glasses that were forever slipping down his skinny nose. He had a lock of salt and pepper hair that kept falling in his face, only to be raked back with a swift, tiny hand. He smiled in a way that suggested he really had nothing to smile about in his life but knew it was the right thing to do.

The class dragged on forever, finally ending with a bell and a whimper. Erica's whimper. She walked over to her sixth and final class, Science with Mr. Rice. Lacy was in that class, which now seemed like the light at the end of a very long, dark, sustenance-free tunnel. When Erica finally found the classroom, most everyone was already there and seated. She glanced around the room and found Lacy sitting towards the front middle. Lacy had saved the seat next to her for Erica. Thank God.

Looking around Erica saw Brad, the guy who had helped them with gas when they'd run out. She smiled at him and he smiled back at her. She turned back around to see the instructor for this, her final class of the day, walk in looking old and disheveled. He kind of shuffled his Hush Puppies up to the desk and sat heavily. If he was already this worn out on the first day, how was he ever going to make it through the entire year?

"Hello," He said weakly. "I'm Mr. Rice and this, as I'm sure you're aware, is 10th grade Science. Except for Mr. Keaton over there for whom this is eleventh grade Science. How goes it, Mr. Keaton?" he said mockingly. Everyone laughed and turned to look at the kid he'd referred to, a jockish kid with broad shoulders, sandy hair and a huge grin that seemed to convey either a great sense of humor or idiocy. Having gotten a good look, everyone turned back to the man at the front of class and to the matters at hand.

Mr. Rice began to drone on about the importance of science in everyday life such as medicine and travel and all of the creature comforts people took for granted. Erica was happy that both Brad and Lacy were in this class with her. She began writing on the margin of her notebook and turning it towards Lacy, something she'd often done in middle school and found to be a great way to communicate while pretending to listen and still not get caught. She wrote about her cute English teacher (Lacy had already heard about him), and how sorry she was that they'd not gotten more classes together. She wrote about the time Brad had helped them with the gas and she described what he looked like and where he sat in the class. Lacy couldn't help but turn around and look at him, even though Erica had specifically asked her not to do so.

The bell rang, and Lacy and Erica walked outside together. Erica lingered near the door trying to still be there when Brad walked out but he was in conversation with some kid at the time and didn't even notice her.

As they walked out to get on the bus, Erica noticed she

was starving, her stomach feeling like it was eating itself, but she dared not confess this for fear of lunch questions so she suffered in silence. They climbed aboard the good ship Lollypop. They'd gotten a bit of a jump on the other riders so the two of them were nearly the first to light upon the bus, save for a few dorks (for whom a choice seat on the bus was second only to a re-viewing of Star Wars) and the handful of elementary kids who'd been picked up prior, among whom was Erica's little sister Ellie, looking forlorn and sad. She'd been crying, one could tell by the streaks running down her face that she had neglected to wipe away and the fact that she was still crying. Ellie sat in the same seat she'd ridden into town. Erica stopped to ask what was wrong.

"Nothing!" she said loudly, turning her little face towards the window dramatically. A lone tear traced down her pudgy cheek where it sat contemplating for a split second then jumped to the neckline of her blouse. Erica debated briefly whether she should sit with her instead but, knowing that she'd shun her at this point, (Ellie being as stubborn as a blood stain), she elected to stick to her original plan and sit with Lacy.

She walked back the three seats to where Lacy sat waiting for her. "What's wrong with your sister?"

"Who knows?"

"Maybe you should sit with her or ask her to sit with us."

"She'd never do that. She's too upset. She'll just pout for the next hour or so."

"Oh."

They talked at length about their classes and the boys in those classes. Lacy already liked a boy in one of her classes. Erica worried that maybe she'd end up being one of those girls that always has a crush and never stops talking about it. She hoped not. Katie got on board. "What's wrong with Ellie?" she asked.

"I don't know. She's always crying about something. She wouldn't talk to me when I tried to find out."

"I feel sorry for her. No friends here or anything," Lacy said.

"Yeah, she's so young," Katie agreed. Erica sometimes forgot that Ellie was only ten. Katie got up and walked over to where Ellie was sitting nudged up against the window as if afraid she'd fall off the other side and down a precipice. Katie sat next to her and began to talk but neither Lacy nor Erica could make out what was being said. Katie seemed to be asking questions and Ellie would respond to her with long tearful answers during which Katie kept nodding her head, interjecting something here and there. Eventually Katie stood up and Ellie watched her as she walked back towards the others.

"I asked her if she'd like to come sit with us but she said you didn't want her to," she said to Erica.

"I never said that!" she protested. "She can sit here with us if she wants."

Katie walked back to Ellie' seat and said a few words and then headed back with Ellie a few steps behind. Katie sat in her seat and then Ellie slid in next to her. Erica turned around to address Ellie, "I never said you couldn't sit here," she said. Ellie just looked away. "How was school?" Erica asked her, trying to make light of the situation. "Fine," she said curtly.

"She doesn't know anyone and she didn't make any friends today," Katie said.

"Well, it is awfully soon, Ellie. It's only the first day," Erica said encouragingly. She was being a lot nicer to Ellie around her friends than she ever would have been at home because she knew they felt so sorry for her. She also knew she would look like a real bitch if she wasn't sympathetic. If they only knew what a brat Ellie was!

"That's easy for you to say! You already have two friends! I don't have any here!"

"You will," Lacy said gently. Katie just nodded her head.

"She's only being nice to me 'cuz yer here," Ellie whined, looking at Erica. She was trying to turn them against her! What an ungrateful little shit! This is why she hated her! She knew she had to choose her words carefully here so as not to get them to feel even more sorry for her younger sister and begin to vilify Erica.

"Shut up you little shit!" Erica said contemptuously. So much for discretion. Well, the hell with her, the little manipulator!

Several kids came on board, Erica recognized some of them from her classes. She wondered if they'd ever end up studying together.

The bus filled up and the driver ascended the stairs and sat down. He started the engine and got on the p.a., yelling at everyone to take their seats. He then shifted into drive and began pulling out of the lot.

The ride home was grueling because Erica was pissed off at Ellie for trying to turn her friends against her and also because she was absolutely famished, which put her in an irritable mood. She and Lacy talked about school some more and she occasionally turned around and asked Katie a question about this or that. By the time they pulled into the lot to change buses they had exhausted several topics.

"So is Brad kind of tall and dark haired? Works at the gas station here?" Erica asked Katie.

"Yeah, his dad owns it. He's cute, isn't he?" she smiled

They all got out of the big bus and crossed the lot to the little bus, (which now seemed even smaller than it had that morning). The ride seemed longer than it had that morning, at least to Erica.

They dropped a few kids off here and there before finally reaching their stop at the top of the hill. Erica said goodbye to Lacy and got off. She stood and talked to Katie briefly while Ellie got off. Everyone said goodbye and headed for home.

Reaching their little trailer, Ellie ran ahead and bounded up the two stairs and into the front door, apparently completely over the angst that had so enveloped her just moments before.

Erica made herself a sandwich and wolfed it down in less time than it took to make. Feeling better, she went back into her shared bedroom, changed into her tennis shoes and took Alias for a walk, reassuring him throughout that, though school would take her away each day, she would always come back. She was certain he understood her.

Later that evening her mother asked Erica about the wedding. She wanted to know what she was planning to wear and how she felt about the whole thing. Erica thought her mother also wanted to talk to her about her own feelings. After all, he was the father of her children. Erica knew she had talked at length with Jillian about it. It had never occurred to her before that moment that her mother may still have had some feelings for her father. She'd just assumed her mother hated him for what he'd put her through, although she never said anything disparaging about him. She actually defended him whenever Erica said anything negative about him (which was a lot) but Erica always thought it was because her mother didn't feel it was appropriate to say anything negative about him to her children, not because she didn't have anything bad to say but because he was their father, at least technically, and she didn't want them to think ill of him.

Erica showed her mother what she planned to wear, floral chiffon dress that came to her knees and buttoned up to her clavicle. Her mother thought it was pretty and appropriate for a wedding. "What was your wedding dress like?" Erica asked carefully.

"Oh, it was simple but pretty. We didn't have much money but my mother indulged me a bit so she spent more on it than we really could afford. It was kind of creamy white with a sash at the waist and it was tea length, you know, to the ankle. I wore white gloves with it and a strand of pearls. It was nice."

"Did Dad like it?"

"Uh huh," she said quietly, looking up at the closet.

"How do you feel about this wedding?"

"Well, I guess I'd prefer he were marrying someone else. Someone who actually liked kids. Also, it makes me feel like we should have tried harder to work things out. You were right, I should have fought harder to keep it together. I was naïve and headstrong at the same time, not unlike yourself. You'll need to be careful and not make the same mistakes I made." She paused briefly. "We never should have gotten married, though. We had nothing in common except that both of our fathers were alcoholic and made everyone else miserable. That's what brought us together and it's what helped pull us apart."

"When do we leave for Bellevue?' Erica asked.

"Well, the wedding is Saturday afternoon and your dad wants you to be there by one, so we should probably leave here by, say ten or so."

"Oh. So then do we come back here the next day?"

"Of course, you have school Monday. We'll try to leave before three or four so as to be home before dark, Okay?"

"Okay. I hate most of Dad's friends. They act like we're low class or something."

"We are low class, dear," she smirked at her a little, then she smiled, "Just be polite and prove them wrong."

"Yeah," said Erica unconvinced.

Erica went to bed that night thinking about the events of the day. The various classes she'd gotten, the conversations with Lacy, Mr. Peters and her mother, and of course, the wedding. She fell asleep, utterly exhausted.

7

The rest of the school week went along pretty well as Ellie and Erica began to grow accustomed to the long bus rides and their new schools. Ellie made a friend who happened to live somewhat nearby. She lived in a large log cabin on the river, about two miles away. Close enough to ride a bike but too far to walk really, especially with the days shortening so quickly. As Ellie had no bicycle, her mother had to drive back and forth to the girl's house several times a week, slowly befriending her mother who was married to a very scarce traveling salesman.

Erica spent most afternoons with Lacy those first several weeks. They would study Science together and chat about the boys and clothes. Erica saw Katie only occasionally because she had gotten her car started and had driven back and forth to school every day since, often staying in town to be with her friends after school.

Erica had dreaded the day that she would have to show Lacy where she lived but she knew it was unavoidable. So one day after school, she just took her there and got it over with- like ripping off a Band-aid laid over hairy skin: quick and painful. She was polite, saying hello to her mother and complimenting the few nice things about the place. Erica was embarrassed and anxious to leave as soon as they'd gotten there so they didn't stay long, electing to walk down to the café while the weather still allowed it. On the way down Lacy tried to reassure her that the trailer wasn't so bad and that she was certain someday Erica would live in a palace. Erica thanked her for lying so convincingly and they moved on to more pressing matters, namely Lacy's latest crush, an intellectual type from her English class whom she admitted was not conventionally attractive but by whom she was nonetheless enchanted.

Erica liked her classes well enough, even Mr. Simpson hadn't turned out to be so bad after all. He was kind of creepy, though, in that he seemed like he could be a pervert. She wondered if she'd have felt that way had the idea not previously been planted so emphatically by Katie.

That first week of school Erica spent a great deal of time thinking about what it would be like going back to Seattle. Would people be happy to see her? Would her dad talk to her much? Would anyone?

Saturday arrived and Erica woke up in a good mood. Although she dreaded going to the wedding, she was still anxious, nervous and excited to go back to civilization and see everyone. Even though she was not looking forward to seeing all of those people getting drunk and asking questions they didn't really care to know the answers to, she was looking forward to going back and seeing everyone. She hoped she'd get the chance to see her old larcenous friend Marcy.

One thing she was not looking forward to was seeing Karen, her father's betrothed. Erica knew Karen would give her a hard time about needing a haircut or an iron or a manicure. Karen always found something to criticize about Erica. Erica determined to avoid her.

The drive over was uneventful and Erica slept a good part of the way. They pulled in to some country club and their mother, looking tired and a little sad, kissed her young daughters, waited for them to get their bags, and bid them good luck before she drove away. Her mother never mentioned it and Erica never asked but dropping her two young children off to attend her ex-husband's wedding could not have been easy for her. Only later in life did Erica come to appreciate the courage it must have taken for her mother to do so without so much as a tear or a disparaging word.

Erica and Ellie went inside and found the dressing room where they quickly got dressed. The wedding would start soon and Erica did not want to be accused of being tardy as well as foolish and unkempt.

The club was nice. It had a big pool and a pretty restaurant that overlooked the lake. There were tennis courts strewn around, here and there. The wedding itself was outside, under a tent. There were already lots of people there by the time the two girls found their way outside. Some guy in a black tuxedo took one of Erica's arms and one of Ellie's and escorted them to their seats, which were surprisingly near the front.

The weather was beautiful and warm. There was a quartet playing something classical and people were beginning to quiet down in anticipation. Then a hush fell over the crowd as Karen appeared with some man in a tuxedo. They walked up the aisle towards Erica's father who was standing up at the front with the minister, both smiling.

"Who giveth Karen James away on this day?"

"Her father," the man next to Karen said and he pulled away and sat down.

Karen had on a short ivory dress and a fishnet veil. Erica's father wore a black tuxedo. Karen reached where he stood and they both turned to face the minister. The rest was a blur for Erica, save for the part about love not being selfish where Erica had to stifle a laugh. It was over before it began and everyone made a beeline for the bar. It was some enchanted afternoon.

Erica meandered up to the buffet and found something edible, which she took to a chair hidden back behind the stage where no one was likely to find her. She ate a little but struggled to swallow due to an unexplained lump the size of a child's fist in her throat. She listened to the conversations she could make out, but, not recognizing the voices, she found them boring. After about ten minutes of sitting there, she overheard a man and a woman talking. They must have sat down near the stage because she could hear them pretty clearly. The man was saying something about children and a divorce and the woman was trying to make a point about something she'd heard.

"Frank, yes, I understand divorce happens but nevertheless."

"He seems happy with her," the man said.

"What does that have to do with anything? Don't you remember what she said about his children? I mean, she actually said that she didn't allow the kids to come over without prior permission. Remember she called them scavengers? Remember?"

"She said that?"

"Don't you remember?!"

"Wow! She's in for a rude awakening."

"I don't know. I didn't hear him protesting."

"Well, the kids are here today, aren't they?"

"Who?"

"The kids, his kids. Who else?"

"Yes, but that may be just for show."

"How old are they?" He asked.

"I'm not sure, maybe nine and twelve."

"That's too bad," the man said.

Erica listened a while longer, fascinated, but they soon moved on to other topics and she again grew bored sitting there all by her lonesome. Eventually she left the protection of her little spot and headed for the ladies room whereupon she found some women she didn't know chatting in front of the mirror. They seemed to be between topics just then and there was an awkward silence.

"Hello Erica. Nice wedding, wasn't it?"

"Uh huh." she said politely.

"So how long are you in town for?" one woman asked. She seemed to know Erica but Erica had no idea who she was.

"Just 'til tomorrow."

"Well, won't that be nice for you?" she said condescendingly. What did that mean? Erica wondered.

"Uh huh," was all she could think to say in all her confusion.

The women departed and Erica briefly had the room to herself. She looked in the mirror and realized that she really needed to fix her hair. She had no hairbrush but one had been provided so she used that, brushing her hair out and making it shiny again. She was lucky in that she did have good hair. Unfortunately her luck had stopped there, as far as she was concerned. She peered into her watery blue eyes. They had potential. Her skin was still tan and her nose slightly pink but not too pink. She looked okay. No boobs yet, though.

Someone came in and broke her stare so she left. She

walked out to the main ballroom where all the guests were milling around talking, drinking and eating. Erica could see her father standing with Karen at the other end of the large room. They were talking to another couple in line. She watched as that couple moved on and the couple behind them came up to talk. Erica realized that it was a receiving line. She meandered through the crowd, still seeing no one she knew. Looking outside she saw Ellie running around on the huge lawn with some other kids. The sun lighting up her white-blonde hair like a big florescent bulb. Erica walked outside and sat on a bench as she squinted in the bright sunlight. She wished she'd brought her sunglasses.

After a while Erica decided she'd better go in and at least say hello to her father and Karen. She walked in out of the sun and waited for her eyes to adjust to the comparatively dim room. She saw that Karen and her father were over near the cake now and she made her way over. "Hi Dad," she said brightly.

Both Karen and her dad shooshed her with their hands as they smiled for the camera, which Erica just then noticed. The photographer took a few pictures and they then stood up straight and turned towards the cake. They cut it together and everyone watching clapped so Erica clapped nervously, as well.

Eventually her dad turned around. "Erica!" he threw at her. C'mere. Gimme a hug! How'd you like the wedding? Nice, huh?"

"Yes, very nice," she said politely.

"You look nice. Doesn't Karen look beautiful?"

"Yes, she does. I mean, you do. Congratulations."

Karen nodded and smiled. Then she turned to talk to her

new husband and Erica became invisible. She walked away without their noticing. She decided to try to find a phone to call her mother. Maybe she could come and get them early and they could go back home that night. Finding a phone became a mission for her once she realized just how badly she wanted to get the hell out of there. She didn't know anyone. Hadn't really spoken to anyone and hadn't much enjoyed the little conversation she had had.

She finally found a phone tucked away near the men's bar and she dialed information. They gave her the number for the Motel 6 where her mother was staying and she dialed it.

"Motel Six"

"Hello, hi. I am trying to reach my mom who's staying there. Her name is Jean Tambo. I don't know which room she's in."

"I'll ring that room for you. Please hold." Muzac came on for about a minute.

"Sorry, no answer in that room. Can I take a message?"

Erica thought about this option for a second or two, and then noticed there was a number on the face of the phone. "Yes, please have her call Erica right away at 425-817-0675."

"I'll give her the message when she returns."

"Okay, thanks. Bye."

Erica loitered by the phone for a while, hoping for a ring and getting none. Finally she tired of waiting and wandered off towards the main dining room where most of the guests had congealed like blood to a wound. She saw people in various conversations and she could see her dad and his new bride standing at the far end of the room, talking to another couple that she didn't recognize. She didn't know where to go or who to talk to. She was disappointed that there weren't more people she knew. She looked around and saw no one she knew well enough to go up and talk to. She felt just as invisible out in the open as she had behind the stage, listening to other people's conversations. No one saw her and she did not exist. Like a phantom she could knock over the entire buffet and no one would be the wiser. Like Ellison's 'Invisible Man' she was there but she was not seen and she was not seen because she was not acknowledged.

Erica decided to go back to where the phone sat not ringing (funny how she suddenly really needed her mother, she actually couldn't wait to see her and how often did she feel that way anymore?) She sat down in the tiny cushioned chair provided near the phone and waited. She could feel the tears welling up in her eyes and she was angry because she didn't want to cry. She wanted to cry to her mother. She wanted to cry in private, but not there. She wasn't even sure why she was crying in the first place.

The phone suddenly rang. It jarred her and at first she didn't even know what it was. She grabbed it and fumbled it like a garden hose gone loose, finally getting a grip on the thing. "Hello?"

"Erica," and the dam broke and the tears flowed, her throat constricting, her voice wavering. "Mommy?"

"Hi! What's the matter? It can't be over yet."

She felt her throat tighten, her speech unrecognizably garbled, "Could…Could…you please come get me please?"

"What's wrong, Honey?"

"I just wanna go home. Please?"

"Where's Ellie?"

"I don't know. Please can you come now?"

"Okay. I can be there in about twenty minutes. See if you

can find your sister and if she wants to go, too. If not, I guess I can come get her later."

"Kay," Erica said quietly. She felt exhausted from crying but relieved to have her mother coming soon and to be getting out of there.

"Alright. I'll be there shortly. Find Ellie and meet me in front where I dropped you. Okay?"

"Okay."

Erica hung up and continued crying for a few minutes. She didn't want anyone to see her for fear of being accused of creating a scene so she stood up facing the wall and stayed turned towards it as she walked to the ladies room where she proceeded to dart into an empty stall and tried to compose herself.

"Erica?" It was her sister Ellie "Whatsa matter?"

Erica said nothing, hoping Ellie would think she was mistaken and go away.

"Erica! I know you're in there! I saw you walk in, you idiot."

"Whadaya want?"

"Are you crying?"

"No!"

"You are so! What's wrong?"

"Nothing!"

"Then why are you crying?"

"Leave me alone!"

"Well, you better stop."

"I know! Mom is picking us up out front in about ten minutes. Otherwise, if you wanna stay, she'll come get you later."

"Why are you leaving?"

"Cuz I want to. Are you coming or not?"

"No! I'll stay at Dad's, tell her."

"Fine," Erica said curtly. She just wanted to be left alone.

Erica heard the restroom door open and close. She crept out slowly, making sure no one was there. She looked in the mirror only to see a reddish, tear-streaked face staring back at her. The little bit of mascara she had applied that morning had become a thin black stream down her cheeks and neck, dried up like a narrow creek in the middle of a drought. Her lips, nose and eyes were swollen and red and her eyes stung from so many salty tears. She looked a fright. She splashed cold water on her face and re-brushed her now limp hair. She used a wet Kleenex to wipe off the caked mascara. Fresh tears began appearing as pools in her eyes but she wiped them away before they could fall, willing herself to stop already.

When she felt somewhat presentable again she left the ladies room and dashed quickly up the nearby stairwell leading outside. The bright late day sun hit her full in the face and she could scarcely see for a few seconds as her already sore eyes adjusted to yet another indignity. She sat on the cement wall encircling the turn-around drive. She again wished she'd thought to bring her sunglasses. A few minutes later Ellie showed up, standing directly in front of her, blocking the direct sun and temporarily relieving Erica's eyes.

"Dad's gonna be pissed you left so early."

"He won't even notice. Your staying then, I take it?"

"Yeah!" she said with obvious disdain.

Just then their mother's car drove up, which, under any other circumstances would have embarrassed Erica to no end but, on this day, it was a welcomed sight. She stood up, walked over and began opening the passenger door well before the car had an opportunity to stop. She slid in and shut the door, sinking down into the seat as if to hide. Ellie went over to her mother's side of the car as she rolled down her window. "Aren't you coming?"

"No! Nobody's leaving yet, except her," She said disgustedly.

"How'd it go?"

"Can't we just leave?" Erica begged, looking at her for the first time since she'd gotten in. She looked somewhat cheerful and, for a split second, Erica wondered if maybe calling her mother and asking her to come so soon had made her feel needed.

"Okay. Okay. We're going. So you're going home with your father, right?' she said to Ellie.

"Yeah."

"Okay, I'll call you there. Let him know Erica's with me. Bye Honey. Have fun."

She watched her youngest child as she walked back into the club and then they pulled away. As they drove out the gate Erica felt a tremendous sense of relief and she was never so happy to be alone with her mother in her entire life. Her mother began asking questions about the wedding, which she answered monosyllabically until, flabbergasted, her mother finally complained and insisted that Erica go into more detail. Her mother's mock irritation cheered her and she was able to forget her misery for a moment and talk about what had transgressed. She told her about the walk down the aisle and all of the people there. She grew a bit quiet as Erica spoke and that made Erica feel a bit funny relating all of this to her but she had insisted.

They reached the motel and Erica got out, only then

realizing that she had forgotten her bag at the club. She went in to the lobby and asked if she might use the phone. She called the club and asked if they could get her bag and leave it at the front desk. Erica waited on the line as the girl went to fetch it. "Here it is. I've got it." the girl said breathlessly.

"Great. Thanks." Erica said relieved that she wouldn't have to sleep in what she was wearing.

Her mother, perhaps sensing that she would rather die than go back there, volunteered to go pick it up for her and Erica loved her for that. She *would* rather have died than go back there for her bag. Certainly she'd rather have done without it. The thought of seeing any more of those people at that point was simply more than she could stand.

Her mother took her to the tiny room they'd be sharing for the night and then left to retrieve the bag. She returned, bag in hand, almost before she'd left. It was starting to get dark and Erica was exhausted so she changed into her cotton drawstring pajamas with matching powder blue top and then sat on one of the two twin beds to watch TV with her mother, there being nothing else to sit on but a tiny wooden chair in the corner.

"So what on earth upset you so badly?" her mother asked. Erica explained that she had just felt very unhappy there and that no one talked to her and that she couldn't wait to leave, especially once she'd begun crying. "But why were you so upset?"

"I just told you."

"But you were so upset. Did someone say something to you? Was it Karen?"

"No! That's just it. No one said anything to me. I felt invisible, like I wasn't even there!"

"Didn't you talk to anyone you know? What about your dad?"

126

"Barely. He just said how great Karen looked."

"Well, maybe they were just caught up in the moment," she said gently.

"Sure."

"Well, tell me more. What was it like? Was it a nice ceremony?'

"It was okay. She wore a short dress with a veil."

Erica didn't want to talk about the wedding anymore so she deliberately changed the subject to their return trip, asking when it was to take place.

"I thought we'd shoot for around noonish, okay?" her mother replied.

"Okay."

"Well, I'm sorry you had such a terrible time, Erica."

"Could it be that you just didn't want them to get married?" her mother asked a little while later, broaching the subject yet again.

"That's not it. I'm just tired of feeling left out all the time."

"Well, you do kind of keep to yourself a lot."

"So?"

"So, maybe if you were more outgoing and talkative..."

"I talk!" she said indignantly.

"I know you talk. I mean you should smile more, engage people. Don't assume they don't want to talk to you."

"I don't assume that!"

Erica quickly grew very tired and laid her head down on the pillow. She overheard her mom on the phone with Ellie, asking her if she'd had a nice time and then defending Erica for having left so early and being so upset at the wedding.

"Ok. Good night, Honey." I'll see you in the morning,"

her mother said gently. She hung up. Then Erica heard her pick up the phone and dial it again.

"So, as I was saying, I have been feeling very tired of late and I spent most of the day in bed. I only went out to get some lunch and later to pick Erica up from the wedding."

"…Of course it was! Very difficult," her voice cracked a bit and Erica thought she might be starting to cry. "Well, Erica said she wore a short white dress with a veil…Yes, I agree, she should have worn something with color instead… Yes, they did for a year or so…not as far as I know or that he ever admitted to…Erica said she didn't say anything to her. I don't know about Ellie…She's fine, staying with her dad and his new wife, I guess…Feels weird to say that…Anyway, I am feeling just exhausted tonight so I'm going to let you go, if it's okay…Okay, talk to you then…Bye" and she hung up the phone. Erica heard her mother sigh a kind of pained sigh. She readjusted herself in the bed and turned out the light. As she fell asleep, Erica thought she heard her mother crying but she wasn't sure.

Erica lay in bed, looking at the flowery pictures hanging on the walls and the ugly floral bedspread rolled back at the foot of the bed. The room was completely devoid of charm, just a muddy oatmeal and purple slur. Erica's thoughts returned to that day and the wedding. How odd it had been that she had scarcely spoken to anyone. She'd barely even spoken with her own father and not at all to any of the relatives. Not a word to them, nor them to her. Nor had she cared to, mainly because she barely knew them, just an aunt here and a cousin there but no one she'd really spent any time with. They were related but the connection ended there. Laying there in that dreary room awaiting sleep she realized that, while they had all ignored her, she had avoided all of them and that there was a certain strength in not trying to be liked and not trying to please people, in not even talking at all. She felt somewhat empowered with this thought and decided that she would, theretofore, opt for indifference with anyone who tried to make her feel small and inconsequential. With that resolution, she fell asleep.

The next day Erica awoke to the sun streaming in through a narrow crack in the faded floral curtains which mostly covered the window and matched the hideous bedspread. She looked over and saw that her mother was already up. Erica could smell her mother's coffee but she did not see her anywhere so she poked her head out the front door and there she was, sitting outside the door on the little wooden chair from the room, sipping her coffee and reading the paper.

"Morning," Erica said in a broken, sleepy voice.

"Oh, good morning, Sleepyhead!"

"What time is it?"

"bout nine"

"Wow! I guess I was tired. Now I'm starving. Can we get breakfast soon?"

"Sure. Why don't you go in and get dressed and we'll get going, okay?"

They went to a cute little café near the mall and Erica ate like a brontosaurus. Her mother just marveled.

"So I was reading an article this morning about this new disease called AIDS. It can be spread through the air and by touching someone who has it and it's fatal and incurable," she said.

Erica's mother was forever quoting articles she'd read about the environment, medicine and politics, always managing to stay on top of current events. It made for some interesting, if somewhat disturbing, conversations.

"We're picking up Ellie at eleven-thirty so we have some time."

"What time is it?"

"It's about ten."

"I thought you and I could go to Seattle and look around," her mother said rather weakly.

"You mean and not buy anything?"

"You don't have to be bratty. I just thought it might be nice, while we're here."

"Okay," Erica said, realizing that she was being a brat.

They got back in their little Pinto, (which Erica noticed could really use a wash), and her mother aimed the car towards the freeway and downtown. Being that it was Sunday, parking was impossible and they found themselves walking several blocks to get to Pike Place Market. Once there, they looked at the people and bought a little fruit here and there. The weather was clear and warm and the mountains were in full view.

"Do you mind if we sit for a while? I'm feeling a little tired," her mother said. Erica just shrugged. She's always tired, she thought.

They sat outside on a bench in a park, eating fruit and watching the ferries go by on Puget Sound. It was a nice day and Erica was sorry when they had to leave to pick up Ellie.

On the drive back Erica remembered that she thought she heard her mother crying the night before. "Were you upset about the wedding last night?" Her mother nodded her head.

"It's been difficult for me. I mean, there is no question that your father and I married too young and for all the wrong reasons, but I still have feelings for him because he's

130

the father of my children. I know you can't understand that."
And she was right, Erica could not understand.

They picked up Ellie and drove the long way home
because, as her mother put it, "It was far too beautiful of a
day to spend on an ugly freeway."

Once home, they unloaded the car and went inside.
Erica had asked Katie to come by and let Alias out and feed
him while they were away, in return for which she gave her
a black and white polka-dotted top that Katie loved. Alias
came running out and went straight for the bushes to relieve
himself so Erica questioned how consistent her friend had
been. She decided to take Alias on a nice walk just in case
Katie hadn't been by.

When she reached home her mother was there but not
Ellie. Ellie had gone to Katie's to borrow some mayonnaise for
tuna sandwiches. Erica proceeded into her room with Alias
and sat on her bed to start her homework. She was in there
working for about thirty minutes when Ellie burst through
the front door, out of breath and screaming something about
a bear. Erica went out to the living room to see what all the
commotion was about. Ellie looked positively terrified, her
eyes wild, her hair matted with sweat from running. She'd
seen a bear, a big, brown bear.

"Where?" Erica asked her.

"On…the way…home from Katie's… top of the trail!"
she said breathlessly.

"Holy shit!" Erica said.

"Erica!' her mother protested.

"Well! Did you know there were bears around here?" she
asked her mom.

"Well, I guess I assumed there would be bears in the area,

just not so close." She picked up the phone and began dialing. "Hello, Jillian?... Yeah I know, she just got back and she saw a bear! A big, brown bear!"... "No, on her way home, at the top of the trail...Oh...oh... okay, well, if that's the case then I guess we'll just...the garbage...Oh...so we shouldn't leave it out...I guess that makes sense. Alright, well, thanks. Okay, bye" and she hung up the phone.

"Well?" Erica asked.

"Jillian says that it's common to see a bear around here this time of year and that they'll soon be hibernating and not to go near them."

"No shit," Erica said.

"Erica!"

"Why didn't she tell us this before?" Ellie asked.

"She just assumed we knew," her mom said.

"Or she didn't want you to change your mind about moving here," Erica said

"Anyway," she said with a dismissive shake of the head, "We can't leave garbage out anymore or they'll smell it and come up here. Erica, will you go haul in the garbage, please?"

"What? Where are we going to put it?" she asked incredulously.

"We'll have to leave it inside for now and I'll take it to the bin tomorrow."

"Great," Erica said sarcastically, stepping outside. She brought it all in and stowed it under the table. Oh well, she thought, better to live with a little garbage than a lot of bear.

That night they had tuna sandwiches, watched a little television and talked of the wedding. Ellie told her mom all about the cake and the people dancing and who she'd seen there. Erica just listened. Ellie tried to make her feel like she'd missed out by not staying and she made it clear that everyone thought it weird that she had left so early and that she'd been crying (apparently it hadn't gone unnoticed as she'd hoped, so much for being invisible!). Ellie went on to say that everyone was asking if she was okay and that she'd made a fool of herself and that it had been embarrassing for all of them. Had her mom not been there Erica would have beaten the crap out of her, but alas, she was, so Erica held back, choosing instead to go to bed early. Erica always went to bed early when she felt down about something. It was comforting for her, lying down, hugging a pillow and thinking. She supposed it made her feel protected and warm when she needed it. So there she was, lying in bed and thinking about what Ellie had said, fresh tears streaking down her face, dampening her pillow. When would she ever stop crying?

Sleep eluded her that night for quite some time, fatigue finally outwitting distress and coaxing slumber. She dreamed that men in tuxedos and women in white gowns threw her in a lake and were pushing her under the water, holding her down. She tried to scream but nothing came out. She couldn't remember anything else then.

8

It was September and the weather had begun to change. It was a little more crisp in the morning and it got dark a little earlier at night. Erica was finally getting used to her new school as well as the long bus ride to and from every day. She was happy to have made friends with both Katie and Lacy and was relieved that they lived nearby because it promised to be a long, cold winter. There were some people in school with whom she got along but had yet to make any extracurricular plans. And Brad was in a few of her classes. Brad was very popular (one figures out who's who in high school pretty quickly). He was all-American cute and he smiled constantly, flashing his white teeth and deep dimples. He sat next to her in Science, purely because he'd been assigned to sit there and be her lab partner. However, Erica chose to see it as fate. He often asked her opinion about whatever assignment they'd been given and she would try her best to give him an intelligent response, often failing miserably. He would just listen to her and smile, nodding his head, making her feel important. She found herself thinking about him a lot, especially when she was deciding what to wear to school each morning. It became of utmost importance to her that he think she was pretty. She began to notice when his name would come up and due to his overwhelming popularity, it often did.

One day, in early October, Erica was in the girl's locker room when she overheard two girls talking about him. She recognized the girls but did not know them. She had seen them come in and she could hear them clearly because she was just one aisle away and yet hidden from sight. Ever the eavesdropper, she listened intently:

"I hear he likes Erica."

"Really? Well, I guess that fits. She's pretty."

"I thought he was seeing Jill."

"No, they broke up."

Their voices trailed off as they headed outside so that was all Erica got. Had she heard correctly? She couldn't believe it! He'd actually told people he liked her? Wow. So it wasn't just her imagination! She peeked around the corner to make certain they'd left. They had. She walked out into the breezeway, her feet, it seemed, were not touching ground.

For the next week or so she waited for Brad to say something to her about getting together, perhaps for a Coke or to go to a football game. Anything. But he never did. He just smiled and asked her opinion on class work. She would occasionally overhear people ask him who he was taking to the Homecoming dance in November. He'd always avoid their question, never giving anything away, just smiling his winning smile and flashing his rolling dice teeth. Two weeks went by and still nothing.

While on a walk with Lacy one day, Erica asked her what she thought.

"Well, you're sure they said he liked you?"

"Positive."

"But he hasn't said anything?"

"No, but he always talks to me and asks me questions. He acts like he likes me, you know, smiling at me all the time. I just get this feeling he does."

"Plus what you overheard."

"Well, yeah! But he hasn't said anything about Homecoming or anything."

"Well, I'm sure he'll come around eventually," Lacy said reassuringly.

"Are you going to Homecoming?" Erica asked.

"Yeah, Andy asked me and I said yes."

"Oh. He did? You must be happy about that."

"Yeah, but I kinda like David now."

"You're fickle!" said Erica with a smirk.

"Yeah, I know," Lacy replied breaking into her gorgeous smile.

They made their way back to Lacy's house where they sat in the living room and watched TV until her father came in and changed the channel to a football game. Erica took this as a cue to leave and quickly made her exit. The walk home was definitely chilly and she wished she'd had brought a warmer jacket.

Right around this time, about a month or so into the school year, the little bus was on its way to meet the larger bus when it made an unexpected stop at the bottom of the hill near the café. Everyone looked around at each other and then out the window to see why they were stopping. After what felt like a very long time punctuated by the bus driver occasionally honking, a figure came running out of the little yellow house that sat a few hundred feet off the road. This house had always intrigued Erica because it was so cute. It was surrounded by property that contained a corral, a barn and, recently, some horses. She'd always wondered who lived there and was about to find out. Watching the figure run towards the bus she realized that it was a girl with long blond hair wearing a red down jacket and really tight jeans. As she got closer Erica began to recognize her. She realized it was the waitress that Katie knew. The one she'd said was really slutty. Erica noticed she was wearing cowboy boots and, once on the bus, her open jacket revealed a huge silver belt buckle and a plaid flannel shirt unbuttoned to reveal more cleavage than Erica had ever seen. The girl was breathless and, smiling a crooked smile, took a seat near the front. Everyone stared. She sat down right in front of Lacy and Erica and immediately turned around and spoke.

"Hey, I know you! Yer Katie's friend," she said. "Erica, right?"

"Uh huh," was all Erica could think to say.

"I'm Jenna, remember?" she said smiling broadly.

After a few minutes of bouncing on the country roads, the bus pulled in to the vacant lot and everyone unloaded from the small bus and re-loaded on to the larger bus. Erica sat next to Lacy as usual and Jenna again sat just in front of them by herself. She looked out the window for a bit and then, just as the bus began to pull away, she turned to Lacy and said in a low- pitched Southern drawl, "What's yer name?"

Somewhat stunned at first, Lacy, finding her composure, said "Lacy. Lacy Edwin."

"Howdy," Jenna said with a nod. "You're new huh? When did you move here?"

"We both just moved here this summer," said Lacy struggling to not stare at Jenna's open flannel shirt.

"We lived in town last year and just moved out here. It's

the goddamn boonies out here! My dad just got back in town. He's been in Cle Elem for the last month or so. My dad trains horses. Race horses. We race all over, California, Oregon. Where y'all from?"

"I'm from Bellevue and Lacy's from all over," Erica explained.

"Oh yeah? Me too. I lived in California before movin' to Cle Elem. I like California better but I gotta follow my dad and this is where he came. So you guys date'n anyone? I got a boyfriend. He's gonna come visit me all next week when my dad's outta town. He works at a lumber mill. He's twenty-two."

"I'm not going with anyone," Erica volunteered.

"How 'bout you, Lacy?" the girl asked with a half smirk.

"I'm going to Homecoming with Andy, this guy in my English class," Lacy said demurely.

"Now she likes David, though," Erica said, shaking her head.

"Is he cute?" Jenna asked pulling out a wallet sized photo. "Cute as this?" she asked holding up a picture of a blonde man with big teeth and tan skin. He looked younger than twenty-two.

"Oh, he is cute!" Lacy said.

"Yup! And he's all mine. I sure miss him. My dad hates him so we hafta wait until next week when my dad hasta be in Cle Elem. Then my guy's gonna come stay with me all week. He buys beer, too."

"How old are you?" Lacy asked incredulously.

"I'm seventeen next month, start'n eleventh grade. What 'bout you?"

"Erica and I are in the tenth grade, we're both going to be sixteen soon."

"My dad's gonna take me in to get my license when he gets back," Jenna bragged.

"How come you aren't already driving?" Erica asked.

"My dad keeps putting it off," she said with a frown.

The three girls talked the rest of the way to school with Erica asking Jenna all about her horses and her boyfriend. Jenna did most of the talking. Jenna liked to talk, mostly about herself. Actually, she liked to brag. She bragged extensively about her dad, who was evidently a larger than life cowboy. She bragged about her boyfriend, her horse, her ability to attract the opposite sex, anything and everything. By the time they'd finally reached the school Erica was captivated by Jenna's seemingly glamorous life. She found her to be loud and histrionic and yet intriguing at the same time. She hoped they could be friends, although she wasn't sure why.

Erica went to her morning classes as usual then headed for the lunchroom. She was curious to see if Jenna would be there. Erica went to the end of the line and waited her turn while anxiously looking around for Jenna. She had made arrangements with the lunchroom cashier a few weeks prior so she didn't have to be embarrassed in line. Erica could get her lunch from the lunch counter like everyone else, then, when it came time to pay, she'd give the woman twenty-five cents (lifted from her mother's unsuspecting purse), which the woman kept for herself. That way, Erica appeared to be paying full price for her lunch while actually saving fifty cents a day. Plus, she had the satisfaction of having corrupted the staff. Lacy walked in just as Erica was attempting to find a seat.

"Hi!" she said brightly.

"Hi."

"Where are you gonna sit?" Erica shrugged in response

looking around the crowded room. "How about over there?" She pointed to a table only half full near the back door.

"Okay, I'll see you in a minute." Lacy went off to get her lunch and Erica walked over to the table. She'd always felt awkward eating alone so she took out her book, Joseph Heller's *Catch 22*, and began reading while working on her turkey and cheese sandwich.

"Hey, hey!" a voice said to her left. Erica looked up to find Jenna looking down at her and smiling her crooked smile. "Okay if I sit with you?' she asked while taking a seat. Erica nodded.

"I didn't bring no money today so I don't get to eat nothin," she said feigning sorrow with an exaggerated frown. Erica marveled at her excessive use of double negatives and wondered if it wasn't an act.

"Well I'd loan it to you if I had it, but I don't have any money on me today either. You can have some of my sandwich if you want," Erica said feeling generous.

"Don't you want it?"

"I'm okay with half. Here," she said handing Jenna the other half. Jenna took it and thanked her with a shrug.

Lacy came over, said hello to Jenna and sat next to Erica. "So how are your classes?" she asked.

"Fine. I got a coupla classes I didn't want and I'm havin some trouble in math."

"When do you think your dad will take you to get your license?" Erica asked.

"Probly not until he's back from his trip next month." Jenna said with her mouth full.

"Too bad," Lacy said. All Erica could think was how this postponed her plans to bum rides to and from town from Jenna. Jenna had already bragged about her Dad giving her his old car to drive. Now it would sit idle while they sat on the stupid school bus day in and day out. It was bad enough she couldn't ride in with Katie each morning.

"Hey, do you think Brad's gonna ask you today?" Lacy asked her.

"I don't know," Erica responded throwing her hands up.

"I think he'll ask today," Lacy said, ever the optimist.

"Who's Brad?" Jenna asked.

"He's in our Science class and she's waiting for him to ask her to Homecoming."

"Hey, I've got an idea…why don't you ask him? Guys love that," Jenna suggested.

"No way!" Erica said.

"Why not?"

"Because, I'd be too embarrassed. Besides, what if he said no?" Erica's heart started pounding just thinking about it.

"Maybe he's worried that *you'd* say no," Lacy said.

"I don't think so," said Erica.

"What does he look like?" Jenna asked. Erica described him a little, not wanting to sound too enamored.

"I agree with Lacy. You should ask him," Jenna said . Erica just shook her head.

The bell rang so they went their separate ways. Walking into her science class later that day, Erica felt nervous. She felt sure today would be the day. She took her seat next to Brad's empty chair, her hands feeling clammy and her heart racing. Brad walked in, smiling as usual, and took his seat just as the bell rang. He smiled at Erica and pulled his books out of his knapsack.

"So, you planning to go to Homecoming?" he asked, grinning at her.

"Um, I don't know. I haven't really decided yet." Here

it was! She waited for him to go on. Silence. "Are…you planning to go?" she asked sheepishly, her head down.

"I dunno. Maybe. We'll see."

The teacher walked in just then and began talking about the homework assignment. Erica pulled her books and listened to the instructions for the lab work. Brad took his books out and he and Erica began discussing their work. She was distracted by Brad's apparent indifference and had trouble concentrating. Why hadn't he asked yet? Was he just being cool?

"Miss Tambo?!" It was Mr. Rice, looking at her, acting flustered. He'd asked her something but she hadn't heard the question.

"Uh..um…Could you repeat the question?" Erica asked. Everybody laughed.

"Sure. It's a tough one. Could you read the first question for us, aloud. Page 19." he asked impatiently.

"Uh, sure." she was frantically flipping through the pages in her book trying to find page nineteen. She found it and began reading, her face red hot and her hands shaking with embarrassment.

When the class finally ended, she took her time leaving, pretending to get her books in order so she could time her exit with Brad's. He started out the door and she followed him. Nick Jamison was in the hall and saw Brad walk out. He yelled to him and they began walking and talking and that was that. Erica's heart sank as she headed for the bus. She didn't see Lacy so figured she must have already gotten on the bus.

Why hadn't he asked? She knew he liked her, what was he waiting for? She climbed aboard and glanced at Ellie who was sitting in her usual front row seat. Erica sat in her usual seat. The bus soon filled up and Lacy came aboard, then Jenna. Lacy sat down, looked at her and asked, "Well?"

"He didn't ask. He brought it up but never asked. He said he wasn't even sure he was gonna go." Erica said dejectedly.

"He brought it up? You mean Homecoming?"

"Yeah, he asked if I was planning to go and I told him I wasn't sure."

"And?"

"And, that was it. He never said another word about it."

"That's weird! Oh well, he may still ask. Maybe he'll call this weekend."

"Yeah," Erica said, unconvinced.

The bus eventually pulled away from the curb and began heading out of the parking lot. She was looking out the window and saw Brad still with Nick, walking to Nick's older brother Mike's car. Mike was a senior and drove to school every day. The younger boys would often bum a ride home. Erica didn't like Nick very much because he possessed such a superior attitude, as though he owned the town and what the hell was she doing there? Actually, according to Katie, his family did nearly own the town.

She watched Mike's car as it pulled out of the parking lot.

"Didn't ask yet, huh?" Jenna said her voice low. Erica just shook her head.

"You gotta ask him!" Jenna proclaimed loudly.

"No way!" Erica said, feeling she'd made her position abundantly clear at lunch.

"Whatever!" said Jenna, frustrated

Erica glanced up at Ellie who was sitting next to her friend Jennifer. They'd become inseparable by this point so Erica no longer had to hear about Ellie not having any friends. Thank God! Ellie and Erica pretended not to notice each other when on the bus but at home it was as it had always been; fighting one minute and laughing the next. Now that Ellie had a friend there was a lot less pressure on Erica to make her happy.

"You wanna come over for a little while?' Jenna asked both Lacy and Erica.

"I can't. My dad's expecting me," Lacy said.

"I can come, for a little while," Erica said.

The remaining kids transferred from the big bus to the little bus and, when they reached the foot of the hill where Jenna lived, Erica got off with her, telling Ellie to tell their mother she'd be home soon. She waved to Lacy who waved back reluctantly.

Following Jenna to her little house, Erica noticed how large the barn was and she wondered how many horses they had. Jenna opened the front door to the house and walked in, casually throwing her knapsack on a kitchen chair. The furniture was rugged looking. The chandelier was made from antlers and there were cowboy artifacts everywhere. All of it seemed out of place in such a small yellow rambler. Pictures of a blonde man with a scruffy beard wearing dirty jeans and standing next to various horses hung on the walls. It smelled a little musty but not bad. There was a good size kitchen and three small bedrooms. There was a large TV in the living room and two full sized bathrooms. Jenna showed Erica her room, which was a mess, the walls covered with pictures cut from magazines and her pine bed covered with clothes. Shoes were strewn about and her bed looked as though it hadn't been made in days, maybe even weeks.

"Have a seat," she said, pushing a load of clothing off the bed onto the floor. Erica looked around at Jenna's pictures, mostly of men and horses. Men and horses, that pretty much summed up Jenna's life.

"Can we go look at your horses? I'd love to see them."

"Okay," she shrugged, obviously not in the mood to look at horses. "Hey, do you smoke grass?" she asked with her back to Erica. Somewhat taken aback by her directness, Erica hesitated. She knew what it was but had never tried it. She chose to feign ignorance. "Grass? What's that?"

"You don't know what grass is? How old are you?"

"Well, I guess you mean marijuana, right?" Jenna looked at Erica with such disdain that she knew she wouldn't be getting an answer from her. "No, I've never done it."

"Try it, you'll like it," Jenna smiled as if she were the first to use that phrase and thought it so clever.

"No thanks," Erica said, trying not to sound too inexperienced. She knew that Katie had done it a bit, but she had never actually seen her do it. Erica assumed the older high school kids did it, at least some of them. Erica wondered if Brad and Nick had done it. Probably, she decided. She knew his brother did it. Erica knew what it was because of movies she'd seen. The smell is distinct, apparently.

"Let's go look at the horses," Erica said, changing the subject.

"Alright," Jenna said begrudgingly.

They walked across the circular driveway and out to the barn. Erica felt invigorated by the smell and the sight of all those horses. There were four in all and seeing them made her long for one of her own. She knew how to ride because her friend Marcy had a horse and had taught her to ride the previous year. She hoped to ride one of Jenna's horses but she was informed that they were racehorses and far too spirited for an inexperienced rider like herself.

"You could maybe ride my horse Mocha sometime. But not today," Jenna said.

She introduced Erica to Mocha, a tall bay. Erica liked him immediately. He ducked his head down for her to pet him. Erica thought he seemed lonely. She wondered how much time, (between boys and school and smoking weed), Jenna actually spent with him. She noticed that the stalls looked pretty dirty.

"The stalls look a little dirty," Erica said quietly.

"Yeah," Jenna said gruffly. She paused, looking at Erica for a moment, then she said "Hey, if you clean 'em for me, I'll let ya ride Mocha!"

"Really? You mean today?"

"Well, yeah. Maybe you could do it every day, then you could ride all you wanted and I could give you lessons."

"Okay," Erica said without a second thought.

"You can start today."

"Right now?"

"Why not? I'll show you what ta do."

"Okay," Erica shrugged.

Jenna proceeded to walk her through it, showing her how to clean out each stall. She also threw in feeding, which they hadn't agreed to but Erica did not have the assertiveness to point out. Once she'd been apprised of the task, Jenna left Erica, walking back into the house. Erica pictured her lighting up a doobie while Erica was out there doing her dirty work. She wasn't angry. In fact, she was grateful. She loved horses and felt it was worth the effort just to be around them.

She finished the stalls and the feeding in an hour and fifteen minutes, (a time she would soon improve upon greatly). Walking outside, she realized that it was already getting dark and that she'd better get going if she wanted to make it home before it was completely dark. She went inside to say goodbye to her new friend and to let her know she'd finished. Erica found her in her bedroom, prostrate on her bed amongst her clothes. "I finished the barn. I've got to go now, before it gets too dark." Jenna said nothing.

"Are you okay?"

"Uhhhh huhhh," she said, turning her face towards where Erica stood in the doorway. Jenna's eyes were closed and she had a devious smile on her face.

"When will your dad be home?"

"Someday," she purred.

"Okay, well, bye." Jenna turned her head back into her pillow, saying nothing. Erica walked home.

When she got home, her mother was irritated with her for not calling but she seemed too tired to deal with it. She's always tired, Erica thought again.

"Lacy called you," Ellie informed her. Erica dialed her number back.

"Hi, Lacy?"

"Hi Erica. Did you just now get back?"

"Yeah."

"What was she like?"

"Weird."

"Really? How?"

"She's just different. I cleaned her stalls for her."

"What?"

"Well she said that if I did, I could ride her horse."

"Oh."

"Took forever."

"Is that worth it?"

"To me it is."

"Do you have any homework?"

"A little. I can do it on the bus, though. That's the one good thing about the stupid bus ride."

"Yeah. Well, I'll see you tomorrow on the bus."

"Okay. Bye"

"Bye."

She hung up and thought about how badly she'd wanted to tell Lacy about Jenna smoking grass but couldn't because her mother was right there. If Jean thought for one second that her daughter was hanging with a drug user she'd freak out. Erica couldn't exactly go to the far wing to escape her prying ears. Erica knew she'd only have about five or six minutes to discuss it with Lacy before Jenna got on the bus the next day so she'd have to get right to it. She made a sandwich, took a quick shower and then, utterly exhausted, fell into bed.

The following morning Erica told Lacy all about her visit with Jenna.

"So I go back to her room and there she is, semi-passed out on her bed. Can you believe that?" Erica said wide-eyed.

Erica had expected Lacy to just shake her head and express surprise but instead she got kind of quiet and seemed somewhat shocked by the story. Erica began to worry that Lacy might think she had tried smoking it with Jenna, even though she made a point of telling her she had not. Then Lacy asked her if she still intended to work there for Jenna in return for riding. When Erica replied yes, Lacy seemed disappointed, as though she felt Erica was destined to become a druggie herself. Lacy turned to her homework and Erica turned to the window where she sat looking out. Neither girl said anything. When Jenna got on, Lacy scarcely acknowledged her, which was disconcerting to Erica. She worried that Jenna might figure out that Erica had exposed her. Jenna plopped down in the seat in front of them and instantly turned around to look at them.

"Hi," she said, chipper as ever. Not a hint of the previous night's lethargy. Erica said hello back and buried her head in her books, hoping Jenna would get the hint and leave her alone. She felt guilty ignoring Jenna but she also didn't want Lacy drawing the wrong conclusion. Lacy was more important to Erica than any potential friendship with Jenna.

When they'd reached the High School there was an awkward pause after getting off the bus, then Lacy began walking by herself. Jenna seemed to be waiting for Erica to walk with her. Erica sped her pace up and began walking next to Lacy, ignoring Jenna altogether.

"Hey! Remember me?" Jenna called. Erica almost turned to look at her but Lacy's lips were pursed tight and her eyes narrowed at her, wordlessly willing her not to look back at Jenna. Erica pretended not to hear and kept walking. Lacy and she parted near Lacy's first class and Erica headed for her class a little further down the hall. Jenna rushed up from behind her and grabbed her arm. "Whatsa matter with you?"

"What? Nothing." Erica stammered.

"I was yelling at you back there. I know you heard me!"

"No, I didn't," Erica protested. Jenna looked irritated and shook her head, "Whatever. Hey, you gonna come clean the stalls today? I'll give you a lesson if you want."

"I can't today. I gotta go right home after school. My mom

wants me to help her at the Laundromat tonight before it gets dark."

"You don't have a washer dryer?"

Erica looked at the ground. "No," she said quietly.

Jenna's face contorted as if she were puzzled about something, thinking something through. Then she looked up at Erica, her eyes wide. "Hey, why don't you guys do your laundry at my house while we ride?"

This sounded a lot more appealing than driving to the Happy Clown and waiting for the laundry. "Okay, I mean maybe. Let me ask my mom when I get home and, if it's okay, we'll drive down. I'll call you." Jenna knew she'd gotten Erica with her modern appliances and horses if not her winning personality and she acted victorious.

"See ya after school then. Bye." Jenna turned and walked to whatever class she randomly attended. Erica headed for her class.

At lunch she sat with Lacy. Neither girl made any mention of the conversation earlier that morning. They discussed the Homecoming dance and what Lacy planned to wear.

"Do you think he's gonna ask you today?" Lacy asked her.

Erica just shook her head no. She didn't hold out much hope at this point. The bell rang and they parted again.

In her science class, Erica sat down next to Brad. He smiled broadly at her like he always did.

"Hey! Finish your homework last night?"he asked.

"On the bus, actually."

"Ohhh."

"Yours done?"

"Yep."

"What did you come up with for an example of how to

apply the scientific method?" she asked, trying to keep him in conversation with her for as long as possible. They talked about homework until the second bell rang and the instructor told everyone to shut up.

On the bus ride home Erica sat with Lacy. She began worrying that Jenna would make mention of their tentative plans for later that afternoon She tried frantically to think of some way to acknowledge Jenna while discouraging her from mentioning their plans. Jenna got on and sat in front of them again, turning her body around to face them and forcing a greeting from Erica.

Erica spoke before Jenna could, asking her if she were planning to go to the Homecoming dance with her boyfriend.

"I might go with Brian Summerfield. He's a senior," she said proudly.

"What about your boyfriend?" Lacy said, breaking her inner promise not to speak to Jenna.

"So? He doesn't wanna go to a high school dance."

"Do you think you'll go with him then?" Erica asked, hoping to remain on this topic for the whole ride home. Anything to keep Jenna from talking about the laundry and riding lessons.

"I dunno, maybe. That guy ask you yet?" she asked turning towards Erica.

"No," Erica said with resignation.

"Why don'tchya just ask him if he's taking someone else?" Jenna asked, annoyed at the redundancy of the conversation.

"I asked him if he were going and he said he wasn't sure, so…"

"He'll ask you," Lacy said, trying to be reassuring.

They proceeded to talk some more about who was going with whom and what they planned to wear for the rest of the way until they finally stopped at Jenna's stop.

"Call me," Jenna said to Erica as she exited the bus. Thank God she hadn't said anything about their plans Erica thought.

Erica called once she'd gotten home and had convinced her mom that doing laundry at Jenna's would not only be more pleasant but quicker, closer and free. Erica told Jenna they'd be there soon and hung up the phone. They loaded the car and were there inside of a half an hour.

Erica's mother pulled their crappy little car into the gravel drive, kicking up some dust in the process. Jenna came out and greeted Erica's mother cheerfully and offered to show her and Ellie around the house, especially the laundry room. They toured the little house while Erica carried in the laundry in large plastic bags.

"This is nice. Now you live here with your father, is that right?" Erica's mom asked.

"Uh huh."

"Where's he?"

"Oh he's in Cle Elum getting the horses."

"I see," her mom said throwing Erica a suspicious look.

Erica and her mother loaded some clothes in the washer. Then Jenna gave Erica a riding lesson as her mother and little sister looked on. Erica had forgotten a lot but it started to come back to her the more they worked. Mocha was pretty tame. In fact, he mostly just seemed tired, possibly from lack of exercise. Jenna worked with her for about an hour or so and then, having loaded the clean clothes in the car, their mother said they had to go and they thanked Jenna and left.

Erica promising to do the stalls the following day.

When they arrived home they put all of their things away and then Erica made them some soup from a can and some sandwiches. They watched Battle of the Network Stars, which was totally lame.

Erica went to bed with her latest book, Milton's *Paradise Lost*. She eventually closed her eyes and, as she drifted off to sleep, she vaguely felt her mother stoking her hair, her familiar perfume and cold hand on her cheek being the last semi-conscious thought she had that day.

The following morning on the bus Jenna made a point of telling her that she owed her a few stall cleanings for her lesson. Erica nodded her head and pretended to busy herself with homework as Lacy looked at her disapprovingly.

She went to her usual morning classes and then met with Lacy in the lunchroom, as she did ever day. About halfway through lunch Brad's friend Nick came up to their table with one of his dopey friends, laughing about something.

"Hey Lacy, how you doing?" Nick asked sarcastically. He was mocking her and she knew it but his will was too strong and hers too weak so she smiled and said, "Fine. How are you?"

"I'm great! How are you doing Steve?" he asked his friend.

"I'm great!" the idiot beside him responded, trying not to laugh.

"How about you, Erica?" Nick asked.

"Great," she said snidely. What the hell were they up to?

"So, Erica, you goin to the Homecoming dance?"

"I don't know, maybe."

"Cuz I know someone who said he'd really like to take

Erica to the dance."

Her heart started racing. Brad?

"You know my buddy Brad, right?"

"Yes," she said not wanting to appear as eager as she felt.

"Well, he said he was gonna ask Erica, so…"

"He better hurry up," Lacy threw in.

"Oh, wait a minute! He already asked her, didn't he Steve? Yeah!"

"Yeah, he already asked her."

"No he didn't!" Erica said, beginning to get a bad feeling about the entire exchange.

"Oh, no he did, about a week ago. She said yes." The two boys looked at each other and burst out laughing and holding their stomachs as they walked away.

"What was that all about?" Lacy wanted to know. Erica was beginning to understand. Jenna walked in just then, looked at her and said "Yer not the Erica Brad likes. There's another Erica. A blonde girl. She's gorgeous!"

"How do you know?" Lacy demanded.

"'Cuz Nick and Steve told me. They're in my math class and I was asking them about Brad and why he hadn't asked you yet. That's when they told me. You're not the one."

"Okay! I get it!" Erica said, feeling nauseous and defensive.

"I got another guy who wants to go with you. Brian's brother. Brian is a senior. He's kinda cute. We can all go together."

"I don't think so," she said, numb from the blow.

"I already told him you'd go!"

"What?!"

"C'mon. It'll be fun!"

"She doesn't want to," Lacy said.

"We'll talk after school. You need to clean the stalls anyway. You owe me."

Jenna walked away before Erica could think of a rebuttal.

"Why do you owe her?"

"Oh, my mom and I did our laundry over there yesterday and she gave me a riding lesson while we waited so now she wants me to clean her horse stalls in return," she said sheepishly.

"I can't believe you hang out with that druggie!" Lacy said, a look of disgust on her face.

"I don't hang out with her," Erica said defensively.

"Well, did you do it? Ever?" Lacy asked.

"NO!"

"Well don't. It's terrible."

"I know," Erica said irritably.

"Good."

Erica shook her head. She was tired of this conversation and wished to move on to any other subject. What a rotten couple of days she was having! The bell rang and they went their separate ways.

Erica almost skipped Science that day. She so dreaded seeing Brad, having to sit next to him, knowing he knew. She walked in and noticed he wasn't there yet. She took her seat and plunged her head into her textbook, trying to become invisible (again). Brad walked in and sat down, smiling. She looked up and smiled at him then dipped her head back down into her book. The bell rang, followed by Mr. Rice walking in, talking about the homework assignment and relieving her of any need to talk to her desk mate/ Science partner/ heart breaker.

The class went by quicker than she had thought it would and she darted out as soon as the bell rang. As she was gathering her things Erica foolishly glanced at Brad. He looked at her sympathetically. It wasn't a look of condescension or arrogance. Just a look that suggested he felt bad about the confusion and her resulting embarrassment. She would have preferred indifference so she could hate him. But instead he seemed understanding and regretful. How could she hate that?

On the bus ride home Erica was silent, not talking to anyone. Jenna got off and she followed her, electing to ignore Lacy's glare. She owed Jenna and that was that. She went straight to work on the stalls, saying nothing. The nights were getting longer and it got dark sooner. If she wanted to get the stalls done before darkness fell she'd have to hurry. Also, she simply didn't care to speak to anyone. Working out in the barn she realized that toiling away made her head feel clearer and she found she didn't mind it so much. She thought about Brad and wondered why she had been the victim of such a cosmic joke. Why me? she thought. This was a question she asked herself a lot, never really getting a satisfactory answer.

9

The night of the Homecoming dance came and went. Erica had considered going but, in the end, she just couldn't quite bring herself to go alone or as a third wheel with Lacy and Andy (although Lacy did offer). Jenna tried in vain to get her to go with her date's brother but Erica did not want to go to a dance with some guy she didn't know and then have to watch Brad with the most beautiful girl in the school. So instead she spent that Friday evening at home, watching television with her mother and sister. Her mother made hot chocolate and burnt popcorn to cheer her up and it worked (a little).

They spent that weekend attempting to winterize the trailer. They bought a big closable bin where they could store garbage outside without attracting bears or other scavengers. The leaves were beginning to turn and it was really a beautiful sight driving down the hill towards Plain. The mornings had become decidedly chilly, making the donning of a coat less an option and more of a necessity. Erica often went to Jenna's and cleaned the stalls in return for riding Mocha on the trails nearby. She really liked riding alone. It was peaceful and it gave her time to think about her life and what she wanted to be when she grew up. She once thought she wanted to be a veterinarian and then a tennis pro, then a teacher and even a pilot. But, around that time she began to realize that what she really liked was solitude. Being alone and thinking. She liked to read a lot and she thought about reading for a living but decided that was unrealistic. One thing she knew for sure was that she did not want a regular nine to five job or, worse yet, to find herself doing odd, menial jobs just to get by like her mother. She vowed never to end up like her mother.

As the days grew shorter and shorter, Erica had to shorten her rides to make time to clean the stalls before dark. She managed to make it home most days before dark but occasionally she would misjudge it and she'd end up running the last few blocks home in complete darkness, certain she'd heard a bear just behind her.

Every once in a while, Erica would go to Katie's after school or on the weekend. Katie didn't like Jenna and she would encourage Erica to stay away from her. She told Erica that Jenna had a bad reputation and that she'd been to Juvenile Detention more than once. Erica felt somewhat defensive of Jenna. She knew Jenna was demanding, arrogant, obtuse and debauched but Erica felt sorry for her because her mother had run out on them when Jenna was very young and her father had seemingly abandoned her, as well. She was practically an orphan! Besides, she was kind of fun and she had a much more interesting life than Erica. Besides, Jenna let her ride Mocha. Despite the fact that Jenna actually benefited more from Erica's regular visits by not only avoiding having to clean the stalls a good deal of the time but also not having to ride her horse to keep him from going lame, giving Jenna more time to get high and service her various boyfriends. Erica had begun to realize pretty quickly that having horses for Jenna was more a means of attracting men than anything she actually cared to participate in. It was all an act, a charade. It was her attempt at being both different and desirable.

Jenna mentioned going to Oktoberfest, which was supposed to be pretty fun. Katie had also mentioned something about it, and Erica began to think she might like to go. Lacy said she was going with her father and said Erica could tag along if she'd like but Erica realized she'd rather die than be stuck with Lacy's stern father all day and night. Katie was planning to go with her new beau, John the bartender from the Cougar Inn. That left either going with her mom and sister (ugh!) or with Jenna.

On a Saturday afternoon, Jenna, (still not driving), had arranged for Brian, the guy she went to the dance with, to pick them up. He pulled in to Jenna's driveway in a red Ford truck. There was another guy in the cab with him.

"Who's that?" asked Erica.

"It's Brian and his brother, Mike."

"You never said his brother was coming too!" she said, suddenly worried she'd made a horrible mistake.

"He's nice. Relax."

Mike got out so the two girls could get in, then he jumped back in, giving Erica about three and a half inches on which to sit.

"Hi ya! I'm Mike," he said cheerfully, smiling broadly. Too broadly, thought Erica.

"Hi," she said timidly. She was trying to convey politeness along with trepidation to distance herself from Jenna's reputation while avoiding being labeled frigid. Not an easy task with one simple two-letter word.

"How old are you?" Mike asked her.

"Fifteen," she said with emphasis, as if to say "Stay away."

"Fifteen! I thought you were sixteen!"

"She's almost sixteen. She's actually fifteen going on twenty-five," Jenna said.

"You're not even legal!" Mike said, obviously concerned about this.

"I'm not illegal!" Erica said, apparently missing the point because they all laughed.

Brian was a cute cowboy type with reddish blonde hair and faded jeans. His face was boyish yet defined and his blue eyes were kindly if a bit furtive. Mike, on the other hand, had the greasy look of a used car salesman. His hair was long and slicked back save for the forelock which eluded his attempts to tame so it kept falling over his glassy gray eyes. His face was pockmarked from years of picking at adolescent pimples. He wore a faded blue plaid shirt and too tight jeans. His teeth were crooked which gave his esses a slight whistle. He wore some kind of foul smelling cologne and, as if all that weren't enough to turn a girl on, his breath wreaked of tobacco and lack of hygiene. Erica thought that this was probably much like how her dirty old ex-clarinet instructor must have looked and smelled at that age.

They sped to town, Brian apparently in some sort of hurry to get there. Mike had opened a can of beer and downed it plus two more in the fifteen minutes it took to get to town. Brian and Jenna each had one. Erica declined, despite Mike encouraging her. "C'mon, try it, you'll like it," he said laughing, thinking himself witty just as Jenna had with that line.

Erica marveled at how quickly they'd arrived compared to how long it usually took when her mom drove. She longed for the day she would have a car of her own.

After hunting for a place to park, they finally found a

spot about ten blocks from town. They all got out and walked towards the main square. There were lots of people milling around, mostly tourists. A grandstand had been set up in the little park in the center of town and the large white gazebo was nearly capsizing with men in lederhosen and women in dark blue woolen dresses adorned with red and white zigzagged piping. They were playing oom pa pa music and their dancing consisted of repeatedly bending at the knees. There was a beer garden set up nearby which Mike bolted for. Brian had filled Jenna's bag with beer and a large bottle of vodka.

They eventually made their way to the larger park just behind the hotel. They saw several people from school there, all of them older than Erica. Seeing a few guys from band she nodded her acknowledgment. The four of them found a spot under a tree and they spread out a large blanket and sat. Jenna passed around her stashed bottle hidden in a brown bag. Erica once again declined. Brian passed out cigarettes which both Jenna and Mike accepted and lit up. They smoked as though they'd been doing it their whole lives. Erica had never even seen Jenna smoke before. She began to feel she was out of her depth. They talked about who was dating whom and who was breaking up. Erica didn't know any of the people they were talking about.

Katie came by with John and they sat and chatted for a bit, smoking and drinking some of Jenna's bottle. Katie and Jenna talked like old friends and Erica wondered why she was suddenly being so nice.

Katie offered the wrapped bottle to Erica and Erica decided that, if Katie thought it was okay and if she wanted to fit in at all, she'd better indulge. She took the bottle from

Katie and took a tentative sip. She swallowed it quickly in an attempt to get the foul-tasting stuff out of her mouth without spitting it out. It burned as it went down and she felt her face and neck flush red. Katie was smiling at her, amused by her obvious revulsion.

Erica talked to John for a while about playing the clarinet, which he thought was very cool. She liked John. He was nice.

It was getting dark fast and Erica began to wonder when they'd be heading back. Jenna seemed unconcerned, even charged up by the waning light. It cooled off quickly and Mike put his jacket over Erica's shoulders after seeing her shivering in her too thin jacket. Someone brought over a big metal garbage can and started a fire in it. Several people gathered around it for warmth as the night air got colder and colder. Erica knew she should really call her mother. She tried asking Jenna if she'd help her find a phone but Jenna was intertwined with Brian at this point, apparently unaware that they were in a public place.

Katie and Jenna offered Erica the bottle several times and she had swallowed a bit each time, loathing the taste but loving the effect. She felt relaxed like never before.

Mike had been sitting across from Erica. Every time she looked up he was staring at her and so she avoided looking at him. She inadvertently looked at him again and he took this as a cue to get up, sit down next to her and put his arm around her shoulders. Erica felt herself tense up and she looked around for some excuse to stand up.

"So, what's your favorite subject?" Mike asked with his face too close for comfort.

The sun had gone behind the hills for the night and the only light came from the garbage can fire and the windows of the restaurant. Jenna and Brian stood up together, a plaid blanket tucked under his arm and the bottle wrapped in paper in her hand. They walked down the hill and disappeared into the woods. Erica could hear them giggling and laughing as they walked further into the woods. She kept staring at the break in the trees where they'd entered, long after they'd gone. She couldn't believe it! She couldn't believe Jenna would go off and have sex in the middle of town with so many people around!

Mike continued looking at Erica, making her feel most uncomfortable. She avoided his gaze as best she could but he seemed to be on all sides of her, staring her down. Suddenly, he leaned in and kissed her. She pulled back but he was pretty intent on it and fell over her, pinning her down. She felt nothing but disgust.

"Get off of me," she said pretty loudly. Everyone nearby was looking at them. Mike stood up, swiped his jacket from Erica's shoulders and stomped of angrily yelling "Thanks a lot, Brian!"

Erica, stunned by what had just transpired, just sat where she was, mouth agape and wide eyed. Katie, sitting nearby, said to her, "Are you okay? Mike is such an asshole!"

"I'm fine."

"Who is that guy?"

"I don't even know him. He's Brian's older brother," Erica said, looking disgusted.

Erica decided to go find a phone to call her mother. She walked back to where the tourists were milling about, some stopping to warm their hands over fires set in large cans along the sidewalk and scattered throughout the park. Erica found a pay phone and she dialed, her hands slow due to the cold.

"Hi, Mom?"

"Erica! Where are you?"

"I'm in town still. I just wanted to call and let you know I'm okay," she said, feeling like a ransom victim.

"When will you be home?"

"Soon, I think. I need to ask Jenna."

"Isn't she there with you?"

"Uh, well she went to get something to eat. She'll be right back."

"Do I need to come get you?"

"No, not now. I'll call if I need you to. I should be home in a couple hours."

"Okay, no later."

"Okay. Bye."

"Bye."

Erica hung up and began walking back towards the little park behind the buildings. She wondered where creepy Mike had gone. Probably off scaring children, she thought wryly.

As she neared the circle again she saw Katie and John talking to two boys who were standing in front of them. Erica realized as she approached that it was Nick and his dopey friend from school. They turned and saw her and smiled. She instantly became flustered and wanted to run away.

"Erica!" Nick shot at her. He was smiling his snide smile and she hated him. She half nodded and sat down. To her surprise, so did Nick and then his friend.

Nick turned to her and said, "Hey, I'm sorry about the other day. That was not cool."

"Yes, I'm sure you really feel terrible," Erica said sarcastically.

"No, I do. We were just giving you a hard time. It was just a joke."

"Yeah, joke's on me. I didn't even know there was another Erica. I'm new, ya know."

"I know, I know," he said, pretending to be understanding.

Katie and John were kissing heavily and no longer aware of other people and Jenna had not yet come back.

"Do you wanna drink?" Nick asked, holding out a bottle cleverly wrapped in paper.

"Ok," Erica said taking the bottle. It once again burned as it went down her throat but not as badly as it had before.

"So, are you going to the game next Friday?" Nick asked.

"I hadn't planned on it. I take it you're going?"

"Of course!"

"Why aren't you on the team? Or are you?"

"Nah. Takes up too much time. Practice every day and weekends."

"Really?"

"Yeah! It's a bitch. I did it last year. That was enough!" he said, smiling at her, handing her the bottle once again.

Erica had begun to feel a little dizzy. She stared into the fire.

"Hey, there's Mia. I'm gonna go talk to her," Nick's friend said, getting up and running off.

"See ya," Nick said.

"Hey, you should come to the game Friday," Nick said to her.

"Okay," she said with a slight shrug. "Maybe Lacy would want to go."

"No, I mean you should come with me."

Erica thought she'd misunderstood him. Had he really said that?

"With you?" she asked, knitting her brow.

"Sure, why not?"

She looked at him, saying nothing. He leaned in toward her and kissed her. Erica couldn't believe it! Nick Jamison kissing her! She'd never even kissed anyone before! He's way too popular to like me, she thought. She was caught off guard and unclear as to how kissing was done. He didn't seem to notice her inexperience as he slipped his arms around her waist and pulled her towards him. He became somewhat more aggressive, his tongue slipping furtively in and out. Is this normal, Erica wondered? Her heart was beating very hard and she felt a kind of giddy nervousness she'd never felt before.

He suddenly pulled back from her and stood up.

"Come on," he said, holding out his hand for her. Erica reluctantly took his hand and stood up next to him. He started pulling her towards the woods where Jenna and Brian had gone. She hesitated but he pulled her out of it and she followed him, holding on to his hand. The woods were large but she still wondered if they would stumble upon Jenna and her beau or perhaps someone else. Nick seemed to know where to go and they didn't see anyone.

"Here's good," he said, sitting down on what appeared to be a large patch of grass. He pulled her, gently but firmly, down next to him. He leaned in and rolled on top of her, pushing her back, her head now resting on grass. He was all breathy as he began kissing her again while fumbling around with her sweater, trying to get his hands underneath. He eventually found his way and began squeezing what little breast she had to offer. This went on for some time as he continued to kiss her more and more frantically.

"Take this off," he said, pulling her sweater up.

"I don't think…"

"Here," he pulled the sweater up over her nearly unnecessary bra and started trying to undo the bra. After some fumbling, he realized that the bra clasped in the back, and he pulled her up a bit so he could reach around and unclasp it expertly. He let go of her and she fell back down to the grass. His hands kneading as he went back to kissing her. He was directly on top of her now and pushing her legs apart.

"Erica? Erica?" a voice rang out. They both sat up, Erica pulling her sweater back down and then, trying to re-clasp as she stood up, she straightened her hair in an attempt to appear less guilty.

"We couldn't find you. We're going now," It was Katie.

"Oh, ok," Erica said, trying to sound nonchalant. She looked at Nick who was dusting off his jeans. He just shrugged and said "See you at school."

"Kay. Bye," Erica said quietly. She and Katie headed back out towards the park. They could see the light coming from the various cans still burning strong.

"Jenna took off so we're gonna take you home," Katie said. John looked at Erica with what she thought was disproval. It was fleeting but she thought she saw it.

"She left without me?" Erica asked.

"No, she asked if we'd take you."

Erica was angry at Jenna for abandoning her and for leaving her with that loser Mike but at least she'd asked Katie to take her home.

Erica followed them to John's car and climbed in the back. It was a tiny sports car so she hadn't much room but she was so grateful for the ride. She'd have ridden in the trunk if they'd asked her to.

Katie fell asleep and John hummed to his James Taylor tape so Erica was alone with her thoughts in the back, her head jammed into the roof so tightly that she had to kink her neck sideways. She was surprised that John liked such mellow music. She had always thought of Katie as being kind of wild and so she assumed her boyfriend would be, as well. Actually, next to Katie, he seemed almost Amish. Still, Erica was surprised by John's maturity, all things considered.

Erica wondered if Jenna would even make it home that night. Her father was never around so he wouldn't even know if she had come home or not. Where was he anyway? Did he even exist? How come he was never there? Maybe she was like Pippy Longstockings, living alone, fending for herself, but then where did she get her money? Maybe he just sent her money occasionally and left her to her own devices. What about the horses? He must be concerned about them. These were Erica's thoughts as they rode back to Plain, listening to James Taylor sing 'Walking Man' and 'How Sweet It Is.' They turned on to her driveway and drove up the hill. John let her out his side so as not to disturb Katie's sleeping. She thanked him profusely and waved goodbye. It was late. She didn't know what time but it was very dark and cold and she was ready for bed.

Erica's mother was so glad to see Erica that she put aside her anger at her tardiness. Erica told her a little of what went on, the 'G Rated' version. Her mother just shook her head and told her to get into bed and not to forget to brush her teeth. Erica was, at that moment, happy to be young enough to still be told to do that.

10

The rest of October went by without much excitement. A boy in Erica's Science class missed a week of classes and became the talk of the school when he accidentally sawed off all four fingers on his right hand while helping his dad cut wood at the logging mill they owned just outside of town. Doctors had tried to sew the fingers back on but they'd quickly turned black with gangrene and he was dismembered anew. Upon his return to school you'd have thought he'd come back a war hero for all the fanfare he received. He suddenly had his pick of girlfriends. This, in turn, prompted a brief increase in hand injuries amongst the Leavenworth High School boys, be they factual or fictitious, eventually forcing the school's principal to ban all bandages not deemed absolutely necessary by a doctor (either one of the two in town). Perhaps Van Gough should have mailed off a few fingers instead, he might have had more success with that woman.

As for Erica, she continued to work a few days a week cleaning stalls in return for riding privileges. However, with the weather getting colder and the days shorter, the arrangement began to seem a tad one sided, especially since the skies would usually be getting dark long before she'd even finished cleaning, which didn't leave much of an opportunity to ride. On weekends she would go down to Jenna's to clean stalls and ride Mocha. This gave her time to think about the encounter she'd had with Nick Jameson. She had thought of little else since it happened. He never called her after that and, when she saw him at school he just kind of smirked at her like he knew some terrible secret about her. Erica eventually realized that he had no intentions towards her. This became abundantly clear when she went to the football game alone on the following Friday and he was there with another girl from school. She caught him looking over at her once or twice but he never acknowledged her. She hated him now.

Erica often went to Jenna's room to listen to her eight track tape of Supertramp's *Breakfast in America.* She listened to that song over and over again. When she wasn't listening to Supertramp, she was listening to the Eagle's *Longrun* or The Cars *Candy-O*. Erica would sit in there for hours, with the headphones on, drumming on her lap at first, then eventually turning the desk into a drum set, pens into sticks, books into tom toms. She'd bang away, forgetting where and who she was. It was weird, she really didn't even like Jenna but she didn't mind being there because, between cleaning (by herself), riding (by herself) and listening to the stereo (again, by herself) she scarcely noticed her.

On weekends, Erica sometimes stayed overnight at Jenna's and smoked weed with her. She didn't do it a lot because it made her too dizzy. Jenna, on the other hand, was like a chimney, constantly lighting up. Erica wondered how she paid for it but didn't dare to ask. She suspected it was some sort of arrangement she had with a guy in town.

Jenna's father did eventually make an appearance. He

showed up one Sunday in a white pickup with a silver horse trailer in back and a blonde lady in front. The woman's name was Val and she couldn't have been more than twenty-five (which at the time seemed plenty old to Erica). Jenna's dad looked to be about forty-five. He was small in stature and the few days' worth of growth on his face betrayed his red-headedness despite the golden locks falling down over his ears and forehead. He looked like a tough pony. He was loud and gregarious and his presence filled the tiny house, his voice, much stronger and deeper than his size would have predicted, reverberated off the thin walls, shook the roof and rattled the windows.

"Jen! How're the boys doin? Ya been workin 'em like I told ya?"

"Yeah," Jenna responded defensively. She'd been working them, my ass! Erica thought.

Val disappeared into the back bedroom unnoticed while Jenna and her father sparred over the care of the horses. Jenna didn't mention Erica's hand in keeping the horses exercised, fed and the stalls clean. Jenna had done almost nothing but throw grain and hay at them on the rare days when Erica wasn't there to do it. Feeling uncomfortable, Erica began to make her exit when Jenna's father called out after her, "Hey, where you going? You don't gotta leave. Hey!"

Erica turned and looked back to where they sat in the small living room. "I should go," she said meekly.

"Jenna! Ain'tchya even gonna innerduce me ta yer friend?" he asked incredulously, his eyes wide, and eyebrows raising so high that his forelock nearly obscured his bulbous nose. His accent sounded phony, as if he'd decided that an accent was needed to be taken seriously as a genuine cowboy. It sounded like a bad John Wayne impersonation.

"Oh yeah. This is Erica. She lives up the street. This is my dad, Jack," she said, bored with the whole thing.

"Pleasta meetchya!" he said smiling broadly and displaying a mouth full of half finished gold dental work and several brownish teeth. Erica smiled back. "Nice to meet you, as well," she said, trying to establish her superiority over his daughter with good manners (not hard to do).

"Stick around. We'll have some dinner, and then I'll drive ya home. Yer mom waitin' on ya, is she?"

"Yes, she is," Erica said, playing along like she was reading a script in a bad movie.

"Well, call her up!"

Feeling like she had no choice in the matter, Erica walked over to the phone and dutifully dialed home.

"Hi Mom. I'm still at Jenna's. I'm…I know, but her dad's here and he's going to drive me home after we have dinn… Oh. Well, there's some stew in the fridge, just heat that up. I'll be home in about an hour or so. Okay, bye."

Erica hung up and looked over at the others. Jack was smiling but looked indifferent, even irritated.

"Jenna, did you remember to take some meat out of the freezer so we can have some hamburgers?"

Jenna got up slowly, and nodded like it was a lot of effort. She walked into the kitchen and started to make hamburgers. Her father stocked the freezer with all kinds of meat and bread so that Jenna had plenty of food while he was away. Erica was, however, surprised that Jenna had remembered to thaw some meat out ahead of time. Erica went in to the kitchen to help while Jack and Val went to the back bedroom to unpack.

"Your dad seems nice."

"He's okay."

"Do you like your step-mom?"

"She's not my step-mom!" She said fiercely.

"Oh."

"And no, I don't like her. She's a pain in the ass."

"Oh," was all Erica could think to say.

Erica set the little table and they all sat down to hash browns and hamburgers. The conversation centered around the horses and where Jenna's dad had been, then how much money he'd made and eventually, as an afterthought, how was Jenna doing in school and did she have any boyfriends yet. Jenna told him about a boy she knew in class that she liked. Not the boy she'd been with the night of Oktoberfest. He was history, as was another boy she'd met in town. Now she liked this senior in her gym class. Erica had long since come to realize that these guys only liked Jenna for what they could get from her, namely sex. She was too stupid to realize the insult and was instead foolishly flattered by the attention, however short-lived. None of this did she mention to her father who wouldn't have cared anyway. He did, however, take an inordinate interest in Erica, asking her how well she did in school, if she liked horses and whether or not she had a boyfriend (which caused her to blush intensely). He laughed at her discomfort and praised her for everything including playing the clarinet and cleaning his stalls, adding predictably that his lazy daughter couldn't be bothered (which was true). He asked about where she lived and about her family. She told him that she lived with her mother and her sister, which prompted him to ask if her dad lived nearby. She quietly admitted that her father did not live close by. Jenna sat stolidly as her father quizzed Erica and Vapid Val

177

complained about everything, including the drive over, the house, the weather and the dinner.

When they had finished dinner, Jenna and Erica did the dishes until Jack came in saying that he wouldn't have Erica, their guest, doing dishes. If only you knew, thought Erica.

"Come sit in here with me," He beckoned from the living room.

"Actually, I really should get going, if that's okay."

"Oh, sure. I'll git my coat."

Erica said goodbye to Val and Jenna, neither of whom could muster up more than a nod. Walking outside it felt really cold and damp. It was early November and Erica wondered if snow could be coming soon. Jack started the truck up and then ran around the other side to open Erica's door. She stepped up into the cab and was overtaken by the smell of tobacco and stale food. The windshield was so dirty she could barely see through it. There were all kinds of wrappers and cans on the dash. She noticed that he had removed the trailer from its hitch. They drove out onto the main street and up the hill towards her home.

"I live just at the top of the hill, 'bout a mile or so. You don't have to drive me up the driveway though, I can walk," she said wishing to keep their little dwelling a secret from him. He began asking her significantly more personal questions like whether she ever drank alcohol, how much freedom her mom gave her, and if she was close to her father? As he questioned her, the truck began to slow until it finally came to a stop at the side of the road. He set the brake and put the truck in park. It was pitch black outside.

"What's wrong with the truck?" Erica asked, concerned it had stalled.

"Erica," he said, looking straight at her and putting his hand on her thigh "I like you." He smiled showing his beige teeth. His hand left her thigh and went up to where her hair hung around her face. He started stroking her hair. Embarrassed, she put her head down and looked at her boots as if they'd suddenly become fascinating.

"How old are you? Sixteen?" he asked.

"Fifteen," she answered quietly, beginning to get a really bad feeling.

"Fifteen! You look older. I'da taken ya for sixteen or seventeen," he said shaking his head. "Do'ya like older guys? I betchya do! Smart, mature lady like yourself."

Erica didn't know what the hell to say. "I'm...I don't ..." she stammered.

"Well, I think you should think about it." He was looking at her the same way Nick had looked at her that night on Oktoberfest. She suddenly felt very nervous and scared. She could feel her heart pounding and wondered if he ever going to take her home?

"You've had boyfriends before, havn'tchya? Pretty gal like you?

"No," she said, shaking her head but keeping it down.

"Good lookin' girl like you? I don't believe it!"

Erica just shook her head again. His hand went back down to her thigh then moved to her knee where it began tightening and loosening its grip. She was nervously biting her lower lip at this point. She could feel him looking at her but she couldn't bring herself to look up. She just kept staring at her stupid boots, waiting for him to restart the truck and take her home.

They sat there on the side of the road, him squeezing

her knee and her looking at her boots for what felt like an eternity. Finally he lifted his hand from her knee, restarted the engine and pulled back onto the road. They drove the rest of the way in silence until they reached her driveway.

"Here it is, right here. You can just drop me here and I'll walk up. It's pretty steep.

"I can take you up. It's no problem."

"No, that's okay. Here's fine," Erica said, desperate to get out of the truck. Her hand was on the door handle ready to release it.

"Well, thanks for dinner and the ride," she said, trying to relieve the awkwardness.

"Anytime. You come by the house anytime it suits ya, alright?"

"Okay, thanks. Bye." She pulled the handle towards her and pressed the door open, feeling the cold night air as she jumped out and bolted up the drive to her front door, a rush of relief over-taking her.

As she walked through the door she could hear the ca-ching ca-ching of the knitting machine. Her mother was in her usual spot on the couch, working away on a ski hat.

"Hi Honey. You were more than an hour," she said without anger.

"Yeah, I had to help with the dishes and stuff."

"Well, you have school tomorrow so you'd better get to bed."

Erica nodded and walked back to where Ellie was already asleep. Ellie looked kind of cute with her wavy blonde hair all around her chubby red cheeks. Nevertheless, she was hogging the bed so Erica pushed the little shit over to her own side, waking her in the process.

"Hey!"

"Hey yourself. You were on my side, you Bed Hog!"

"You're such a brat!" Ellie mumbled and turned her back to her older sister.

"You are!" said Erica. Even as it was happening, Erica couldn't believe she was indulging in such a juvenile conversation when just moments before she had felt so grown-up.

As she crawled into bed, her thoughts went to Jenna's dad and how oddly he'd acted in the car. Had he been coming on to her? How could that be? He was so old! And he was her friend's father! Besides that, he had a girlfriend. So why had he acted so weird? She couldn't figure it out. She thought about Nick again and how uncomfortable and yet excited she'd felt with him. Was there something wrong with her or was it just the wrong guy in the wrong situation? She was pretty sure, had it been Brad and not Nick or Jenna's dad, she would have felt differently.

Later that week, Jenna's dad took Jenna to get her license. Surprisingly, she passed. Jenna was so excited she could hardly stand it. Her dad gave her a crappy old Ford to drive and she was thrilled. She started taking it to school. In order to get a ride in, it made more sense for Erica to stay overnight most nights. She would go home occasionally to get some things or to appease her mother but she'd always go back down to Jenna's.

One Friday in November, Erica and Jenna drove to the Leavenworth High football game. Erica saw Lacy but Lacy ignored her. Lacy had practically stopped talking to Erica since she'd begun spending so much time with Jenna. On the rare occasions when Erica would ride the bus to school,

181

Lacy would sit way back, far from Erica. It made Erica sad because she really liked Lacy. But then, Erica did have more fun with Jenna. Besides, Jenna had a car and Lacy didn't."

When they got to the football game, they purchased hot chocolates at the concession stand and went behind the bleachers where Jenna poured Schnapps into each of their cups. She put the bottle back in her purse and they walked out among the throngs of fans. The alcohol artificially warmed them as they strolled around.

Eventually, they found a seat near the top of the bleachers. They sat sipping while watching the game and commenting on the cheerleaders and the people as they passed by. Halftime came and Erica went to go find a bathroom, (cursed with a tiny bladder she was always looking for a bathroom). On the way, she ran into Nick and Brad on the track that encircled the field. They stopped in front of her, blocking her way.

"Where ya goin'?" Nick threw at her.

"The girl's room," she answered brilliantly.

"Who ya with? Jenna?" he asked mockingly. She nodded her head at the truth of it.

Brad just looked at her, smiling as always.

"Where ya sittin'?" Nick asked.

"Near the concession stand, at the top of the bleachers."

"See ya," Nick said abruptly. Brad just nodded and smiled.

Erica headed for the bathroom, not quite sure what to make of the exchange. She still hated Nick, but when she saw him, she just froze and couldn't think fast enough to be rude to him. Erica still really liked Brad but it was obvious that the feeling was not mutual. Well, at least Nick had shown interest.

When Erica returned to her seat in the bleachers, she found Nick and Brad sitting with Jenna. Her heart quickened and she tried to keep her composure. Just be cool, she thought to herself. Jenna was sitting next to Brad so Erica went to sit next to Nick. He nodded to her as she approached.

"Hey," he said.

"Hey," Erica said back, taking the seat next to him The guys watched the game and discussed it loudly through handfuls of popcorn. After a few minutes, Nick's hand fell onto Erica's lap and stayed there.

"What are you doing after the game?" he asked at one point.

"I don't know," she said.

"We're going to the diner. You hungry?" he asked. It was a small town so it only had one diner so she knew which one he was referring to.

"Well, I'd have to ask Jenna."

She leaned over him a little further than distance and noise level would have necessitated, "Jenna? Do you want to go to the diner after this? With them?"

"Sure," she said, smiling.

"She said okay," Erica said to Nick.

"I can hear. Thanks," he said sarcastically.

They sat watching the game until it ended and then walked the two and a half blocks to the diner, where they got a table right away. The irritated waitress led them to a booth. Erica sat down first and slid over. Nick sat next to her and the other two sat across the table.

The waitress came back and Erica suddenly had a wave of fear overtake her as she realized that she had spent most of her money on the stupid hot chocolate. She would not have enough to pay for anything but maybe a cup of coffee, which is what she ordered (feeling too nervous to eat anyway). Nick ordered half the menu. Jenna ordered a milkshake and Brad ordered a hamburger and fries.

They talked about the game and school and who was dating whom. Nick's arm was around the back of the booth, just above Erica's shoulders and her heart skipped a beat.

When the waitress brought the tray of food and laid it out on the table before them, Nick ate like a starving wolf while Jenna drew on her straw diminutively. Erica knew Jenna was on her best behavior because she'd seen her suck down a lot of food in the past and diminutive was not the word that came to mind when Jenna ate. It was easier to look straight ahead at Jenna and Brad than it was to turn and look at Nick. Both boys made her exceedingly nervous but, at this point, Nick more so.

Eventually the check came and the boys paid it (thank God!). Walking outside Nick took her arm and started walking back towards the school. She liked it. It made her feel taken care of for once. She wished she'd felt that way more often. They walked back to the school.

"Are you going to Tom's party?" Nick asked Erica.

"I didn't know he was having one. Actually I don't even know Tom."

"Tom Monahan? It's at his house tomorrow night. You should go."

"Kay," was all Erica could think to say. What was this hold he had on her?

Nick let out a huge, bellowing burp and then laughed. "C'mere. I wanna show you something," He said, pulling Erica along.

184

"Hey, I need to go home soon. My dad's waiting," Jenna said.

Erica looked at Nick. "We'll be back in ten," he said to Jenna as he pulled Erica's arm. He walked her towards the back of the school and once they had turned the corner he stopped fast and pushed Erica against the wall. It was dark and quiet except for their breathing. No one else was around. He began kissing her hard, like the night of Oktoberfest. His hand behind her head, gripping her hair. His other hand once again groping her chest. Erica's heart pounded in her ears. He had her pinned against the wall like a starfish suckered to aquarium glass.

Erica finally broke away. "We should get back," she said.

"Soon," he said, going back in.

"No, she'll leave me here," Erica said. "Really."

That seemed to convince him. He pulled away from her and began walking back to the school parking lot. She followed him while re-adjusting herself. Neither of them saying a word.

Erica saw Jenna and Brad in Jenna's car, the motor running and exhaust trailing up like a huge tobacco pipe. She walked up to the driver's window and tapped on the glass.

Jenna cranked down her window part way. "We gotta go. Get in," she said. Brad got out of the car, his breath trailing in the cold air like smoke.

"See ya Monday," Brad said, flashing his winning smile.

"Okay, see ya," Erica said, trying really hard to sound both sweet and nonchalant at the same time but succeeding at neither.

"See you tomorrow," Erica said to Nick.

"Yup," he said with a half smile.

Erica turned and talked to Jenna about nothing in an attempt to quell the awkwardness of their leave-taking.

Erica slept at Jenna's that night after calling her mother first to let her know she was alright. She went to the little bed in the guest room which she'd become so accustomed to sleeping in. Lying there, she went over the events of the night in her head. She felt so confused. How could she hate Nick one minute and then make out with him like that the next? He had some kind of power over her that she couldn't seem to resist. Like Kryptonite, she thought. She fell asleep thinking about what she'd wear the following evening.

The next morning Erica walked home early. She wanted to see her mother and feel normal again and she also wanted to look at her clothing options.

Ellie and their mother were in the living room watching television. "Katie called you," Ellie called out as soon as she walked in the door. Katie? I haven't seen her in forever, Erica thought.

"Erica, I don't think I like you spending so much time over at Jenna's. You're hardly ever here!" her mother said, sounding out of breath.

"What's wrong? You sick or something?" she asked her mother who looked really tired and pale.

"Oh, I'm ok," she said weakly. "Can you please stay home tonight? For once?" her mother pleaded.

"I have plans tonight. Jenna and I are going to a party."

"No you're not. You are to stay here tonight. I'm not having you going all over town with this girl."

"Why? What's the big deal? Everyone is going!"

"Not you, young lady!"

"If we lived closer, I could walk there and it wouldn't matter."

186

"Well we don't live closer."

"I know. I hate it!" Erica said disdainfully.

The phone rang then and Erica picked it up.

"Hello?"

"Erica. It's Jenna. My dad won't let me go tonight. He's pissed 'cuz I stayed out so late last night."

"Oh no!"

"Yeah. Sorry." she said, sounding dejected. "You coming over to ride later?"

"Maybe. Depends. How much longer is your dad in town for?" Erica asked.

"'Til next week," she said.

"Ok, maybe I'll see you later today."

"OK, Bye." Erica sighed and hung up the phone trying desperately to figure some other way to the party.

"Can you drive me in to town tonight? Then you could go read somewhere and have dinner and coffee. That way you'd be close by and wouldn't have to worry about me!" Erica asked hopefully.

"Well, I guess that would be alright," her mother replied thoughtfully.

"Great!" Erica loved her mother right then. She called Katie and asked if she'd be there. She said she and John might go, but she wasn't sure. It all depended on whether or not her friends were going.

"Do you wanna come over?" Katie asked.

"Ok. When?"

"Any time."

"Ok. I'll come over soon."

"K. Bye." As she hung up the phone, Erica felt guilty not seeing Katie much lately. She was glad to be asked over and she looked forward to seeing Katie again.

Erica went in to her room to find something to wear. This took her over an hour. Then she walked to Katie's house. It was really cold and she hadn't been doing much walking of late because she'd been driven everywhere by Jenna. Arriving at Katie's she found the familiar odor of their house oddly welcoming. She and Katie talked for hours about school and John. Erica told Katie about what had happened with Nick. Well, the edited version. She was far too embarrassed to tell her what really happened.

"Yeah, I knew something was up when you were with him in the woods that time," Katie said with a knowing smile.

Erica just shrugged, feeling foolish.

"Be careful. He's a Jameson."

Erica suddenly felt sick. Was she once again the butt of some joke?

"What does that mean?" she asked fearing the worst.

"Just don't let him break your heart. He's probably just like his brother."

"I thought you said they were fun?" Erica said, flustered.

"They are but they're not exactly altruistic."

"What does that mean? Altruistic?

"I mean they are not looking out for anyone but themselves and they don't care who they hurt."

Erica just nodded her head, feeling too numb to respond verbally.

Just then Erica's mom telephoned and asked Erica to come home. She said she had something important to tell her.

When Erica returned home she learned that her father had called when she was at Katie's. He would be passing through Leavenworth the following day on his way to a nearby ski resort and he planned to stop by.

"Didn't he even ask to talk to us?" Erica asked.

"He said he'd see you tomorrow," her mother said. She seemed a little nervous. Erica wondered again if her mother didn't still have feelings for her father. How could she? After all that had happened? However, her nervousness was unmistakable and it happened every time she spoke to him.

"When's he coming?"

"Tomorrow morning. Around ten or eleven."

"That means one or two," said Erica with disgust.

"We'll see," her mother said half smiling.

So he's going to pay us a visit, Erica thought wryly. She didn't like the idea. She didn't want him coming up and seeing where they lived, and yet she couldn't help but think that viewing up close the extent of their poverty might finally shock him. Perhaps it would spark some long awaited concern and guilt. Maybe he'd be moved to help out a little.

Later that evening, Erica started to get excited for the impending party. She had carefully dressed and she went out to get in the car. It was snowing a little, and she waited nervously for her mother and sister to come out. She hoped her mother wouldn't let the snow keep her from taking her in to town. Erica looked down at her outfit. She'd chosen a fitted blue sweater and dark jeans with black boots. Such a simple ensemble had taken her hours to decide upon.

Her mother came out to the car wrapped in a giant coat. The coat appeared to be swallowing her whole. She looked so frail and walked so slow that it concerned Erica. She looked so sick and seemed so weak lately.

They drove in to town, slowly of course. Her mother

didn't say much, probably thinking about her ex-husband coming the next day. Erica was distracted by what Katie had said about Nick. She was nonetheless anxious at the prospect of seeing him that night. She was fidgety and nervous about getting there, like a racehorse at the gate.

"It's here, right here!" she said eagerly.

"Calm down, Erica!" her mother said sternly. "What are you so nervous about?"

"Nothing," she said, fooling no one.

Her mother pulled up in front of the house and Erica got out quickly.

"Ok, I'll be at the Inn if you need me. I expect you there no later than nine. I mean it young lady. No later or I'll come over here and find you!"

"OK! OK! I get it. Nine o'clock," Erica said irritably. She shut the car door and walked towards the front door, a lump the size of Kansas in her throat.

It was a huge log house with a manicured lawn. It had big windows and two huge front doors. There were some cars already parked in the drive so she knew she wasn't the first to arrive (which would be disastrous). Just as she was reaching for the doorbell, two girls opened the mammoth doors from the inside and walked out. They sat down on the stoop and lit cigarettes.

"What're you waitin' for? Go on in," one of the girls said. She giggled and took a long drag on her cigarette. Erica recognized them from school but they were seniors and she didn't know their names. She walked in tentatively, like the mouse she'd chased out of the trailer a few months back. The entry was large and rustic, like the old Ponderosa lodge only cleaner and shinier. In the entry, there was of course the requisite antler chandelier and a huge coat rack hanging over a large pine bench. Beyond that was a sunken living room and an enormous stone fireplace. Above the fireplace, hung a formidable looking gun rack complete with guns. The far wall consisted of grand arched windows featuring the snow-capped hills that surrounded the town. There were some kids hanging out on the dark leather sofas and chairs in front of a roaring fire. Erica looked around, somewhat in awe. Then she turned and walked towards the voices coming from the kitchen. Once in the kitchen, she saw lots of people standing around talking but no one she knew. She found a chair in the far corner near a door leading out to the patio and sat there by herself, waiting nervously for someone she knew to arrive.

After a few minutes, Erica stood up and headed for the bathroom. She knew where it was as she'd passed it on her way into the kitchen. She made her way past the group of people hovering around the kitchen island, with her head down. She was trying to avoid drawing attention. When she got to the bathroom, she could hear voices near the front door. As she listened she heard a familiar voice: Nick's. Then she heard a female voice but she didn't recognize it.

"Hey," she heard Nick say.

"Hi," the girl said.

"You made it," he said.

"I said I would."

There was a brief silence and then another voice.

"Hey, none of that!"

"Hey, Tom," Nick said

"Hi Tom" the girl said.

"Whataya got to eat?" Nick asked.

"I dunno. Chips and shit like that," The new voice answered.

"Mmmm. Shit," Nick said.

"Krissy!" a female voice shot out from the kitchen.

"Hey Nancy!"

The group headed towards the kitchen, past where Erica was standing in the bathroom listening, her ear pressed to the door.

The voices began to blend in with the din of the kitchen chatter so she could no longer make out what was being said. She stood there by the door, looking at her reflection in the pine framed mirror hanging above the copper sink. It was difficult to see in the dim light of the powder room. She was horrified to be there now and wondered how she might escape. She could dart out the front door and run to the Inn and the reassuring arms of her mother but she remembered she'd left her coat in the kitchen on that chair. What to do? Finally she decided she'd better get out of the bathroom before people began to notice the lengthy occupation. She walked out with her head down and her eyes looking only inches ahead of her feet. She turned the corner to the kitchen. In her rush to get out of the there, she stumbled into someone....a girl, blonde, yellow sweater...her glass of pink liquid bouncing off her ample chest and spraying its contents down the front of her v-neck yellow sweater. Erica gasped, shocked and horrified.

"I'm so sorry," she began to apologize.

"Look what you've done, you stupid bitch! You've ruined my sweater!" the girl began screaming at her.

"I'm sorry. I...I didn't see you," she stammered.

"Well, why don't you watch where you're going? God! Look at this!" Her face was turning bright red as she screamed.

"Here Krissy, some other girl said and threw a towel in Krissy's direction. Erica's mind was racing. Should she run for the door? Should she get her coat? Yes, she'd need it. These girls seemed older. Why didn't she recognize them? She looked up to see Nick looking at her, shaking his head with a look of amusement. He was handing Krissy another towel. As he looked away, Erica reached for her jacket and darted out the back door. She ran as fast as she could around the back of the house and down the street towards the Inn. When she reached the Inn, the sight of her mother sitting there so calmly drinking her coffee and reading the paper made Erica feel so much emotion that she started sobbing. Rushing in, her face contorting uncontrollably, Erica collapsed in a heap next to her mother. Her mother, incredulous, just kept asking what was wrong and what had happened. Too choked to talk, Erica said nothing, just held on to her mother as she wept.

That night as Erica lay in bed, she continued sobbing off and on. She ran through the course of events, trying desperately to understand why everything bad always happened to her. Why her? Why did it have to always be me, she thought? And Nick just stood right there, and didn't do anything! Why couldn't her life just be normal? Her mom came in several times to check on her. She sat on the edge of the bed stroking Erica's hair. She tried to reassure Erica that accidents happen. It would soon be forgotten. She was saying all the things a mother was supposed to say but didn't really ease the pain. Erica just looked at the walls and cried anew, saying nothing. It seemed like all she ever did anymore was cry. Lie in bed and cry. She began to wonder why Nick had told her to come to the party if he was going to meet someone else there. Why had he insisted Erica come? Or had he? She couldn't figure it out. She didn't know how she was going to face going to school on Monday. She finally decided that she would call Katie in the morning and ask her advice Katie always had good advice. Exhausted from crying, Erica fell asleep.

That next day she called Katie as planned. Katie told Erica to come over. It was pretty cold and there was a heavy layer of frost on the ground but not much snow. She wore a heavy coat and her beat up old mittens but she was still chilled to the bone within blocks of leaving her house. Alias seemed to thrive in the cold, must have been the sled dog in him. When she arrived, Katie was on the couch reading some trashy novel. Erica let herself in after knocking as she always did. Erica sat down across from Katie on the beat up old chair and Katie dog-eared her book and sat up, looking at Erica with mock concern, barely concealing her amusement.

"So what happened?" she asked as if Erica were six and had merely skinned her knee.

"Well, I was at Tom's party and…"

"By yourself?' she asked, shocked.

"Well Jenna couldn't go and I thought you might go so I figured I'd know people. Also Nick had asked me to go."

"So? What happened?" She said impatiently.

"Well, I was walking back from the bathroom and I ran into this girl, I think her name is Krissy. She was there with Nick."

"Why was he there with her? I thought you said you were meeting him there."

"Well, I thought so too. Well, sort of. We hadn't set it up like that. He just encouraged me to go. But I certainly didn't expect him to be with anyone else. I was in the bathroom when I heard their voices through the bathroom door. That's when I realized he was there with someone else. I was so upset that I just wanted to get out of there. I don't know why he acted like he wanted me to come."

Katie dramatically rolled her eyes at this point. Erica pressed on. "Anyway, as I was walking back from the bathroom, I accidentally ran into the girl Nick was with and I spilled her drink all over her sweater. She screamed at me and called me a stupid bitch. I couldn't move and…." her throat started to constrict again and she could feel her eyes welling up with fresh tears.

"So you were back up."

"What?"

"You were back up. Nick didn't know if Krissy could make it so he arranged to have you there so he would have someone to talk to and maybe scam on."

"What?"

"C'mon. You know what I mean. He's a guy. That's what they do."

"No, I don't believe that. He seemed to really want me to be there and…"

"I rest my case," She said authoritatively.

"Now everyone thinks I'm a total klutz."

"You know, they may think you did it deliberately, I mean, you do like him."

"But I didn't. Do you really think anyone would think that?"

"Maybe, if they knew you liked him."

"No one knows except Nick."

"This is Nick Jameson we're talking about?"

"Yeah."

"Then everyone knows."

"Oh crap."

"Well, it's better to be a vindictive bitch than a clueless klutz, don't you think?"

"Yeah, I guess."

They sat and chatted for a while and Katie told her to just make light of the situation on Monday. Erica thought that made sense but she didn't know if she could do it. I'll try, she thought.

They had talked about this and that for an hour or so then Jillian came in from the bus and Erica decided to take her leave. Walking back home she remembered that her dad and his new wife were going to stop by that day. Dread suddenly overcame her. Would mom stick around? Would she take off and leave us alone with them? Erica wondered. She couldn't blame her mom if she elected not to be there. It had to be awkward for her.

Glancing at her watch Erica noted the time, 10:30. She had two hours or so (her dad had never been on time in his life). She'd have just enough time to clean things up a bit and make some coffee. She didn't want them to think they were hillbillies.

When she got home, Ellie was sweeping the entry and her mother was cleaning the kitchen counters. Most of the snow had melted so Erica began cleaning up the yard, putting away Alias' toys and picking up loose branches. The place would never look good but she at least wanted it to look clean. Apparently, her mother felt the same.

When she finished the front yard, Erica changed her clothes and straightened up her room. Then she came out and made some coffee. The clock informed Erica that it was 12:30 pm. They all sat around looking at each other expectantly for a while but as the time passed 1pm then 1:30,

2:00 they grew tired of waiting. Eventually Erica went to her room and began reading. Finally, when everyone had given up on their father showing up at all, a car pulled into the drive. It was after 4pm.

Alias heard them first and began barking. Visitors were rare so he was just happy to have something important to do for a change. Erica stepped outside just as the Mercedes came to a stop behind the Pinto.

Her dad got out of the driver's side and Ellie came running out to hug him. Erica remained at the top of the steps, her mom in the living room, pretending to read the newspaper. He looked up from Ellie and beckoned her with his free hand so she walked over to him in no hurry. As she did Karen opened her car door and began to get out. Erica reached where her father stood and he put his arm around her shoulders and pulled her towards him in a kind of sideways hug.

"Hey hey. How are my girls?" He asked gregariously. Erica thought about how different it felt to have him there, as though they were safer somehow. Protected, if only for the moment. She wondered why she felt that way.

"We're fine, Daddy," Ellie said, smiling broadly. Daddy's little girl. Erica still said nothing.

"John, I gotta take a pee," Karen cooed to him. Seeing Karen brought Erica back to earth and she no longer felt protected. She felt vulnerable.

"Uh, oh yeah. Hey, any chance we could use your bathroom?" he asked. Erica considered telling him they didn't have one, which would accomplish two things: 1) He'd really think they were roughing it and 2) Karen wouldn't have any reason to go into the trailer. She hesitated and, just as she was about to speak, her mother poked her head out the front door.

"Hello John. Of course you can use our bathroom, Karen. Come on in." Why was she being so nice? Erica was shocked by her mother's graciousness and it threw her. She looked at her mom in astonishment. Karen scampered up the stairs and into the trailer like her life depended on it. Her mom walked out and sat on the steps. It was all very awkward and Erica hoped they would leave soon.

"So, I hear the wedding was nice," Mom said, trying to break the glacier.

"Yeah, real nice. I guess not everyone thought so," he replied, throwing Erica a look.

"Well, Ellie said they had a nice time."

Alias was hiding in his doghouse. The door opened wide and smacked the aluminum siding. Karen sidestepped Erica's mom before she could get up. She walked to the car, opened the door, got in, shut the door and sat staring straight forward. The car was still running.

"So, how's school going?'" he asked, trying to keep things upbeat.

"Fine," Ellie said proudly. "I have five new friends here."

"How about you?" he asked Erica.

"Okay," she said.

"Good. Well, that's good. I'm sorry we're so late but we got a late start. Unfortunately, now we gotta go or we'll be late for Karen's friends at the resort."

"You have to leave already? You just got here!" Ellie whined, crocodile tears forming.

"I'm sorry Pumpkin. But we'll see you Christmas, alright?" He looked up at their mother who nodded affirmative.

"Oh, hey, do you need some money? You look like you

could use some money," her father said.

"Well I haven't received a check from you this month, if that's what you mean," their mother said. He was always acting like the measly child support ($150 a month) was some kind of favor he was doing for them out of the goodness of his heart. He took out his wallet and began folding back bills. He counted it out and reached it out towards his ex-wife without taking a step. It forced her to stand up and walk over to get it. Erica hated him for that and she resented her mother for letting him get away with it. She never says anything, Erica thought.

"Well, we'll see ya in about a month, huh? Probably be snow here by then, huh? Happy Thanksgiving."

He got into his car and began to turn it around. As they passed, he lowered his window and said "Bye" then quickly raised it again and they were gone. They would see them again at Christmas.

"How much did he give us?" Erica asked.

"A hundred and seventy-five. A tip! For raising his children, I guess," her mom said contemptuously.

So they'd waited all day for them to show up and they stayed for all of five minutes. In spite of her outward indifference, she had nevertheless held out hope (as she always did) that her father would show some genuine interest in her, a modicum of concern, a hint of love. But, alas, she received none of that, only ambiguity and apathy, and, as such, she conveyed nothing in return, (tit for tat and all of that). If he didn't care about her then fuck him! She didn't give a shit about him, either. So there!

11

Erica awoke to snow one day in late November. It snowed the entire day and into that night. When she awoke the following morning it had nearly reached the windows of the trailer and made opening the front door next to impossible. The steps were covered and she could see only the very top of the doghouse. It must have snowed at least three feet. The boughs of the trees dipped low under their new burden and the lower ones dusted the top of the snow or were swallowed by it altogether.

She let Alias out and he danced around in the snow biting at it like it were a giant snow cone just for him. His white fur blended with the snow so well that only his blue eyes and gray trim gave him away. Eventually he grew tired and came back to where Erica stood in the doorway watching. She wondered if the road had been plowed or if they'd get to miss school that day. It was early, just 6:00 am and it was still dark so she had no idea of the condition of the road below. She went to have a look at it. After putting on a few layers and some snow boots, she negotiated her way down the steps with Alias leading the way. They trudged down the steep drive out to the street, which as it turned out, had even more snow due to a lack of tree cover. The chances of going to school that day were slim to none, which was just fine with her because school had taken a definite turn for the worse since the punch spilling fiasco. Apparently Krissy had gotten wind of the fact that Erica had a thing for her beau and logically deduced that Erica had deliberately defaced her sweater that evening. As such, she had made a point of telling everyone what had happened (her version) and why and Erica, in turn, was abruptly ostracized, (even more so than she'd already been by virtue of being new and somewhat of a dork). So now she was new, somewhat of a dork, vindictive, scheming and devious.

Erica welcomed any number of snow days, but unfortunately the next day, the snow was plowed and the bus got through. They only missed one day of school, which Erica spent reading, watching TV and sledding down a nearby hill with Katie. Erica had used a garbage can lid as a sled.

Her sixteenth birthday came and went without much ado. Her mother made a cake and an attempt at a roast. As mentioned, her mother was never much of a cook and most of what she made was a burnt offering, this case being no exception. Once they had cleared out the smoke, they sat down at their makeshift table to eat. Her mom brought out the cake and lit its sixteen candles. Erica blew them all out quickly, wishing desperately for someone or something to come save her from her life. Her mother gave her new leather gloves which she loved and Ellie gave her sox which Erica knew she'd gotten from Dad but hadn't worn yet. That was okay with Erica. It wasn't as though Ellie had any of her own money.

Thanksgiving was only three days away and the snow day had shortened the school week so Erica only had to worry about Tuesday and Wednesday. The ride to and from school on those two days were even more treacherous than usual due to the excessive snow. Both days the long bus seemed to stall and almost roll on a particularly tight, steep hairpin turn. On both occasions, everyone aboard gasped and grabbed on to their seats with white knuckles.

Erica had returned to riding the bus when she stopped going to Jenna's. Erica had stopped because she had decided that Jenna was not only morally bankrupt but also because Jenna wasn't much of a friend. She had set Erica up with that gross Mike guy and then had left her there in the park. Plus Jenna let Erica clean the stalls all the time when she knew it would be too dark to ride afterwards. Also, on weekends, Jenna always had some excuse for not giving Erica a riding lesson. But probably most damaging was Jenna's growing reputation as a skank. It wasn't good for Erica's social standing.

Lacy no longer sat next to Erica and hadn't for some time. One day while they were waiting in line to get off the bus, Erica had said hello.

"How's it going?'" Lacy asked but hadn't looked at Erica.

"OK," Erica said nervously. "How are you?"

"Good," Lacy had replied and that was the end of the conversation.

The Tambos went to The Cougar Inn with Aunt Jillian for Thanksgiving. Her mother and Jillian spent most of the dinner discussing her mother's health. Erica had not been the only one to notice her mother's decline in health.

"You look like shit," Jillian said halfway through dinner.

"Thanks a lot," her mother replied sarcastically.

"I'm sorry. I just mean I'm worried about you. You don't look like yourself these days. You look tired."

203

"I am tired. All the time," Jean said with frustration.

"Maybe you should go see your doctor again."

"What are you saying? You think it's come back?"

"No, no. I just think you should get checked out. That's all."

"Yeah, well I can't afford it."

"Yeah, I hear ya," Jillian said. The topic of Jean's health was dropped and they all focused on enjoying the rest of their Thanksgiving dinner

Monday came and it was back to school. Two weeks left before Christmas break began and Erica had plenty of homework piled on by her various teachers. Plus, the Jazz Ensemble had a stupid concert scheduled for the evening of the last day of school before the break. Much to everyone's dismay, it was mandatory. Erica's mother was, of course, thrilled as she foolishly held out hope that Erica might one day become a professional jazz musician. Erica didn't have the heart to tell her mom that there was almost no chance she would ever get even the lowliest gig as a jazz musician but, Erica figured her performance (or lack thereof) would clear the air of any misplaced dreams her mother held for her. It might even be fun watching her mother grope for reassuring adjectives after the show.

She went to science class every day only because she had to. Brad was cordial but distant. Erica felt bad about this because she had really liked him. She missed their open banter.

As for Nick, Erica felt ambivalent about him. On the one hand, she hated him for using her and yet fantasized about the next time he would. She had no illusions about him. She knew he was a jerk, and yet she was drawn to him somehow. He never called her and scarcely acknowledged her but that only served to fuel the fire.

The last week dragged itself out. Finally the last day of the semester and the night of the jazz ensemble concert arrived. Erica had decided to hang out downtown and wait until show-time rather than take the bus all the way home after school only to have to return with her mother an hour later. Also, she enjoyed walking around town by herself. She got to check out the Christmas windows and browse through the stores without much risk of seeing anyone from school because nobody cool ever went to the tourist trap stores unless they absolutely had to.

After wandering the streets for a while, Erica landed at the Inn. She went into the café. There was a pretty good chance of seeing someone from school because the Inn was considered so lame that it became cool. Erica asked to be seated in one of the back booths. She didn't see anyone she knew. She sat there for about an hour reading Henry James' *Daisy Miller* occasionally looking around the room to see if anyone she knew had come in. She began to feel a few butterflies in her stomach thinking about the concert and the fact that she would have a short solo (everybody did, the teacher/conductor being an equal opportunity exploiter). She began to dread it terribly, and tried desperately to think up ways she might get out of it. Fake a stomachache, fainting spell, brain tumor? Anything that would get her out of having to perform in front of all of those people. Oh what the hell? she thought. She could do it. Just go in and get it over with. It wasn't Carnegie Hall, and it was just a short solo for a bunch of parents. After that, she could just blend in with the other musicians. No one would even notice her.

Looking at the cuckoo clock on the wall, Erica noted the time and realized she'd better make her way over to the school gym for the concert. As she approached the school, she saw a lot more cars than she would have expected for such a minor event and she got nervous all over again. Her stomach started doing flips, which stirred up the hot chocolate she'd downed into a frothy, acidic meringue that constricted her every breath.

She reached the gym, which was darkened for effect. There was only a spotlight beaming directly on the heavy black curtain hiding the stage. It gave the gym an air of expectation and anticipation. Erica's attitude towards the Jazz Ensemble had gone from naïve hopefulness to humiliation to out and out hatred for the lot of them. Especially the other clarinet players who had taken to alternately ignoring her and prodding her (literally, with their instruments and figuratively with mock enthusiasm for her ability). Needless to say, she had not elected to take the class again the following semester.

Erica found her way back stage to where the rest of the students were already assembled. Her instructor was at the podium addressing his students.

"So, just remember to keep one eye on the music and the other on me or, more to the point, my stick." A few students giggled at his accidental double-entendre. He looked perplexed.

Earlier that day, they had all come over to the gym and set up their equipment and instruments so the stage would be all ready to go when they returned for the performance. All they had to do was walk out on stage. The crowd quieted down and the instructor was at the microphone, hitting it with his finger, blowing on it and actually saying "testing, testing." He was playing the role of the misunderstood musical genius all the way. "We thank you for coming to tonight's concert and we hope you enjoy it." He went on about what they would be performing and who would have the solos, naming the first chairs for each type of instrument, blah, blah, blah. Then, finally, he said, "Enjoy the show." The curtain went up and the concert commenced. The students played through the first few songs and everything was going okay. Then he turned to face the audience at the end of "Green Onions" and said, "For our next piece, we will be doing a series of solos, one for each member of the ensemble." With that he turned back towards his students and rapped on the podium. Erica's turn came after the three other clarinet players so it was easy for her to remember where to come in. The baton went around to the brass and on to the piano and finally to the clarinet section The first chair began his solo. This sent her stomach whirling and her heart pounding. Her turn was drawing close. Erica despised the first chair. He acted as though he were Benny Goodman incarnate. After he was done showing off, swinging his head around and side to side unnecessarily, the next kid went, and then the next and finally it was her turn. She kind of went through the motions, just trying to get through it without screwing up. She managed to finish and even got a little applause at the end. Everybody got applause. Whew! Her heart was racing and her face was flushed. She hadn't realized how nervous she was until she actually had finished it. She was glad she'd shown up and not faked a stomachache.

Afterwards, her mother said she'd done well and was proud of her. Erica merely shrugged as she always did when paid a compliment. She had never been very good at accepting compliments. She knew her mother had to say something encouraging, but she appreciated it anyway.

12

Christmas break was twenty-three days long, part of which Ellie and Erica were to spend in Bellevue. They'd planned on leaving two days before Christmas and coming back two days after. They would stay with their mother's friend Phyllis because Erica's dad said it would be inconvenient to have the girls stay with him this year. After all, he had just gotten married and the new couple had not even put all of their wedding gifts away yet. Arrangements were made to stay with Phyllis and she was happy to have them. Erica and Ellie's school lunches were usually their main meal for the day. That made weekends tough for lack of food, and both girls worried about this long holiday stretch. They had some food in the house but not enough to get by for that long. Their mother hadn't sold enough knitting to cover the rent so no money would be coming in until more sold. Erica suggested that Jean ask the store owner for an advance, especially since it was Christmas. Surely more of her knitting would sell during the holidays.

"Don't you think I already tried that?" her mom asked irritably. "She said no because she has no guarantee of future sales and because it's against store policy to advance money. She even went on to say that I should have saved for a rainy day. Can you believe that?"

"So much for her Christian spirit," Erica said wryly. Despite a plethora of crosses throughout the store and one perpetually around the owner's neck, this woman seemed to have missed the whole Golden Rule part of Christianity. She was, in fact, a judgmental bitch with a 'What's in it for me?'attitude. The owner had even scammed Erica's mom in the past by undercounting the inventory and pocketing the sales. This and other similar experiences had helped form Erica's own opinion of religion. She became extremely untrusting of anyone who touted their religious beliefs. She even began to feel that often those same people used religion merely to gain credibility instead of actually living by it. Also, she wondered if there was a God, why do some people suffer so much while others live easy?

As far as money was concerned, Erica did have a little babysitting money saved up from watching two little brats down the street once in a while. It was money she'd earmarked for her lunches as well as for any other stuff she might need.

It was a terrible thing, and even at the young age of sixteen, Erica knew it had to pain her mother to ask. But Jean did ask how much money Erica had. Erica told her mother she had thirty dollars but she really had closer to forty. She handed it over for groceries, saying nothing, surprising even herself.

They managed to get by on those thirty dollars.

Erica often met Katie for walks to the café. She'd order a thirty-five cent small coffee each day, having calculated in her head that at that rate she could make it to Christmas having only spent a few bucks.

As for Christmas gifts, she'd drawn a picture of her sister Ellie and framed it with colored cardboard from school.

For her dad, she made him a pair of donkey bookends in ceramics. (Since he was such an ass) and, for Jean, Erica made a ceramic bust of her mother. She'd used black glaze as it seemed fitting. The high gloss of the glaze looked almost like onyx. When Erica gave it to Jean on Christmas her mother said she loved it and placed it above her bed as soon as they returned home.

They drove to Bellevue and went directly to Phyllis' house. Phyllis lived in a quaint little brick home southeast of the downtown area. She answered the door wearing a red apron and pearls. Phyllis was tall with short, white, curly hair. She was rather rotund and her face was always flushed red. Erica thought she looked like Mrs. Santa Claus. Erica vaguely remembered her since Phyllis and her mom had lost touch for quite a while. They had recently become reacquainted due to Phyllis' own impending divorce.

"Come in. Come in," she beckoned, scooping the air with her arms. "Jean, your daughters are lovely. How old are you girls now?"

"Sixteen," Erica blurted out.

"Almost eleven," Ellie said. Yeah, in five months! Erica thought.

"My goodness! How quickly time flies!" Phyllis said. "Well, you three must be exhausted! Come sit down in the kitchen while I make us some tea."

It struck Erica how odd it was that most of her mom's friends were so domestic. It seemed odd that none of them were still married. It seemed that all of Jean's divorced friends had continued on relatively unfettered financially, living in the same house they had lived in when they were married and able to afford to live a comfortable life style. So what had become of her family? She hadn't a clue.

Phyllis brought out tea for herself and their mother and cocoa for Ellie and Erica. She put each of the girls in their own room because she had two guest rooms. Erica felt so happy to have her own space and her own bathroom. The room was kind of girlie, as was the rest of the house, but she didn't mind. It was comfortable and huge.

That evening, Phyllis made dinner while talking with Erica's mother. Jean offered to help but Phyllis just sent her a comical look by way of answering. Apparently Jean's reputation as a terrible cook went well beyond their kitchen. Predictably, Ellie called their dad as soon as she had the chance. She had been talking with him for a while when Erica overheard her ask "Do you wanna talk to Erica?"

There was a pause, and then Ellie continued. "Oh, okay. I'll tell her. I love you, too. Bye." And she hung up. Erica returned to her book, pretending not to notice the slight.

Dinner was four courses. It started with salad and ended with chocolate cake. But Erica's favorite part of the meal was the roast beef and potatoes. It was heaven to have a full meal with all the fixin's. Even hot rolls and steamed vegetables. Having lived on rations for several days, Erica ate like she was a member of the Donner Party.

The conversation centered on Leavenworth, knitting and the weather. Ellie and Erica high-tailed it to the TV room as soon as they'd finished stuffing themselves. Phyllis had cable and a big screen TV and they couldn't wait to see all the shows they'd been missing. They sat glued to it for hours.

The following few days went by quickly. One day they walked around downtown Seattle, window-shopping and visiting another friend of their mom's. On another day they saw the movie 'Nine to Five' with Dolly Parton, Jane Fonda and Lilly Tomlin. Erica thought it was hilarious. They stopped in a different coffee shop each day. Jean loved to sit in a coffee shop with a hot cup of coffee and a good book to read. She could do it all day without getting the least bit anxious to leave. Even despite the caffeine. Ellie and Erica, on the other hand, felt quite the opposite about sitting for so long.

On Christmas Eve day they had a spare but pleasant lunch downtown. Her mother seemed happy and looked better than she had in weeks. She paid the bill and seemed so confident that Erica elected not to take that moment to point out that she was still owed thirty bucks.

Christmas Eve night was spent at their father's house just outside of town. Ellie and Erica plopped down in front of the TV and began fighting over the remote. Eventually they opened presents and had dinner. Erica couldn't remember ever enjoying herself with her father and Karen. For the first time ever, the time seemed to fly and before she knew it, their mother was there to pick them up. Erica left feeling as though she'd just arrived.

Christmas day they had always spent at home with their mother, but since home was now about a hundred miles away, they decided to go to a hotel coffee shop and then go see a movie. They saw *Arthur*, which Erica decided was the all time funniest movie ever. All in all, they had a nice time and things went relatively smoothly. They drove home the following morning after being fed a giant breakfast by Phyllis, much of which went back home with them in Tupperware. Erica suspected that Phyllis felt sorry for them.

"Phyllis is nice," she volunteered on the ride home.

"Yeah," Ellie echoed. "How'd she get so rich?"

"She's not rich, Ellie. She's what you'd call comfortable."

"How'd she get so comfortable?" Erica asked.

"Well, people build up a nest egg over time. They invest well, buy a house, get promotions. You know."

"How come you and Dad didn't do that?"

"Well, we did but we got divorced. Divorce changes everything."

"Isn't Phyllis divorced?" Ellie asked.

"Yes, but…"

"So, how come she got so much and we live in a trailer?" Ellie asked, genuinely perplexed.

"Yeah, how come?" Erica asked, similarly mystified.

"If you'd let me answer!" their mother said in a stern tone her children had long ago realized would go un-enforced. "The reason we are in the predicament today is because I foolishly agreed not to get a lawyer. I thought your father and I would save both time and money by settling on our own. Unfortunately, that ended up working against me. I agreed to things I didn't realize I would regret and I signed things I shouldn't have signed. Okay?!"

"What does that mean? Why couldn't you just say you didn't mean to sign them?" Erica asked.

"It doesn't work that way. Unfortunately. Once I had signed, I was legally bound. There was nothing I could do. So here we are," she said with a heavy sigh. Erica had always found that sigh irritating. It seemed to imply that Jean accepted being a victim and believed there was no other option. Erica couldn't believe her mother had just accepted it.

"Why didn't you fight it? Is it too late to get a lawyer? Can't we get a lawyer now?" Erica kept firing away.

"Erica! Stop it! Don't you think I tried?"

"No, I don't!" Erica said like the brat she truly was.

"God damn it! You're wrong then. You don't know, you're too young and you don't know. I did everything I could." Jean began sobbing and was on the edge of getting hysterical. "I…I did everything I could do. Don't you understand that? Do you think I like living like this? Do you think I liked working menial jobs just to pay the mortgage only to lose the house anyway? Well, you'd be wrong! Your father went off to have a party and I stayed to raise you kids. I've done the best I can. Why don't you get on him for a change? Why don't you ask Karen to sell one of her fur coats so we can buy some groceries for a year or two?" She was sobbing so hard at this point she nearly hit an oncoming car. The car fell silent. Neither Erica nor Ellie dared say another word. They both knew whatever they said wouldn't help.

The second semester at Leavenworth High started much as the first one had, minus the trepidation. Erica knew most of the people in her homeroom now and no longer felt intimidated by them. Mr. Jones looked even more bedraggled than he had prior to Christmas break, something Erica had not thought possible.

Erica and Jenna had stopped speaking altogether. Jenna would often make a point of sneering at her whenever she thought Erica was looking. Erica learned to simply ignore her. She had begun to feel rather sorry for Jenna because Jenna had no friends and was quickly establishing quite a bad reputation for herself. Katie told Erica that Jenna was known as "Five Finger Jenna" and there was a rumor that Jenna bedded nearly every guy on both the football and basketball teams. Erica didn't doubt the rumors but she couldn't see how that could make Jenna feel too good about herself. Who knew though, maybe she was a nymphomaniac, and with baseball season fast approaching...

Erica and Katie spent some time together here and there but Katie had her own older friends. Erica never talked to Lacy anymore, although she did try calling her a couple of times to no avail. Both times Lacy's father said she was unavailable. One time on the bus ride home, Erica caught Lacy looking at her but she quickly turned away.

Erica's classes seemed better the second semester and she liked most of her teachers. She'd taken Jazz Ensemble again because it was either that or hear her mother bitch about how much she'd spent on music lessons over the years and what an ungrateful brat she was. Unfortunately, hearing Erica play at the concert hadn't dissuaded Jean as Erica had hoped it would. She also took advanced Creative Writing at the behest of her English teacher, Mr. Peters. Mr. Peters had arranged for Erica to be allowed in the class despite the fact that it was a class reserved for seniors only. She volunteered nothing in class and only spoke when spoken to, mainly because she didn't want to draw attention to herself and feared the others would think she couldn't cut it in a senior class. Instead, she listened intently and drank it all in, learning a great deal more than in any other class she'd ever taken up to that point.

Neither Nick nor Brad were in any of her classes. Nor were either of their girlfriends, thank God! So at least she only had to see them at random in the halls and such. Lacy was in two of her classes but they still weren't speaking. Erica really did not understand why Lacy seemed to hate her so much now. She knew she had been a bad friend by favoring Jenna so much but still, she hadn't been that bad, had she? The ill will flowing towards her in class from Lacy was, at first, palpable. But over time, it became like a bad smell—one eventually grows accustomed and learns to forget.

That spring, Erica went out for the track team and made Varsity. She was really a much better long distance runner than a sprinter and it showed in her times The track coach placed Erica in the mile and the two mile. Further good news, and a result of living way out in Timbuktu, the coach allowed her to skip most practices and just attend meets. He made the exception for Erica because he knew getting a ride home each night after practice would be difficult for her if not impossible. He agreed as long as she maintained or improved her times. Erica thought she'd slough off and not train enough at home but, with the days getting longer again and the weather turning towards Spring, she felt a renewed vigor and a desire to run. She did so nearly every day after school and on weekends, cutting minutes off her time and lifting her, up 'til then, decidedly glum mood.

One Saturday afternoon in March, literally out of the blue, Jenna showed up on her horse at Erica's front door, mud, sweat and tears streaking together on her face and down her neck. Jenna was frantic and wouldn't stop yelling something about her dad and how he wanted to kill her. Erica had already been outside feeding Alias. Her mother, ever suspicious of Jenna and finding her to be both overdramatic and lacking integrity, came outside to find out what was the commotion and, seeing who it was, instantly crossed her arms, looking at Jenna disdainfully.

"Jenna, calm down now. What's going on?" Jean asked with more than a hint of suspicion in her tone.

Jenna took a few theatrical breaths before she responded. "My dad says that I haven't earned my keep and that I've ruined his horses. He says I can't stay there anymore. He's kicking me out!"

"Where does he expect you to go?" Jean asked.

"I don't know!" Jenna screeched hysterically. "He says he wants to kill me!"

"He really said that?" Erica's mother asked incredulously. "C'mon."

"Well, he said that he could kill me for neglecting his horses and to get the hell off his property. So I took off and came here. I didn't know what else to do!"

"I'm sure he's just upset right now. He'll get over it."

"You don't know what he's like!"

"Does he know you're here?" Jean asked.

"No, I don't think so. He knows we don't hang out anymore so he probably thinks I went to Scott's." Scott, was Jenna's latest bed-buddy.

The three of them stood there, looking at each other, not saying anything for a while. Finally, Erica's mom half-heartedly suggested Jenna call the police.

"Well, I don't know what to do with you here. We have no room. I guess I should call your dad."

"No, it's okay. It's cool. I'm gonna go back. It's fine." Now it was okay? Erica thought. What? What happened to Jenna being scared for her life and all that running away stuff? What the hell?! Jenna turned her horse around and clicked her tongue, kicking her horse's sides with her "shit-kickers" as she called her cowboy boots.

"Hey!" Erica called after her as she trotted off down the hill. Jenna didn't turn back, she just lifted her arm, her back to them. Erica listened to the clopping of Mocha's hooves on dirt and then asphalt, growing more faint as Jenna got further down the hill towards her house. Finally, Erica could hear nothing and she began to feel pathetic for trying, so she went inside where she found her mother was on the phone with Jenna's father.

"She said she was going to go back home. She was headed

that way just now when she left." Mom said into the receiver.

"Let me know if there's anything I can do…okay…okay… oh, that's okay. I'm just glad everything's all right. Sounds like typical teenage melodrama. Good luck. Bye." And she hung up the phone.

"Was that her dad?" Erica asked, already knowing the answer.

"Uh huh."

"What'd he say?"

"Well, seems Jenna wasn't entirely forthcoming with us just now. Seems she got caught with some drugs and apparently the horses and stables are beyond filthy. He's worried that the horses may be sick from neglect."

"How long has he been gone?" Erica asked

"I dunno," Jean shrugged.

"Well, I don't think it's fair that he leaves her for such long periods of time and expects her to do all the work."

"In the old days kids did all the work on farms. Why do you think they had so many kids?" Jean said.

"That's dumb."

"Is he really gone that much?" she asked, pressing on.

"Yeah, all the time. He's never home," Erica admitted.

"Hmmmmm." A knowing nod.

"She has quite a reputation, too."

"I'm not surprised. I'd rather you didn't spend any more time over there. She's trouble."

"I don't. We don't even talk anymore, remember?"

"Well, I tend to think that her coming over here had more to do with you than it did her dad."

"Whadaya mean?"

"I think that she had a fight with her dad and used it as

an excuse to come up here. I think that she thought you'd do anything to keep her as your friend and, when you seemed willing to drop her, she didn't know how to win you back. This was her opportunity. Obviously things haven't gone so smoothly without you there to do her work."

"Yeah, I guess. But do you really think that she came up here like that because of me?"

"I think it's entirely possible. Her dad sounded more irritated than anything else."

"I don't think he likes her very much. I feel sorry for her," Erica said, feeling generous.

"Did she ever offer you drugs? Tell me the truth."

"No," Erica shook her head.

Jean seemed to accept that and it was just as well because otherwise Erica might eventually break down and tell her what had really happened.

The following day Erica went straight to Katie's house. Erica knew Katie would be direct and would tell her what she knew and what she thought. Erica also knew Katie didn't trust Jenna and would be eager to hear any kind of dirt on her.

Upon her arrival, Erica noticed that the old purple bus was gone. She knocked softly on the door and Chloe answered.

"Hi," Chloe said demurely, not at all her usual effusive self.

"Hi. Is your sister home?"

By way of answering she turned around and walked into the living room where Katie's voice shot out over the back of the couch.

"Come in. Yer lettin' all the cold out."

"Hi. Sorry I didn't call first."

222

"You never call first." Katie said with a smile. That was only somewhat true.

"Sorry. I…I…" she stammered.

"Uh huh." Katie said nodding her head but not buying it. Erica changed the subject.

"Hey! You're not going to believe this! Jenna came by last night on her horse. She was all upset. Actually, it was late afternoon and she said that her dad had threatened to kill her. She said she was going to run away." Erica felt she needed to pique Katie's interest initially so as not to lose it all together.

"So? Who wouldn't want to kill her? Even Ghandi would strangle that girl."

"Who?"

"Never mind. Go on."

"She was all upset and crying and hysterical. She said her dad kicked her out."

"Really?"

Erica smiled. She knew she gotten Katie's attention.

"Yeah, really."

"So, what happened?" Katie asked and threw her hands halfway up.

"Well, she said that her dad was mad that she hadn't cleaned the stalls…"

"You mean that you hadn't."

"Well, it's her job. Anyway, he said that she wasn't earning her keep and he kicked her out!" Erica emphasized that last word for effect. Katie kept looking at Erica as if she wanted more.

"Well, then she left and my mom called her dad. He said he found drugs in Jenna's room and that the horses are sick because of her."

"Maybe if he stayed home once in a while…" Katie said while wrinkling her nose.

"Yeah. I know! Anyway, my mom talked to him for a while and he said he wouldn't kick her out. He was just mad because she'd been so irresponsible and had been lying to him about keeping the place up when he'd called to check in. I think she went back home after she left our house."

"I'm sure she did." Katie said picking up her book. Erica could see she was losing her.

"Why do you say that?"

"Because it's just like Jenna to be so over-dramatic and show up at your place like that instead of just trying to work things out like a normal person.

"Yeah, I guess that's true." Erica agreed.

"Where's her mother, anyway?" Katie asked.

"She left them a long time ago. I don't know anything about her," Erica responded.

They sat around and talked about school and boys and who was seeing whom while simultaneously looking through fashion magazines, just like the previous summer, before everything got so weird and confusing. Erica stayed and stayed, finally going home after maybe five hours. She found out that the bus was missing because Jillian had sold it, finally coming to the realization that she'd never make it as an artist (though never admitting it—choosing instead to blame it on the low brow taste and utter lack of appreciation for true art in the area). Jillian was now embarking on a brand new career: Vitamin sales. Needless to say, Erica's family was immediately diagnosed as being jaundiced, lacking vitamin C and possessing a milk allergy. Furthermore, they were all in need of riboflavin and whey. Who knew?

14

Mid-March and the weather, though still chilly, had warmed up enough to melt most of the pretty snow, leaving only the dirty slush on the sides of the roads waiting to be put out of its misery. Leavenworth High held a March Madness Dance every year. Erica knew just about everyone was going except her. Katie suggested she ask someone but Erica just couldn't. Besides, who would she ask? Nick? No way! Katie had offered to let her tag along with her and John but Erica just couldn't quite bring herself to go with them. She didn't want to have to see Brad or Nick with some other girl. So instead she spent that Friday evening at home, watching television with her mother and sister., as usual.

The next morning Erica took Alias for a long walk down by the café. The leaves were slowly returning and the mornings had become decidedly less chilly but still required the donning of a coat.

Jenna had begun calling Erica again but merely to re-establish their stall cleaning deal. Erica was hesitant at first because she had really come to dislike and distrust Jenna. On the other hand, she missed riding. In the end, she agreed with certain stipulations: 1) Erica would only clean the stalls as often as she actually rode, 2) Erica could do so as often or as seldom as she wished. She did agree to let Jenna know whether she'd be coming by each day or not. Erica agreed to come the following afternoon.

Erica had missed riding through the nearby trails and she was happy that she would once again be doing so. Riding alone was so peaceful and it gave her time to think about her life.

As the days grew longer, Erica had more time to ride before nightfall. She would come home, eat whatever she could scrounge together, run with Alias down to Jenna's, clean stalls and then she would ride through the woods with Alias tagging along. Afterwards, she'd run back home and do her homework.

15

Back in school, Erica endured yet another peculiar experience in what seemed like a long series of peculiar experiences. This experience was much more disturbing. She was in math class, which was taught by the notoriously creepy Mr. Simpson. The bell had just rung and all the students were filing out the door when Mr. Simpson asked Erica to stay behind for a moment so that he might have a word with her. He always spoke as if he were applying for a job. "Sure," she replied, wondering if he were going to accuse her of cheating, something she was not above doing but hadn't done in his class-yet.

"I wanted to discuss your work. I think maybe you could move up to the next grade level and skip a good deal of this class if you were to get a little help. You seem to grasp the concepts well but I don't think you'd fare well in pre-calculus. That is without some special tutoring. I don't feel you're being challenged enough in this class. Do you see?" He always asked "Do you see?"

"Uh huh," was all she could get out before he pressed on.

"I am prepared to help you get, well, prepared for pre-calculus if you'd be game." He was looking at some papers on his desk, shuffling them around, not looking up.

"Well, I guess that would be okay except that I live out in Plain and…"

"Yes, well, that is a problem." He rubbed his chin. "You know, I…I could take you home afterwards. I live out in the canyon anyway."

"How often would I need to be tutored do you think?"

"Oh, once, twice a week I'd say," he said looking at her.

"Well, I think it would be okay but I'll have to ask my mom," Erica said, feeling ambivalent. On the one hand she wanted to excel and she wouldn't mind skipping ahead. On the other hand, she felt like it was an awfully big commitment of her time. Plus, she hadn't even considered track. She just didn't know. She decided to think about it. She knew her mother wouldn't care. In fact, she'd be all for anything that might eventually lead to any kind of scholarship. But Erica was glad she mentioned her mother in case she decided not to take the tutoring lessons. That way she could blame it on her mother. Erica thanked Mr. Simpson and said goodbye. He nodded as she left.

After much debate, Erica decided that the best thing to do would be to not alienate Mr. Simpson. She agreed to meet with him and see how it went. The following day she got to class early and walked up to his desk. "My mom said it would be okay as long as I didn't let my other work suffer."

"Good," he said, half smiling. "We'll start next week." And that was that. It troubled her a little because she knew she wasn't the best student in the class. There was at least one other student who always did better on test scores than Erica. Why not include him? Also, there was something very awkward about riding in a car with one's teacher. It seemed too familiar. Finally, there was Mr. Simpson's reputation for being creepy and perverted. Erica hadn't seen anything perverted but he was definitely creepy. He had a Playdough mouth and squinty eyes. His jaw was weak and his hands were decidedly feminine. He wore khaki pants nearly every day with Hush Puppy loafers and his hair looked like he washed it with whatever bar of soap was within reach in the shower. He didn't really walk, he shuffled, like a man on a foosball table, unable to pick up his feet or move his arms. On top of all of that, he spoke with a lisp, making his last name a cruel joke. She had heard that his wife was from the Amazon and had wild hair and eight chins. Erica heard that she was always yelling at Mr. Simpson. They had no children, which was just as well. Why pass on those genes? Erica thought to herself. When Erica finally told her mother that she would be staying after school every Tuesday and Thursday for tutoring, her mother asked, "By whom?"

"Mr. Simpson, my math teacher."

"That's odd. The teacher is going to tutor you?" her mother asked.

"Yeah. Why is that odd?"

"Well, usually it's the teacher's assistant or another student that does tutoring."

"Well, it was Mr. Simpson's idea and he said that I could skip ahead to pre-calculus if I did this." That was enough to impress her mother.

"What time will you be getting home on those days?"

"Probably around 4:30 or 5," Erica said. Her mother nodded and that was the end of the discussion.

When Erica told Katie about the tutoring sessions she reacted quite differently. "Are you insane? He's a fucking pervert!" She was almost yelling.

"I've never seen him do anything perverted," Erica countered.

"Well, he is. Trust me. He came on to Jamie Leach last year."

"How?" Erica asked skeptically.

"She said he totally creeped her out. He started off rubbing her shoulders, telling her how tense she seemed. Then he started talking about how much prettier she was than anyone else in the school and, finally, he tried to get her to go to his house after school. Jaimie didn't go so Mr. Simpson turned on her and gave her a lower grade."

"Well, that doesn't prove anything. She probably just wanted to tell people she's prettier without actually saying it herself," Erica rebutted.

"Also Jaimie heard he was kicked out of his last school 'cuz he nailed some girl there."

"Who told you that?"

"It's common knowledge," Katie said.

"Knowledge?" Erica asked incredulously. "You know this for sure?"

"Well, I wasn't there at the time but it did happen!"

"How do you know?"

"Uhgggg!" Katie said with frustration "Do what you want."

"Well, I just won't go to his house," Erica said resolutely.

Katie just shrugged her shoulders and turned back to her book, Sidney Sheldon's 'The Other Side of Midnight.'

"Just be careful." she said.

"I will," Erica answered defensively.

The following Tuesday she stayed after class to be tutored by Mr. Simpson. Nothing out of the ordinary happened. He went over a couple of chapters that the class had not yet covered and gave her some extra work to do. Then they walked out to his car, an old, beat up Volkswagen Bug with one headlight and no seatbelts. He let her in and then he got in, apologizing for the mess which was an understatement. The car looked like a hurricane had gone through it. It was raining and the poorly lit road was slick so the drive was a little scary and rather awkward. Mr. Simpson asked her a little bit about school and how she felt about living in Leavenworth. The usual inane chatter but it did help to reduce her anxiety.

When they arrived at the bottom of her hill, she insisted he not drive up. She explained that it was such a bad road, with the left-over snow and all, that his car might get stuck. Erica hopped out, perhaps a little too quickly, and waved goodbye. She raced up the hill with her books under her arm. She didn't look back but she could hear his car idling for a few seconds before shifting into reverse and backing out.

"How'd it go?" her mom asked curiously.

"Fine."

"Just fine?"

"Well, it is math, ya know. It's not my favorite subject."

"I guess I meant the tutoring. Was he helpful? I mean, do you think you'll be able to skip ahead?"

"I think so." Erica began talking to her dog as she went to feed him which, in turn, ended the conversation with her mom. She took Alias for a quick run before darkness set in and returned with the hope of avoiding further discussion on her tutoring. She didn't know why she didn't want to talk about it. She just didn't. Fortunately her mother seemed to have been satisfied and the topic didn't come up again that night.

That Thursday there was a track meet scheduled. That meant Erica would not have tutoring again until the following Tuesday. She won the two mile run and took second in the one mile. They were competing against some Podunk town she'd never heard of, which showed up looking like the cast from 'Deliverance'. It seemed like the entire track team had a total of twelve teeth between the ten of them, and son of a bitch if they didn't all look alike! However, they could run like the wind! They won every event except the two mile and the long jump.

When it was over, they left in a blue school bus that looked a lot like the one Katie's mother had sold. Could it have been Jillian's bus? Erica didn't think the thing even ran.

Tuesday arrived and Erica stayed after with Mr. Simpson again. She handed him her extra credit work, which she had done over the previous weekend. He was impressed with it (or so he said). He asked if it felt like too much of a burden but he asked it in a way that implied he knew she could handle it. She agreed demurely.

"Are you alright?" he asked, with a look of either concern or constipation, she wasn't sure which.

"Yeah, I'm fine. Why?" she asked quickly as if it were all one word.

"You seem a little tense. Are you sure this isn't too much for you? This extra work?" Oh no, she thought, here it comes. Katie was right.

"I'm fine," she said tersely. He began nervously thumbing through the textbook.

"Good. Good. Well, let's get going, shall we?"

"Uh huh," she said a little too anxiously while looking down at the book and nodding her head.

"All right then. Where were we last week?" He asked flipping through his textbook and arriving quickly at the place where they'd left off.

"Here," she said pointing.

"That's right." He flipped to that section of the book, skimming the pages with his fingertips, reading to himself. He did this for a couple of pages, then he flipped back to where he'd started and began to paraphrase the text. Erica pretended to listen intently but her mind was wandering as it so often did. She was thinking about Mr. Simpson's dubious reputation and whether there was any truth to it. He was kind of creepy, she thought, but he didn't really do anything in particular that one could point a finger at and say "Ah hah!" There was just an underlying, visceral suspicion that was indefinable yet undeniable.

They went over the chapter plus two more when Mr. Simpson suddenly looked at his watch and announced that he had to get going. Startled by his abruptness, Erica stood up too quickly and knocked the papers and the textbook off the desk. The book hit the floor hard while the many loose pages floated down slowly in all directions. She frantically began scooping them up and tried to shape them together. Mr. Simpson picked up the text and brushed it off. "It's no big deal. It happens," He said reassuringly.

"I'm sorry. All your papers!"

"And yours too."

"I know, now they're all mixed together. I'll hurry and sort them."

They began to sort them all by handwriting. His writing was neat and clear, Erica's looked like she had Parkinson's disease. There were pages scattered throughout the room, under desks and chairs. It took a while to find them all. Standing there in front of the desk sorting all the pages out, Mr. Simpson began rubbing her shoulders. "You are so tense. You need to relax a little. You're much too young to be so uptight," He said almost whispering.

"I'm okay. I don't feel tense," Erica said attempting to deflect. He was really kneading her shoulders now, almost but not quite to the point of pain.

"There!" she said triumphantly, spinning around and handing him his pile of papers. "They should all be there."

"Thanks," he said while looking down at her with a faraway look in his eyes. He eventually took the papers from her and began shoving them rather roughly into his case. Erica walked over to the door and waited. It was all very awkward and she couldn't wait to get home but she dreaded the lengthy drive with him.

Once in his car, they drove in silence. He was apparently feeling as uncomfortable as she was. They finally made it to her driveway and she began trying too hard to leave things on an upbeat note.

"Well, thanks again for the ride and for tutoring me today. I feel like I learned a lot. Thanks." He briefly looked her way then faced back forward with a dismissive "Uh huh." With that, she hurriedly jumped out of his car and ran up the drive as fast as she could. As she was running, she was trying to figure out what had just happened and why everything had gotten so weird. It occurred to her that he may have been irritated by her clumsiness but, if so, why had he been so quick to dismiss it? Anyway, he had definitely made her feel peculiar, but why? She couldn't put her finger on it. Frustrated, she quickly decided that it wasn't worth worrying about.

The following day Erica went to math class and Mr. Simpson acted normal She wondered if she was losing her mind. Just because she had felt a bit odd didn't necessarily mean that anything odd had actually occurred. Perhaps she'd imagined the whole thing. If that were true, what else had she imagined or read into? Had she mistaken Jenna's father's intentions, as well? Erica remembered that she had wrongly thought Brad was interested in her. She also remembered the previous summer when she'd freaked out about riding with Mr. Peters when she'd lost Alias. Was she paranoid? Did she conjure up these thoughts in her head to stifle the painful fact that she was utterly undesirable? Oh my God! I've become Janice Ian she thought! That painfully homely singer of the song 'At Seventeen' which is about an unattractive teen with bad skin who has to pretend to have guys calling to say "Come dance with me and murmur vague obscenities."

"For those of us who knew the pain,

Of Valentines that never came

For ugly girls like me, at seventeen."

How pathetic, Erica thought!

Erica resolved to feign ignorance to even the most obvious show of interest. She figured her logic was sound for two reasons:

1) She would never again find herself embarrassed and humiliated for having mistaken the slightest hint of recognition for romantic interest and

2) No one could ever think her conceited if she were oblivious to any kind of attention.

It was days before she could get that stupid song out of her head.

16

March finally came to a close and April started off promisingly. The weather continued to get warmer. In fact, they were having unseasonably moderate temperatures. Erica's mother had gotten a real job in town answering phones for a dentist's office. Jean would need to drive into town every day, thereby alleviating the need for Ellie and Erica to take the bus to and from school. This arrangement suited both girls just fine. Their mom had to leave a little earlier in order for them to get to class on time, but the girls pointed out the wonderful fact that riding in to town together gave their mother more time with her two children. The appeal for them was obvious: no loud, bumpy, slow-moving bus and not having to stand out in the cold. There were other advantages. Jean's new job had medical and dental benefits and paid substantially more than Jean had been making selling knit wear. Best of all, the new job had a steady paycheck.

Jean's mood seemed to change overnight. She went from an oppressed victim of life to a seemingly happy woman. She still looked a little pale and thin but perhaps a little less so. She liked her new job and the people with whom she worked. The regular pay allowed her to upgrade her wardrobe a little and save some money. Two things she wouldn't have dared even dream of doing before.

Things were looking up for Erica too. In addition to the extra hour of sleep each morning, she managed to jump ahead to pre-calculus and she caught up with the rest of the class pretty quickly. Mr. Simpson turned out to be quite a big help and nothing unusual happened during the time he tutored her. She'd joined the Cross-Country running team as her track coach had suggested. She continued to run at home and wasn't expected to stay for practice after school. What the cross-country coach—who happened to be her cute English Teacher, Mr. Peters—didn't know and what she certainly wasn't going to tell him was that, although he thought that she took the bus home directly after school and went running from there, she often elected to stay in town, drinking hot chocolate at the Inn while doing homework or, occasionally hanging out with Katie. Her mother would pick Ellie and Erica up at the Inn after she finished work at the dentist's office. Erica was able to hang around town which was way more fun than Plain, and being in town made her feel a little bit more like part of the community instead of just sitting at the trailer and feeling like an under-privileged minority.

As the semester wore on, Erica started running with the Cross-country team more. Her mother would pick her up after practice. Erica knew she needed to stay in shape in order to do well for the team. Actually, her reason for running with the team was not as pure as all that. In reality, she was becoming enamored with Rick Peters. She had not really thought much about him while she was in his class the previous semester. But somehow, outside, in the cool spring air, running with the team each day, it felt different. Like they were equals. Besides, he was young enough that he could talk to the students without seeming out-of-touch or condescending. He was also pretty funny. Erica began to look forward to seeing him and she paid more attention to how she looked both at school and during cross-country.

All in all, things were looking up. Jean was making pretty good money and the larders were full. Ellie had several friends with whom she could pal around after school which made her happier. The only fly in the ointment was a miserable witch with whom Jean worked. Her name was Patty and she was cruel and tyrannical. She also happened to be Jean's superior. Patty felt it was well within her managerial rights to make Jean, (who was much younger, thinner, and prettier), miserable. She didn't hesitate to do so on a regular basis. Any chance Patty had to undermine or insult Jean she took gleefully and without a hint of mercy or reluctance. Within a few weeks, the situation worsened, eventually turning Jean into a nervous wreck. Making matters worse, was the fact that Jean couldn't go directly to her effeminate, cowardly boss because he happened to be Patty's long oppressed husband.

Being a mere sixteen at the time, Erica was incapable of only having concern for her mother. Erica saw Patty as a threat to her own newfound happiness. After all, what if Patty were to let her Mom go? They'd be back to taking the bus and eating macaroni and cheese. Not to mention the toll she knew it was sure to take on her mother's spirit. Erica wondered if Patty had hired Jean just so she could torture and abuse her. Didn't she care that she was hurting kids as well? Erica decided she hated Patty before even meeting her.

Jean stuck it out at work while Ellie and Erica just tried to enjoy the good life while it lasted since they knew from experience that good things didn't often last too long. Life was fickle.

Back at school, Erica's Creative Writing teacher, Ms. Stoop, asked that Erica stay after one day. Ms. Stoop was an uptight, stiff, frigid type with a long, boney nose and a body to match. Erica assumed Ms. Stoop wanted to talk to her about her horrible penmanship. As it happened, Ms. Stoop had something else in mind altogether and she got right to the point:

"The reason I've asked you to remain for a moment, Erica, is that I wanted to discuss your writing." Ms. Stoop had no facial expression that Erica could see. She maintained a patina of stone at all times. She often wondered how Ms. Stoop would react to winning the lottery or riding a roller coaster. Would she respond with a yelp or a scream? Probably not, but it'd be fun to find out.

"I see a lot of potential in you and I think you should enter the essay contest." What essay contest? Erica wondered. Had Erica heard right? She must have been daydreaming in class again and missed this. Erica nodded as if she knew what the hell Ms. Stoop was talking about.

"With a little guidance I think you could submit a rather good essay." Ms. Stoop said.

"I…uh…my…I…hadn't really thought about it. I don't know what I'd write about," Erica stammered.

"Anything. Any experience you might have had or perhaps a family member's experience. It doesn't matter. What's important is that you give it your best effort. I'll help you, if you'd like."

Couldn't you just write it for me? Erica thought to herself.

"I can't write it for you, mind you…but," Ms. Stoop added, apparently reading Erica's mind.

"No, no, of course not but I don't think …"

"I can assist you in your writing." Ms. Stoop cut in with a magnanimous look down her narrow nose.

"But I don't think…" Erica tried again.

"You don't think what, Erica?" Erica felt trapped like a bug under glass.

"Okay, that sounds great" she heard herself saying. What the hell had she done? Now she'd be stuck with this woman after school instead of doing her own thing in town. What an idiot she was!

As if sensing her discomfort Ms. Stoop added: "The winner gets a five thousand dollar college scholarship."

Like that would happen! Erica thought to herself. But perhaps she'd get extra credit for her efforts. Erica had no idea what she would write about. No idea.

"Good. Then how about you get going on it and we'll meet here after school on Monday?"

"How long does the essay have to be?" Erica asked.

"Weren't you listening in class today at all?" Ms. Stoops asked with a frown.

"Uh, well…"

"Between seventy and seventy-five single-spaced pages. April twenty-fourth is the deadline." She said, beginning to get impatient with Erica's obvious oblivion. Erica wondered if Ms. Stoop had mentioned the five grand in class. If so, how'd she miss that?

"I'll see you in class tomorrow." And with that she turned and walked out the door. Erica caught a glimpse of her walking in a perfectly straight line to her perfectly maintained car. Erica assumed she would no doubt drive to an immaculate home.

Erica began walking towards the lunchroom and thinking about what she'd just agreed to. Seventy pages! Single-spaced! There goes her best writing trick. She could make ten pages look like twenty by widening the margins, enlarging the font, and double spacing instead of single spacing. Erica figured the contest would probably have rules specifying font size and maximum margin width. She began to panic. When would she have the time? Between track practice, band and her regular homework, she wouldn't have any time for socializing. And the essay was due in less than a month!

By the time she had reached the lunchroom and found Katie, she was feeling overwhelmed. Katie immediately picked up on it.

"What's the matter?"Katie asked, looking concerned.

"I just stupidly agreed to write a seventy page, single-spaced essay for the Creative Writing contest. It's due April 24th and Ms. Stoop wants to help me with it which means I have to stay after school again! Can you believe it?!"

"Hey, maybe you'll win! Whaddaya win if you do?"

"A five thousand dollar scholarship," Erica said limply.

"Five thousand! You're kidding?"

"School money only. I couldn't go shopping with it or anything. Not that I'd win it anyway."

"Oh," Katie said. Obviously less impressed now that she knew the money could be only used for further education. "Well, still."

"Yeah."

"When are you going to run and stuff?"

Erica shrugged as if to say she hadn't a clue. And she hadn't.

As usual, Ellie and Erica met their mother at the Inn at

5 pm that afternoon. On the drive home, Erica mentioned the contest. Jean practically threw a party.

"That's wonderful, Honey!"

"You wanna do it?" she asked glumly.

"No but I'll help you if you'd like."

"Well, the teacher, Ms. Stoop is going to help me with it after school."

"Oh. Well, that's great. She'd be much better than me. If you want, I can still take a look at it."

"We'll see," Erica said with a shrug. She was proud to be singled out as having potential and irritated that now she would have so much more on her plate. Plus she still had no idea what she would write about.

"Hey, what do you think I should write about?" she asked, genuinely hoping for a clue...

"Well, let's see..." her mother responded, rubbing that area between her lower lip and chin. "How about the tennis tournament last summer?"

"No, that's dumb."

"Okay. Well, how about our move to Leavenworth? That was a big deal for you. A big change."

"Then I'd have to write about the trailer and everything. What if she makes me read it out loud?"

"You could leave that part out if it would make you feel better. Just write about the move, your new friends, riding horses and running out of gas." She said this like it was so idealic. Erica thought she threw in that last part about running out of gas as a way of making light of her mistake. It was all just one big, wonderful adventure. At least that's how Jean would spin it.

"Nah, I don't wanna write about that."

She was glad when Ellie started a new subject. The rest of the way home she thought about what she might choose to write. She hadn't a clue.

Erica didn't know why or what came over her but, for some reason, she began working on the paper as soon as they got home. She pulled out her legal pad and started making notes. She drafted an outline of what she thought she'd write and where it should go. She planned to write it longhand first and then, after making corrections, she'd rewrite it on her mom's crappy old typewriter. There was no "q" because that key was permanently stuck but at least it would be typewritten. Besides, she thought, how often do you use the letter 'q'?

Erica had decided to write about Jenna. She would change her name, of course, but she would write about the girl she knew. Erica didn't think much of Jenna, but she was the most interesting person Erica knew. Between all the guys, her sad family life and the drugs, she'd have plenty to write about.

Once she'd written an outline, Erica went back and started writing about Jenna. She began with the first day she'd met her at the Inn. Erica knew she'd have to fill in what she didn't actually know with speculation and out and out bullshit but that didn't bother her. She wrote about Jenna's dad and his long absences. She wrote about how being alone had impacted Jenna. As she wrote, it became obvious to Erica why Jenna acted the way she did. Abandonment, loneliness, fear, resentment, insecurity. Jenna had to feel all of this, Erica thought.

Erica's empty stomach finally pulled her away from writing and she went in to the kitchen. She ate some reddish glop Jean had made for dinner and had kept warm on the stove for her. She didn't know what it was and didn't ask. Exhausted she went to bed and fell asleep thinking about what she'd write next.

The next morning, Erica woke up excited about the paper she'd started. She was looking forward to telling Ms. Stoop about how well it was coming along. As the day wore on, however, she began to rethink the idea. She realized that Ms. Stoop would probably think she was either lying about having done so much work on it so soon, or she'd want to see it before Monday. Erica decided not to tell Ms. Stoops just yet after all. She'd turn it in on Monday, after a long weekend of writing and rewriting. Maybe she'd even let her mom take a look at it, she thought. That's when it hit her: Why not ask Mr. Peters to help? He was an English teacher. He could help her and it would be a great way to get his undivided attention.

Erica spent the next few days writing in her notebook after school, getting all of her thoughts down. She intended to go back through it later to give it more structure and direction. It was really coming along and she found herself thinking about her paper, and Mr. Peters in her other classes. By the weekend she had thirty handwritten pages! Thirty! She merely had to go back through, edit and then type it up. After which she would show it to Mr. Peters to get his input before letting Ms. Stoop see it. The problem was that she knew she had gone way too fast for Ms. Stoop to take it at all seriously so she decided to put the brakes on and just show her half her notes, acknowledging that it was only a first draft and needed work.

That weekend she went running a few times to make up for not running the prior week. She visited Katie briefly on

Saturday and they went for a walk but Katie could see Erica was distracted. Instead of getting irritated, Katie chose to ask about what Erica had written and she even made some suggestions. Erica thanked her for listening when they parted and she ran the rest of the way back home. From that day forward she decided that really listening was the mark of a true friend. Katie was indeed a good friend.

Katie called on Sunday and the two of them talked a bit about school and Katie's boyfriend John. Apparently John had become a bit of a shit lately. He wasn't calling Katie back and he'd been cancelling dates. Erica tried to be encouraging because she liked John but she also realized by the signals that John was probably losing interest in Katie. Erica gave her the old 'other fish in the sea' crap while not totally suggesting that Katie throw in the towel on the relationship. When they hung up, Erica happily returned to her essay.

At lunchtime the following day Erica managed to track down Mr. Peters in the faculty lounge. He was there reading James Joyce and sipping on a beige shake.

"Liver and whey," he said, hoisting it like a stein of ale. He smiled at her inability to hide her revulsion. "Your body is the only thing you'll ever truly own, so take care of it. It is a temple," he said this like he was winging poetry.

"Yours may be a temple but mine's just a tear down," Erica quipped.

He laughed. "What can I do for you, Miss Erica?"

"Um, well, I was just wondering…I have this essay that I've been working on for Ms. Stoops. I thought maybe you could help me with it?" she asked sheepishly. She suddenly felt like she was five years old and asking him to help her learn to ride a bike.

"Oh. Well, I can try. Let's have a look."

"I…I don't actually have it with me now. I thought maybe we could meet after school, I mean when we're not running. Like Tuesday…uh, tomorrow maybe?"

"Sure. How about in my classroom?"

"Great. After school tomorrow," she said nodding her head.

"I'll see you then," he replied and went back to his book.

"Thanks. Bye." Erica left with her heart beating insanely and her face flush from embarrassment. She went into the nearest girls' room and looked in the mirror. She was horrified by what she saw. Her entire face was bright red, her neck too. She put her hand to her cheek and it was hot. She looked like a burn victim. Erica thought Mr. Peters must think she was a freak. A bright red freak! She splashed some water on until her temperature came down then she headed for the lunchroom. She couldn't figure out why she was so nervous to talk to Mr. Peters about helping her. It wasn't as though it was so unusual, but Erica's heart was still beating when she reached the lunchroom. Too nervous to eat Erica just sat by herself and tried to calm down. She tried to think of something else but her mind wouldn't allow her to stop thinking about her brief encounter with Mr. Peters.

Erica realized that she couldn't give half of the paper to Ms. Stoop if she was going to give it to Mr. Peters to read the following day so she went to the office and made a copy. The office sat across from the teacher's lounge so Erica was nervous that Mr. Peters would come by while she was making the copy. He didn't. She got the copy and the original and bolted out. She met with Ms. Stoop who, as it turned out, just asked Erica to leave the paper. Ms. Stoop told Erica that she'd read the essay and get back to Erica the next day.

The following day Erica was so nervous that she spent the entire day watching the clocks in each of her respective classes. They all moved remarkably and maddeningly slowly. Erica's last class finally ended and she made her way to Mr. Peters' room. She had taken great pains getting ready that morning and had chosen to wear her best black slacks and a fitted black sweater that made her nearly nonexistent boobs appear to be somewhat significant. She had spent a full forty-five minutes on her hair alone, trying to get it just right. She even used a little blush and mascara that she'd bought at the Safeway in town.

"What's so important today that you're fussing so much?" her mother had asked suspiciously.

"Nothing," she'd said in a way that she knew to be unconvincing.

"Well let's go or you'll be late." Erica took one last glimpse in the mirror as she left and it reassured her. She thought she looked okay.

Walking into Mr. Peters' classroom Erica's heart was beating fast and she felt her face flush again. Why had she bothered with blush? The room was empty and dark. She found the light, switched it on and sat down in the front row to wait. The clock informed her that she was nine minutes over-anxious so she pulled out her pad of paper and started going over her work. As she read she began to get a sinking feeling. He's not going to like it she thought. She worried that he would think she was a complete dolt. Mr. Peters had encouraged her to pursue writing when she was in his class but now she started to think that perhaps he'd just been being nice... She thought about running out and forgetting the whole thing. What had made her think that she could write anything worthwhile? She began to realize that she'd made a huge mistake and that she should tell Mr. Peters she had changed her mind. Erica started to panic. She was unsure of what to do and was just standing up to leave when she heard the door opening. It was Mr. Peters. God he's cute! She thought.

"Hello Erica," he said brightly while smiling broadly. So cute! Erica thought again.

"Hi," she said, looking back down at her papers. She still half wanted to tell him that she had changed her mind, that she didn't want to enter the contest after all but she also wanted to spend time with him. Just be near him.

"That it?" he asked with a nod towards the papers in her hand.

'Oh no,' she thought but she answered with a noncommittal "Yeah."

"Let's have a look."

She handed the papers to him like she'd been caught shoplifting. She immediately started making excuses:

"It's just a first draft and it's not very good. I haven't had a chance to even read over it yet so…."

He shut her up with a wave of his hand as he began to read. Erica sat at his desk feeling incredibly uncomfortable and vulnerable. He occasionally raised an eyebrow, and once or twice raised both brows. Mostly he was expressionless which she took to be a bad sign.

When he had finished reading, he let the hand holding her paper fall to his thigh and he looked up at her. He shook his head. He hates it! she thought.

"I like it. It's good. Better than I expected. I mean from someone so young, that is."

"Really?"

"Really. I mean, it's only the rough draft and it certainly needs work, but it has a lot of potential. I look forward to reading it again when you have finessed it. If I were to extend a criticism it would be that you're too wordy. I would go through and cut out some of your repetition. Also, you may want to narrow your scope since it's a relatively short paper."

"Yeah, I can see where that would be a problem. I'll go back over it."

"But really, it's good for a first draft."

"Alright," she said nodding. Erica was waiting for him to either say more or return her paper to her. He did neither so she extended her hand by way of asking for it back.

"Can I go over it again tonight and get it back to you tomorrow?" He asked, pulling it up to his chest as if he wouldn't give it back.

"Sure." Maybe he wanted to show it to his friends so we could laugh about it.

"Good. Then I'll get it back to you tomorrow," he said with a friendly smile.

"Okay. Well, bye," she said, not knowing what the hell else to say and feeling utterly foolish.

"Bye Erica."

She walked out and shut the door. She ran down the hall and out the main doors finally stopping at the Inn where her mother would pick her up in a couple hours. She sat in the corner booth, trying to calm herself while downing ice water. She kept replaying the exchange in her head over and over again.

Had he said he liked it? Yes, but he also said that it was wordy, a bit redundant and too broad. But he said he liked it. He said it had potential. He even took it home. Erica wondered if he would actually read it that night. He probably had a date, she thought. She wondered if he did date much or if he had a girlfriend. Actually, that was something she wondered about a lot.

Erica was uncharacteristically quiet on the drive home. Her mom inquired as to what so engrossed her thoughts.

"Nothing. Just thinking about my paper and school and stuff," she said.

"Oh," her mother said. "How's that going? The paper I mean."

"Fine." Erica didn't feel like discussing it. At the moment, she only seemed able to think about Mr. Peters.

"Just fine? How about school? Is that okay?"

"Yeah," she said with a shrug.

"Erica, a little more than monosyllables please."

"It's wonderful," she said sarcastically. "And that's polysyllabic."

When they arrived home she went directly to her room and turned on The Eagles The Long Run album. She listened to Sad Café all of the time. It reminded her of Mr. Peters for some reason. Many things made her think of him, actually.

She lay on her bed for a while and then got up and walked to the bathroom. She shut the door leading into the kitchen and locked it as well. This was the only way she could be guaranteed any privacy. She drew a bath and checked out the progress of puberty. She was distressed to see that very little had actually changed. She was getting taller, that was obvious by the fact that all her pants had begun to look as though she was awaiting a flood. But she was still pretty flat-chested. If she squeezed her arms hard against her sides and pushed them forward she had a little cleavage. But, as soon as she let go they'd go right back down flat again. She couldn't exactly walk around like that all day! It's hopeless she thought.

As the mirror steamed up she had only a tiny window of reflection before that too would be gone so she stood on her toes enough to see herself staring back. "Not bad," she thought. Her face had thinned a bit since the summer and she could see more pronounced cheekbones. As her visage became obliterated she stepped into the tub half full of warm water. Being that it was a trailer designed for road travel the hot water tank was about the size of a mini bar so it didn't afford one much of a bath. She had a good trick though. She turned the water temperature up to high so that she would need that much less hot water from the heater to mix with the cold for a warm bath or dishes, or whatever.

In the bath, she thought about the meeting with Mr. Peters and wondered if he was reading her paper at that very minute. Or was he out with a friend? Maybe he was with a girlfriend. She hoped not. If he was reading it, did he like it? Was he marking all over it with his red pen like he used to in class? Erica wondered what he thought of her. Maybe he thought her a bore and a mere child. She was sure he thought of her as just a kid and she hated that. She wanted him to see her as a woman and not a girl. She tried to think about what she could do to seem older and more mature to him. She could stuff her bra and wear high heels to school. Some of the older girls did that but they looked stupid and besides, he seemed like he would like more of the outdoorsy type. I could talk about politics and wine, Erica thought, aware that she didn't know anything about either. So she'd come up with nothing. No foolproof plan to get his attention. No feminine guile. She had no guile. She was guileless and hopeless.

Suddenly there was a loud banging on the door and it startled her out of her thoughts.

"Get out, you jerk! I've been waiting forever," Ellie yelled.

"Okay, okay you little brat!" she got out and toweled off. So much for privacy. Or for maturity.

The next day Erica went to her classes and tried to concentrate but her mind kept returning to thoughts of Mr. Peters, his great smile and his rich brown hair. Eventually she just gave in and ignored class altogether, drawing pictures of him in her notebook. First she only drew within the margins but eventually she filled the entire page.

It seemed funny, even in her own personal thoughts, that she still used his full name. How could she think so much about someone who hadn't even offered his first name? This realization forced another. He had never singled her out in any way. Nor had he ever shown her the slightest hint of interest outside of the teacher/student relationship. This avalanche of reality stung her and left her feeling cold and foolish. She turned to a fresh sheet of paper, determined to listen to Ms. Stoop instead of her own thoughts. But, she was soon daydreaming again. Drawing pictures and weaving scenarios in her mind. It was impossible.

The end of her final class came and she headed for Mr. Peters' classroom. Her heart was beating so fast that her shoulders and arms tingled with the increased circulation. She could feel herself blushing. She went in and sat down, outwardly calm but inwardly in turmoil. She waited for what seemed like hours until he finally came in, smiling and apologizing for making her wait. "I just got here myself," she lied, not wanting to seem over-anxious.

"Well, I had a chance to read over your work again. I have to say I think it shows promise. I really enjoyed reading it and I think that, with a little tweaking here and there, it could be really good."

"Yeah, well, I know it needs work. I...it's just the first draft..."

"No need to qualify it. For a first draft it's fine," he said smiling encouragingly.

"Okay, so what do you think it needs?"

"Well I've made some notes on it, I hope that was okay?" She nodded. Anything you do is okay with me, she thought. "Why don't we take a look at it now and then you can go home and work on it, okay?" Erica nodded again.

He picked up her paper and began perusing it. She could see a lot of red marks all over it. So he had obviously found some problems.

"Right here, where you say that her father abandoned her, do you mean to say that so strongly?"

"Uhh...um...I"

"Because, later, you merely imply it, as if you're not committed to that fully. You may want to just tell what you know and not opine quite so much. Let the reader draw his own conclusions. Also, you're kind of all over the map with the years and places. You may want to simplify it. Just say that she lived in numerous places before moving here. I would either work chronologically, that is start from the beginning, and then carry it through to present day, or just simply tell what you yourself saw when you were with her. Either way, you'll keep your reader more interested if they feel they're not being pulled in all different directions. Do you see what I mean?" Erica nodded. She assumed opine meant to give one's opinion but she wasn't certain.

"Alright. Well, I hope I've been of some help. I wish you luck in the contest." He was ready to go, ready to be with someone his own age. Ready to not be stuck with her, reading her stupid paper (which she was now certain he found laughable). Erica stood up quickly.

"Thanks for all of your help," she said gratefully. She started to leave, grabbing her book bag and coat. She was heading for the door when he said, "I can take another look at it when you've revised it if you'd like. Your final draft maybe?" He gave her a look of genuine interest. Or was it condescension? She nodded, not sure how else to respond.

"Don't forget this," he said, handing her back her dumb paper. She took it from him and thanked him again. "Bye," she said weakly.

"Bye Erica," he said smiling back.

The meeting had not gone at all as she had hoped. She had hoped to resolve something with this meeting. She had hoped that he would either give her some hint of interest, being mildly flirtatious perhaps (which she knew was highly unlikely) or would give her a good reason to believe he saw her as nothing more than another one of his students. As it turned out, even though she knew that the latter was far more likely than the former, she still felt a touch ambivalent when she walked out. Was she reading too much into it? Erica decided she was reading too much into it. He was only trying to be helpful, like holding an elevator or donating a kidney or something. She remembered the vow she'd made to herself to feign ignorance at even the slightest hint of interest. She decided to amend said vow. She would assume a lack of interest thereby avoiding disappointment.

Having a plan made her feel better.

The rest of that week was difficult because she was constantly admonishing herself for thinking about Mr. Peters. Her mind would wonder in class and she would think of him and then she would have to stop and think, No! He barely knows you exist! And this went on for days. She worked furiously to rewrite and perfect her paper, not so she could turn it in to Ms. Stoop, but so that she could show it to Mr. Peters again. In fact, winning the contest had become an afterthought to her. As had Ms. Stoop's offer to help. Erica had managed to put Ms Stoop off for the first few weeks but she eventually put the pressure on and insisted on setting a time to meet with Erica. She wanted to go over what Erica had gotten done on the essay. Erica was sure Ms. Stoop suspected she hadn't even started the essay. Ms. Stoop had insisted on the meeting with Erica the following Monday after school.

On Thursday night, after her mother had driven her back home, Erica went for a short run with Alias. When she got back her mother was upset. She lay crying on the couch. She seemed fine when Erica had left so something had obviously happened while she was away.

"What's the matter?" she asked, somewhat apathetically. Erica had learned to be suspicious of her mother's bouts of despair. They were often more theatrical than legitimate.

"Ellie is leaving!" her mother moaned.

"I never said that!" Ellie yelled back from their room.

"Where is she going?" Erica asked.

"Your father wants her to come live with him," her mother said with so much disdain she practically spat it out.

"What?" Erica was shocked. He wanted Ellie to come

260

live with him? Just Ellie?

"He just thought I'd like to be there more. I mean not with him but in Bellevue," Ellie called from the little bedroom.

"Why? Erica asked Ellie. "You live here." Who am I kidding? Erica wondered. Of course Ellie would rather live in Bellevue!

"Yeah?" Ellie said as if to say, "What's your point?" Erica didn't have one.

Erica's heart tightened and sank a bit. Her whole body felt cold suddenly. She realized that she didn't want Ellie to move back. She didn't want to be here alone with her mother. She felt abandoned by Ellie and her father. Why hadn't he asked Erica to come too? Her mind was racing.

"Did he call you?" Erica asked. It would be worse if it had been his idea.

"Yeah."

Tears began welling up in Erica's eyes. Her throat tightened painfully as it always did when she became upset. It felt like it was choking off her air. And she suddenly felt very cold.

"It's not my fault we live here. If we lived there I could see him more. I mean we could. He wants to see me grow up. That's what he said. I can't help it," Ellie said defensively. She too started to cry.

"All of the sudden he wants to see you grow up? What about Erica? He didn't ask for her to come." Jean shouted. Erica didn't want to hear the answer Ellie would give but she had to. What excuse had he told Ellie to give? Not enough room? Erica's already adjusted? She's too old to change schools?

"He thinks you need her here." Ellie said to their mother.

261

So that was it. That was a good one. He must have thought about it for a while to come up with that one. Too bad he had never shown the slightest inkling of concern for his ex-wife's welfare. Which kind of made this reasoning now suspicious.

"When are you going?" Erica asked Ellie.

"I dunno. I never said I was going to go for sure." This was unconvincing. Ellie had already made up her mind to go and they all knew it. It was just like how their mother had been with them about moving to Leavenworth. Payback time, Erica thought.

Their mother looked up. "She's going. Why wouldn't she?" she said. She looked drained, spent, almost ghostly. Her eyes were red and swollen, her face wet with so many tears. For the first time that Erica could remember she felt truly sad and concerned for her mother. She'd had so much misery and so little joy. It didn't seem fair. How could her father take her youngest away? Hadn't he done enough? Hadn't he caused her enough pain? Erica thought.

It took all the maturity and strength she had to walk over and sit down next to her mother and try to comfort her. It went against every cell in Erica's body to do so. Her natural instinct was to try to talk things out, try to cheer her up. Her mother put her head on Erica's shoulder. Although Erica felt uncomfortable, she stayed there and comforted her mother.

It was late April when Ellie moved back to Bellevue. She acted like she was undecided until the bitter end. After she'd gone, Erica and her mother were left with more room but also with an almost palpable sadness that seemed to envelope the tiny trailer. It felt as if their star player had left for a better team. Ellie's jumping ship had effectively shown a light on the folly of their existence. It was like a child had yelled, "The Emperor is Naked!"

Ellie hadn't wasted much time making her escape, either. She was gone by the weekend. She had removed herself from Leavenworth Elementary School with glee and enrolled herself at Bellevue Elementary. She never actually acknowledged she was moving back, (presumably an attempt to avoid conflict), but the sight of her packing cleared up any confusion in the matter. As did her dad's arrival on Sunday morning to pick Ellie up and take her away from living in squalor. He gave Erica another one of his sideways hugs, not wishing to commit to a full one. He handed her a check, telling her to give it to her mother and not to spend it. He then smiled at what he apparently thought was a funny joke. She looked at it: $75.00. Half the normal child support payment. He made no mention of the fact that Erica was to be left behind and she said nothing of it, either.

Preferring to let it weigh heavy in the air like some deadly gas, unseen but choking the life out of what little relationship they'd ever had. Her mother never came out of the trailer. She just sat on the couch, motionless. Erica had expected a dramatic scene worthy of Tennessee Williams or something. She was surprised when her mother remained very quiet the rest of that day, speaking in a low monotone and only when necessary.

After Ellie had been gone for a few days, her mother's behavior began to vacillate between hysterical, whereupon she would tearfully beg Ellie over the phone to come back, and the nearly catatonic, when she would neither talk nor move, rarely even blinking. It scared Erica to see her that way and she felt very much alone.

To make matters worse, her mother's work life had become increasingly difficult. The office had brought in a new computer system and Jean was expected to learn it nearly overnight. Patty, the bitch, had been especially cruel and it was wearing Erica's mother down. Somehow, it seemed to Erica, wearing her mother down had been Patty's intention from the beginning.

One day Erica was in the school cafeteria and Jenna came up to where she was sitting by herself.

"Did you hear about President Reagan?" she asked, looking at her and then around room to see who had heard her.

"What?" Erica asked.

"He was shot!" she said wide-eyed.

"He's dead?" Erica asked.

"No. I think he's okay."

"Wow," Erica said. "I wonder if he'll be able to work still?"

"Yeah. I dunno."

"Who's Vice President? Bush, right?"

"Yeah, Bush." Jenna nodded. As if she'd know who the Vice President was, Erica thought wryly.

They talked about the shooting for as long as two teenagers were able to converse about such things— which was about two minutes, at which point Jenna sat down uninvited. Erica didn't feel comfortable sitting with Jenna because she worried that Lacy would see her sitting there and that would put the final nail in the coffin that had been their friendship. Erica still held out hope they might one day reconcile. Erica stood up and said she had to get going.

"You coming over to clean stalls today?"

"I can't today but this weekend, okay?"

"Okay. See ya."

"Bye," Erica said sadly. She felt bad about not wanting to be seen with Jenna. She felt bad about Lacy. She felt bad about her sister moving back to Bellevue. She felt bad for her mother. But mostly, she felt bad for herself. She really needed to speak with Katie and soon!

As means of forgetting her domestic and social hell, Erica dove headlong into her schoolwork and, whenever possible, her paper. It was due in just over a week. She met with Ms. Stoop as planned. Ms. Stoop actually claimed to like Erica's work, even though she referred to it as an early draft. Erica, on the other hand, had come to view it as the final draft. She thought it was ready for submission except for a few typos. When first Ms. Stoop pulled it out of her impeccable briefcase, Erica's heart sank. It was covered with red ink. Erica knew this could only mean a lot more work but, as it turned out, most of the red had been suggestions or approval rather than corrections and drastic re-writes (thank God!). After meeting with Ms. Stoop Erica felt more confident and decided that, once she'd had a chance to work on it a little more, she could approach Mr. Peters with it again. She tried reading it objectively and she found several things that needed altering or complete omission. Overall, however, she was relatively pleased with how it had come out. She hoped Mr. Peters would like it as well. She didn't want to take it to him only to have him disapprove of it. She wanted him to be overwhelmed by its insight and wit. She fantasized about Mr. Peters calling it a masterpiece and becoming so carried away that he'd grab her, kiss her passionately and tear her clothes off. Erica realized this scenario was unlikely, but a girl can hope.

She worked on her essay for the rest of that week and then on Friday afternoon she went in to see Mr. Peters to make another date… er, appointment with him. She had hoped to make it for later that day because she figured on a Friday he'd be more relaxed and willing to take his time with her. She knocked on the hollow door to his tiny office off the faculty lounge.

"Come in," he called.

"Hi," she said as she opened the door and poked her head in. She smiled sheepishly, hoping he'd be happy to see her and not irritated that she was pestering him again.

"Hello Miss Tambo. How good to see you!" He smiled back.

Erica nodded, saying nothing. An awkward silence ensued and then he said:

"What can I do you for?"

"Um…well… I was wondering if you could maybe take another quick look at my paper. It's due next week and I 'd like to…well…you know…"

"Win?"

"Yeah, I guess so," she said, feeling a little more at ease.

"Sit." He beckoned her with an inward wave and a welcoming smile. She sat down on the edge of the only available chair.

"Well, let's see it." She placed it in his outreached hand. He had nice hands, large but not too paw-like, tan with pinkish nails.

She sat as he read, making funny expressions now and then. His brows would raise and then lower and sometimes furrow. He even laughed a few times. After about ten minutes he lowered it to his lap and looked at her, smiling.

"So far so good," he said, glancing at his watch. "I'd like to finish reading it but I have to get going now. How about if I make a quick copy of it so I can take it home with me and read it over the weekend?" How about taking me home for the weekend? I'll tell Mom I'm at a sleepover, Erica thought to herself.

"Umm…sure. Okay," she said. No, No, she thought.

"Oh, wait. You probably need to finish it over the weekend if it's due next week. What day is it due?"

"Tuesday," she lied. It wasn't due until Friday.

"Hmmm. That is a conundrum. Well, how about this: I'm supposed to meet with Principal Andrews in about…" he looked at his watch… "Twenty minutes. That should only last about a half an hour and then I really need to hit the bank but, after that, I'm free for a while. You could wait here for me until the meeting is over and then, if you don't mind, you could come with me to the bank real quick. Wait a minute. On second thought, how about if I just meet you at the Inn at around four-thirty?" He probably meant the café at the Inn, not the hotel, she decided.

"That'd be fine," she said with butterflies inside.

"Great. I'll see you then."

"Okay," she said trying to be nonchalant.

Erica couldn't believe Mr. Peters was going to meet with her! On a Friday night! Well afternoon, but still! She wondered what he was doing later that night. Did he have a date? Plans with friends perhaps? Movie maybe? She was sure he had something going on. But he was meeting her at four-thirty and that was all that mattered.

She looked at the clock on the wall and then at her watch, which had stopped at 1:56 two days prior. She had over an hour to kill so she went into the girls' locker room to spruce up a bit. The locker room was empty except for a couple of girls in the far back chatting. Erica was far too excited to think of anything but Mr. Peters. Her heart pounded and she tried to relax. She told herself over and over to calm down but couldn't quiet calm down.

Erica walked up to the large mirror hanging over the sinks. During gym, it was always so cramped with girls, all squeezing in to get a look in the mirror, all trying to apply mascara and blow their hair dry. Erica had long since given up on trying to use the mirrors during gym. Instead she had resorted to a form of hair Braille using a hand mirror she kept in her book bag.

Now, looking at her reflection she assessed the situation. Her hair looked okay but needed a little brushing. Her face was definitely thinner than it had been when they'd first moved to Leavenworth. She looked less child-like than she had that summer. Her cheekbones had become more defined and her nose had lengthened and narrowed. And something else, too...she felt more womanly, if that was the word. It

268

was important because she had never felt that way before. She'd always felt like an awkward child or the half child/ half woman that so confused her. But, this time, on this day, Erica felt …significant.

She left the girls room and made her way over to the Inn, walking slowly to make sure she didn't arrive too early. Erica thought she'd better call her mom and ask to be picked up around 5:45 instead of 5:05 like usual. She found a pay phone and called her mom at work. Jean agreed to pick her up later and they hung up.

Reaching the Inn, Erica slipped in quietly and waited for the hostess to come seat her. Scoping out the room, Erica didn't see anyone she recognized. This was probably a good thing. No sense getting people gossiping. Eventually the hostess came and asked where she'd like to be seated. Erica considered one of the booths that looked out the window but she opted for a table in the far corner of the room.

"You're expecting one more then?" the unfamiliar waitress asked kindly, handing Erica a menu.

"Yes." It was strange but, for some reason, acknowledging that she was expecting him made it all seem very real. It scared her a little.

Erica looked at her watch: still 1:56pm. She looked at the clock on the wall: 4:18pm and counting. She was too nervous to read so she just sat there staring at the menu. Feeling very anxious, she began tapping her fingers on the table to a song they'd practiced in class that day. After a while, she began playing with the spoons, pretending they were drumsticks, clanging them on the table and the condiments. She was clanging them back and forth, using the fork as a spear and the spoon as a catapult for sugar.

"Having fun?" Mr. Peters said. Oh God!

"Oh.... Yeah," she stammered, "I was just...bored." What an idiot she was! So much for feeling womanly.

Mr. Peters sat down across from her, smiling but in a distant sort of way.

"You order yet?" he asked quietly.

"No. I just got here," she lied.

"Oh. Well, let's see it," he said, reaching out for paper. She sheepishly handed it to him. He started reading. Erica tried desperately to sit still while her body fought to squirm.

The waitress came and Erica ordered coffee, trying to seem mature. He looked up and half smiled at the waitress, ordered a beer and resumed reading. Erica resumed nervousness.

"So, here, where you say, 'Her father had been gone for several weeks and Julie had had three different boyfriends in his absence.' Even though it's grammatically correct, it's usually best not to use had twice like that because it doesn't flow well and isn't necessary. And here, where you say her mother must have died,' do you know that for sure?"

"Well, either that or she's extremely sleepy."

He laughed a little and then pressed on. "Do you know that?"

"Well I inferred from what she has said..."

"But she hasn't told you that. We discussed this before. Remember? If you don't know something that's fine but then leave it open-ended"

"Okay," Erica said glumly, disappointed in herself.

"I think you may want to comment on your initial impression of her. Don't tell us the reason she's unhappy yet. You see?"

"Yeah, you mean that I should just say she seemed like

270

she was filling a void but not try to explain why yet."

"Exactly." He resumed reading again. Another several minutes and pages went by before he commented again. This time to compliment her on her use of the word magnanimous.

"Thesaurus?"

"No, thanks."

He smiled. I mean, did you use a Thesaurus?"

"No," she lied.

Erica got the distinct impression that he was enjoying this. Like he found her amusing and even witty. She even thought she caught a glimmer of flirtation. It was subtle but it was there. She remembered her personal vow to not acknowledge such things and tried to tell herself that she had been mistaken.

After about a half an hour of reading, periodically asking her questions and ordering more beer, Mr. Peters finally came to the sixty-seventh and last page. When he finished that last page, he put the essay down on the table and looked at her.

"It's quite good. I enjoyed reading it." He stopped for a long pause as if he were collecting his thoughts. "The... There are a few things that I mentioned that you may want to change but, other than that, it's great. An interesting read." He was slurring his words a little, but with earnest.

Thank you." It was all Erica could think to say. She couldn't look at him for some reason. Embarrassment maybe.

"Well, I hope I've been of some help," he said, downing the last of what she counted as his fourth beer.

"Oh yes. Thank you," she said, trying to sound alluring but instead just sounding phlegmy.

"Yeah? You ah right?" he asked.

"Yeah, I'm fine," she replied, irritated with her inability to appeal to him in the slightest. She wasn't anxious to make a complete fool of herself and she realized she was getting dangerously close so she decided to back away and start to make her exit.

"Well, I really do appreciate all you've done for me. I wish there were a way I could make it up to, you."

"I'll thinka someth'in." he said with an impish smile.

Suddenly feeling uncomfortable she said, "Well, I should go."

"You gotta so soon?"

"Well…"

"Take a ride with me? I'd like to show you something. A young lady such as yerself ought to see this place."

"I…I'm not sure…My mother usually drives me home and…"

"Cantchya call her? I'll take you home, Erica."

"I guess so. Do you know where the phone is here?" She was flustered and her face and neck were on fire. She didn't know why she'd asked where the phone was when she'd just used it. Her heart was pounding and her mouth had turned to cotton. She was sure her nervousness showed but he seemed to be enjoying it. He seemed to find her discomfort amusing, which only served to add to her discomfort.

"Over there," he said, pointing towards the lobby. "How come you don't drive?" he asked. Erica turned back and said, "My mother would never let me drive her car because her insurance only covers the other car. Liability insurance," she said, horrified at having confessed their hillbilly status.

She scurried right out, feeling like a moth caught under glass as she walked away from him towards the phone.

She knew her mom would already be waiting out in the parking lot for her so she went out to find her. She was right where she always parked, the car running. She hadn't wanted Mr. Peters to know that her mother was likely already waiting because it may have changed his mind. She wondered what he wanted to show her.

Erica told her Mother that she needed more help on her paper, and Mr. Peters had offered to drive her home. She promised to be home in an hour or so. Her mother neglected to remind her to call if it was going to be any later as she usually did, which Erica thought was strange. She assumed the fact that her teacher was driving her home had put her mother at ease, making her uncharacteristically consenting. Either that or she was distracted by work and hadn't thought it through enough to question Erica's explanation. Either way, her mother seemed distant and looked terrible. Erica briefly wondered if her mother were really sick and then her thoughts returned to Mr. Peters and the amazing prospect of riding alone with him in his car.

Jean said she'd see Erica at home and Erica darted back into the café. She went immediately into the ladies' room to primp a little. Her face was a little flushed but not as bad as she'd expected. She flipped her hair, tousling it with her fingers. She adjusted her blouse and gave herself a disapproving look and then headed back towards the table and where Mr. Peters awaited her.

As she approached the table she could see that he was paying the bill. Seeing her, he stood up and motioned her towards the lobby. He briefly held her elbow, steering her towards the main entrance, then he let go. She stayed in step with him until he turned sharply towards the parking lot, at which point she stopped. He turned around and held out his hand.

"C'mon, Ah'm over here," he said, motioning towards his car.

She caught up with him, and hesitating briefly, she took his hand and walked with him to his Jeep. It was the same old beat up thing with duct tape holding the back window in place that she remembered from the summer before. He walked her around to the passenger side and opened the door for her. She got in after a brief hesitation and he shut her door. Erica watched him walk around the front of the car and step in. It felt very strange to be in his car with him, like somehow he was more human in this context.

It was after 6pm in mid-April and the sun was beginning to set. It would soon recede behind the hills which made it feel later than it actually was. Mr. Peters started the car and headed toward Icicle Canyon.

"S'not far from here. Ya like Clapton?"

"Yeah."

"Course ya do, yera musician. My little musician girl." He smiled at her and put his hand on her knee and kept it there. "You probly like The Eagles then, huh?"

"Yeah," she said weakly.

"Fleetwood?"

"Of course."

"Hows about a little Fleetwood?"

"Ok," she said.

"It's inna case, down at yer feet. Will you?" She picked up a plastic case made to look like leather. "Can ya fine it in there?"

Erica found it and handed it to him. It was the same one she and played at home all the time. He put it in the tape player and she tried really hard not to drum her fingers. She had always felt secretly that she had a voice just like Stevie Nicks.

They drove along to Fleetwood Mac's Rumors until they reached what looked like a fire road off to the right. He turned off quickly and the car bounced on the dirt road, weaving around holes and rocks. Finally, they reached a point where the road stopped and there was just a trail. He cut the engine as well as the music. The sudden silence coupled with the awkwardness of the situation made Erica's heart jump.

"Less go," he said, opening his door and getting out.

"Where are we?" she asked, really wanting to know.

"You'll see."

She followed him down a path. The terrain became more and more steep and the trail less and less clear as they went along. After a couple of minutes they crested the hill and were in a beautiful meadow. It was twilight and so the colors were muted. There were lots of shadows and yet she could still see the different types of trees and the tall grass. It was beautiful. She swept her hand along the top of the grass blades that were nearly thigh high. She looked over at Mr. Peters and he was smiling at her.

"So, whadaya think?"

"I think it's amazing Why does it feel like spring here and it's still pretty cold everywhere else?"

It's warmer 'cuz ah the treez an the warm springs underground. Didjya know there's warm springs here in Leavenworth, Erica?"

"Yeah, I'd heard that," she said.

The sun had mostly set, and looking around, she saw a light just over the hill that she hadn't noticed at first.

"What's that?" she asked pointing towards the light.

"Tha's ma place. Well, wuz mine. Kinda outta the way, inn'it?"

"You have to walk up this way every time you come home?"

"Na, s'nother entrance 'roun the bend. Not as pretty, though."
Erica nodded her head as if she understood.

"C'mon, I'll give ya a tour."

"Oh, that's okay. I should probably get going anyway."

"C'mon, only take a minute. Then Ah'll take ya home."

"Well…um…" she stammered. If riding alone in the car with him had seemed awkward, the idea of being alone in his house made her downright panic-stricken, He seemed to sense this. "Erica…Erica, Ah'm gunna walk back ta the car and drive 'round to come get you in front so you don't hafta walk back in the dark, k?"

She followed him through the tall grass towards the dim light. As they approached, she could make out a tiny, brown wooden, house with a short set of stairs leading to the back door. The house, like his car, was pretty dilapidated and looked like it wouldn't survive another snowfall. This made her wonder what he meant when he said that "it *was* his house" as if it no longer were.

Mr. Peters started up the stairs and a dog began to bark from inside the house. He looked over his shoulder, "Tha's Fred, ma dog."

"I figured." She nodded.

Erica followed him up the stairs and waited as he opened the creaking door. Fred, a Golden Retriever, ran out past him and nearly knocked Erica over as he bounded down the steps and over to a tree to pee.

"I have a dog, too," she said with a laugh.

"Come on in." He gestured with his arm and let her pass. Walking in, she could see that it was actually pretty cozy. There was a large rock fireplace with a huge overstuffed chair in front of it. It was really dark, even after he turned on some lights, and it smelled of old musty books and damp wood. There was a tattered, old couch, a dark wooden coffee table full of books and a floor lamp, all atop the rattiest rug she'd ever seen, Worse even than the one on their floor.

"Have a seat," he said, once again gesturing with his arm. He had a way of talking and gesticulating that made him pretty hard to refuse. She sat down on the old couch. As she sat, the cushion sunk way down under the unexpected burden and she threw her hands up in surprise as she sunk lower.

He took a bottle of beer from his refrigerator, which was an old fashioned kind that you pull a handle to unlatch.

After a long, awkward pause during which he just smiled at her, she knew that he was enjoying her discomfort.

There was a whine at the back door. "That'd be Fred," he said, getting up to let him back in. "Getchya someth'in ta drink?"

"Liver and whey shake?" she said smiling.

"Funny! Tha's funny. Yer a funny girl, ya know that? Like a drink?"

"No thanks, I'm fine," she said.

Fred came running in as soon as the door had been opened wide enough for him to squeeze through. He ran over to Erica and put his nose on her lap, insisting that she pet him as Goldens do.

Mr. Peters crossed the small room over to where his stereo sat and he put on a tape. She knew within three notes that it was The Eagles' Long Run album. He skipped over a few songs until he found the slow, brooding 'Sad Café'. He then came over and sat next to her on the old, tattered couch and handed her an open beer. Erica's back stiffened anew and her heart pounded as she reached for it, wondering if he just hadn't heard her say no to a drink.

"Erica. How old do ya think Ah am?" He asked looking very serious.

"I don't know, Mr. Peters."

"Guess. An call me Rick, Dammit!"

"Twenty–five or twenty- six?"

"I'm thirty-three."

"Wow."

"Yeah, Ah know. Ya think tha's old now. Jus you wait."

"I don't think that's that old," she said even though she really thought it was.

"Really? Do ya feel like you and I have stuff ta talk about or do ya think I'm too old?"

"No, I like talking to you. You're interesting."

"Ineresting." He repeated with a weak smile. "Ineresting in a teacher sorta way or someth'in else?" He put his hand on her knee again.

"Well, you're interesting as a teacher, too," she said honestly.

"Do ya ever have any other thoughts… 'bout me?"

"What do you mean?" she asked even though she was beginning to get a pretty good idea of where he was going. She was playing dumb. She was scared. He'd gone from cute to scary in less than half an hour.

"Ah mean do ya ever think about me, ya know, outsida school?"

"Uh…I don't know…I guess….sometimes." Erica said quietly. Nervously.

"Whadaya think about?"

Her throat was clenching up and she couldn't talk. She shook her head slowly.

He began stroking her hair and he was leaning in close. "I'd hate yer firs esperience ta be with some bumbling high school kid. Ya need someone with some experience. Dontchya think?"

"I....don't know."

"You'd havta be real discreet, Erica. Canya be? ...discreet, I mean, not tell anyone, not even yer best friend?" He was sounding all breathy as he half whispered this to her. His breath was cold and smelled like beer. Erica nodded and he started kissing her, softly at first and then more aggressively, his tongue going in and out of her mouth skittishly and then loitering there for long stretches. He was sort of pushing her down onto the couch at the same time and she was lying beneath him. He pulled her hand down to his fly, which he must have opened when she was otherwise occupied. She could feel him through his boxers, hard and twitching. She tried to pull her hand away but he, evidently anticipating her reaction, held it there. She felt scared and embarrassed and excited and hesitant all at the same time.

He started struggling with her jeans, trying to unbutton them while attempting to distract her with his tongue some more. He eventually succeeded and moved onto his own jeans, which came off much quicker than hers had. All she could think about was that she couldn't believe she was in Mr. Peter's house in her underwear like that. She wondered what his grandmother would think. What his dog was thinking. He unbuttoned her blouse and undid her bra, pulled it aside and started squeezing her breasts really hard, (at least there was something to squeeze, a month or so prior he'd have had trouble finding them).

He whispered something unintelligible in her ear.

"What?"

He let go and sat up straight and started pulling her panties off. Erica made an unconvincing attempt to stop him, which he quickly brushed off and continued. He fumbled around for awhile, giving her too much time to think and she started to protest.

"Mr. Peters? Rick? I'm...I'm."

"Call me Rick, Jezzus Christ!"

"Rick, I'm..."

"A virzgin, Ah know. It's ahrigh.

"No, I ... I'm not sure...

"Relax."

She hadn't expected it to hurt so much and she screamed a little. It stopped being exciting and she just wanted the pain to go away as he kept going faster. Finally, after what seemed like forever, he groaned and grunted several times before collapsing on top of her.

After a few seconds he stood up and picked up his clothes. He left the room wordlessly and without looking at her at all. Erica didn't know what she was supposed to do. Should she get up and get dressed? Should she wait? What do other girls do? She decided to take the opportunity to get dressed while he was away. She dressed quickly and, not knowing what else to do, she sat back down on his couch. She was pretty shaken and she really wanted to go home. She hated that he would be driving her. She thought about calling her mother but that would be weird. No one in all the books she'd read ever called their mother to come pick them up after sex. They usually smoked a cigarette. Of course, Mr. Peters, Rick, would never smoke. He was too healthy. Erica had been surprised to see him drinking beer. She'd kind of figured him for a teetotaler.

But then she hadn't expected him to deflower her, either, so what the hell did she know?

The dog came over and she started petting him. Just then, Mr. Peters came back into the room. He seemed distracted as he walked around collecting his jacket and then his keys. He looked over at her and smiled. "We should get you home?" He sounded more sober now.

Erica nodded and stood up. He looked at her oddly, kind of hauntingly, and then turned for the door.

The ride home was beyond awkward, almost unbearable. He said very little and she said nothing. He had switched from the Fleetwood Mac tape over to the radio, which was playing Al Stewart's 'The Year of The Cat'. As they neared the point where he would need to turn off she began giving him directions, using as few words as possible. When they finally reached her driveway a wave of panic rolled over her as she realized that he would try to take her up the drive to the trailer.

"No! Um, the driveway is under construction and we can't use it right now. There's a path right over there." she pointed to an opening in the trees where a path led to their little trailer on the hill.

Erica started to get out of the car and he grabbed her arm and pulled her to him and kissed her.

"You okay?" He asked. She nodded. He kind of hung his head then. "I hope we can just keep this between us."

"I know," she said. "I won't tell."

She got out of the car, shut the door and waved just before turning and running through the trees and up the path. As she ran up the hill Erica thought about her mother. She'd be sitting on her little couch waiting for her. What would she tell her mother? She didn't want her mother to know what had happened and yet she wished she could confide in her. Feeling both nervous and exhilarated, she opened the door to the trailer and found it empty. Not even Alias was there. There was a note on the little table that simply red: Call Katie. A wave of panic washed over Erica. She reached for the phone to dial Katie's number, fumbling with the buttons, having to hang up and start over twice.

"Hello?"

"Katie? What's going on? Where's my mom??"

"She's in the hospital," Katie said, her voice cracking.

Erica's heart jumped "What happened to her?"

"I don't know. She called Mom and told her she was sick and need to go to the hospital"

"What?"

"I'm coming to get you right now. I'll be there in a minute." Katie hung up. Dumbfounded, Erica slowly returned the handset to its rightful place. She didn't know what to do or what to take with her. She looked over at the little tattered couch where her mother usually slept and she saw the fluffy yellow pillow that her mother had owned for as long as Erica could remember. She grabbed it and ran out the door, through the trees and down the narrow trail that led to the street below. It was pitch black on the heavily treed street, the only light being the few stars not obliterated by the tall firs.

Katie arrived after what seemed like an eternity. Erica got in the front seat and Katie tore off.

"What's wrong with her?" Erica asked, knowing that Katie still didn't know the answer.

"I…I just know that she was too sick to drive so she called Mom. I'm sure she's fine. Probably just a bad flu."

"Where's Alias?"

"He's fine. He's at our house. We didn't want to leave him at your place alone."

Erica wondered why that should be. Surely they'd be back soon enough to take care of him.

"Where have you been? We've been calling and calling. Mom's calling me wondering where you are."

"Where's Chloe?" Erica asked, wishing to divert.

"She's at our neighbor Jeannie's house.

"Oh."

They reached the hospital in town and Katie pulled in to the Emergency lane where Erica jumped out, throwing the car door shut behind her. She ran through the front glass doors and up to the Information Desk where a chubby, middle aged woman sat dressed in white.

"Where's my mom?" Erica asked breathlessly.

"I'll check. What's your mother's name?"

"Jean. Jean Tambo. She has dark hair," Erica said, thinking that would help them find her quicker.

"Alright, let's see…here she is. Oh…"

Just then, Katie came in. "How is she?"

The woman was on her phone now. "I'll let them know." She hung up the phone. "Her doctor wishes to speak to you. He's on his way down now," she said softly.

"Why? What's wrong with her? Did he say?"

The woman just shook her head. A short time later, a man dressed in loafers and a white lab coat came through the double doors to the right of the Information Desk. He was looking at Erica and Katie as he approached. He held out his hand for Katie's first, "I'm doctor Levin," he said with a half smile and sorrowful eyes that conveyed sympathy.

"I'm Jean Tambo's daughter," Erica said, wanting to get to the point. He shook her hand and then stepped away from her.

The doctor looked at her and took a long breath. "Your mother is very, very sick. Her cancer has returned and has metastasized or moved, if you will. It's in her lungs and lymph nodes and she has pneumonia. She's in a coma. I'm very sorry."

Erica tried hard to wrap her head around everything she had just heard, but it was too much. What had he said? She's in a coma. Oh my God! "Where is she? Can I see her?"

"Yes, of course. Follow me." He turned and walked back through the doors he'd just come through, before Erica's world had come crashing in on her with just a handful of words spoken by someone she'd never met. Erica and Katie followed the doctor. They got in the elevator and the huge steel doors closed after them. The doctor pushed the #2 button and the cables began to lift them to the next floor. Erica stared at the crack between the two doors, waiting for it to open, wanting to see her mother but scared to see her at the same time.

The doors opened and the two girls once again followed the doctor as he walked through white halls and passed through double swinging doors into a dark room with two beds covered in blue sheets. One was empty but the other was not. As Erica approached it she could only see a few short, dark curls peeking out of a kind of shower cap and a plastic mask jutting out where a nose should be. Could this be her? She got closer and saw her mother's closed eyes and long, dark lashes. This was indeed her mother.

Erica started to break down, a huge lump was forming in her throat, her eyes were stinging. She tried to swallow to

284

relieve the pain but it did nothing. Her ears were ringing and she was starting to panic. How could this be? Her mother seemed ok. Erica knew her mother seemed kind of tired and weak lately—but not this bad! She laid her arms across her mother and rested her head on her arms. She could hear the machines breathing air into Jean's lungs and she felt the faint beating of her heart. Tears ran down Erica's face, tickling her nose and dropping to the sheets below. She lay there like that for a long time, sobbing intermittently. Finally a nurse gently pulled her away saying that they needed to tend to her mother for a while and that Erica should go wait out in the other room with her family.

Erica allowed herself to be led out but she turned her head to look at her mother as she walked. Once out in the hallway she saw Jillian and Katie sitting on a metal bench.

Jillian got up and hugged her, saying something about trying to reach her all night. She led Erica over to the bench and sat her down next to Katie who promptly put her arm around her. No one said anything. Hours, perhaps days went by. No one came in or out of the room. Finally Doctor Levin came out with his head low. Erica knew her mother was gone.

"She's dead, isn't she?" Erica said matter-of-factly.

"I'm sorry," he said. "Very sorry." He turned and walked down the long hall, his loafers making no sound on the white tile floor.

Tears began to well up in Erica's eyes. She couldn't believe it! She had to see her mother again. She turned and walked back in to where her mother lay. The machines had all been turned off and it was eerily quiet in the room now. There were nurses walking to and fro, putting things away. Erica looked at her mother's face. She looked ghostly but serene. As if all the blood had been drained from her body and she was finally at ease. God! How can she be dead? Erica wondered. I just saw her! It didn't make any sense. She started sobbing again and hugging her lifeless body. Erica noticed that her cheeks felt cold. She thought maybe if she stayed there long enough she'd come back. But Erica knew this was the last time she'd see her mother.

Later that evening, they all went back to Jillian's house. Katie helped an unstable Erica to bed with some tea. Erica tried to sleep. She certainly was exhausted but her mind was going too fast and she couldn't calm down. Erica kept trying to piece together what had happened. Had she been that sick? For how long? Why didn't I notice? Is that why she'd acted so strange in the parking lot earlier that night? Erica realized she'd picked the worst possible night to be away. Her mother had really needed her and she wasn't there for her And where had she been? God!

Erica began whispering to her mother, sobbing and becoming somewhat hysterical.

"Mommy! I'm sorry! I'm so sorry! Mommy! Where are you? Don't leave me like this. What will I do? Please, Mommy!" And this went on for some time, all to the tune of 'The Year of The Cat' going through her head, over and over again until she finally gave in to fatigue and fell asleep, never having tasted the tea.

18

Erica's dad came out to get her the following afternoon. She was surprised to see him. He seemed upset but also very matter-of-fact about the whole thing. Erica couldn't decide if it was indifference or if he was putting on a brave face. Maybe he just didn't know what to say to her.

Jillian, Katie and Chloe all hugged her goodbye and made her promise to call soon. They all were crying, of course, even Jillian. Erica hugged Alias until her dad finally said "enough" and to get in the car. She got in and they drove off. Erica thought of Fleetwood Mac as she looked out at the snow-capped mountains.

'...And if you see my reflection in the... snow-covered hills, well maybe....the landslide will bring it down. Oh, oh, the landslide will bring it down...'

After signing some papers at the Coroner's office at Leavenworth Memorial Hospital, her father came out to the car, got in quietly and they headed for Bellevue. No one saying a single word the entire drive. Erica sat numbly, an occasional tear forcing its way out and down her cheek. She felt a little groggy from crying.

As they drove in silence, she ran the events of the night before over and over again in her head. Had it all really happened? It was too much for her to grasp all at once so she compartmentalized. First, she thought of Mr. Peters, his couch and what had happened there. She wondered if she'd ever see him again. Had he kept her paper? She couldn't remember. Then, she thought about her mother. Was she really gone for good? How could that be? She was alive and then she was dead. It didn't seem possible. What would happen to all of her things? To Erica's? Would they come back to collect her remains? Her remains! It was so peculiar to think about her mother in terms of 'remains'. Her mother would never kiss her cheek again. Never stroke her hair and reassure her. And she really needed her mother now! Of all times! Erica started to cry anew

"When can I get Alias back?" she asked suddenly.

"After we get you settled," her father said.

Erica couldn't believe she couldn't be with Alias now, either. She missed him already.

When they arrived in Bellevue they pulled in to her father's house. Erica had almost forgotten what it looked like. Had they painted it? It looked different somehow. Her dad helped her to some bedroom and sat her down on the bed. He helped her get her shoes off then told her to lay back and get some rest. She nodded and he left. She figured Ellie must be in some other room because she never saw her. She wondered how Ellie was doing. She curled up in a ball and hugged the pillow and cried some more. The fresh tears stung her eyes.

The next several days, Erica spent mostly lying in bed in what she assumed to be her new room. It was downstairs and halfway down the hall from Ellie's room. It was a nice room. There was apple green wallpaper and a pretty comforter with green and white flowers. She had her own normal-size closet but many of her clothes were still in Plain, along with her dog, whom she missed terribly. Erica's father had thought to grab a few things for her but she was sorely lacking key items, like underwear and socks. Needless to say, she was doing a lot of laundry. Luckily, the laundry room was just off her bedroom so she was able to go in and out without having to see anyone. She could hear if someone was in there and just wait for them to finish and leave.

Erica took a lot of hot baths in her bathroom. She always locked the door so she could maintain her isolation.

She barely spoke to or even saw anyone for days and days. Ellie came to her room crying now and then, which made Erica cry. It sort of forced a truce between the two sisters.

She called and spoke with Katie to see how Alias was doing. Katie said he was just fine and asked how Erica was holding up.

"Okay, I guess," she said glumly.

"When are you coming back here?"

"I don't know. I will let you know as soon as I find out, ok?"

"Okay. Get some rest. You sound tired," Katie said with concern in her voice.

"Thanks, I will. Bye." And she hung up.

A couple of days later, her dad came down and spoke with her about school and such. He said that she needed to get back into school soon. He said he would take her the next day to register. He made a big deal about the school being close enough that she could walk each day. She knew where the school was from when she'd lived there and gone to the elementary school. He also said she could get lunch at school and that he'd leave her money each morning. He told her to try to stay out of Karen's hair because she was none too pleased to have them both there.

Through it all she said nothing, just sat there on her bed, staring at the floor. He started to go and she said, "When can I get my dog back?"

"I don't know, Erica. Karen doesn't like dogs so I just don't know right now."

He left quietly and shut the door behind him.

Erica thought about Alias. She hoped Katie was taking good care of him. She went in search of a phone to call her again.

She thought a lot about Rick Peters, also. She wondered if he'd heard what had happened. Had he inquired after her or had he been too afraid of being found out? Had he made any attempt to reach her? Should she call him? He could have gotten her number from the school if he'd wanted to. Had he called and no one told her? It all seemed so surreal, like a dream she hadn't yet convinced herself was just that, a dream.

Her dad did indeed take her to register at the high school that next day and the lady behind the desk sat her down and went over the classes she needed and the offered elective classses. Erica told her to choose and she looked confused, then flustered and finally sympathetic.

"Art, I guess," Erica said "I like art."

"Ok, great, we can do that." She seemed relieved to have at least some input.

Erica started classes that very day but it was just a blur for her.

She walked the mile and a half from school back to the house. Entering the house (which had been left unlocked) she realized she was famished and that she hadn't really eaten much since moving back. She went to the kitchen, opened the fridge and peered in. There were a lot of left-over take-out boxes as well as milk, different cheeses and eggs but nothing appealed to her. There were some crackers, potato chips and unopened olives in the pantry so Erica just took a box of crackers downstairs with her, mindlessly eating them.

Ellie came home from her school and knocked on Erica's door.

"What?" Erica said.

"Can I come in?"

"Yeah," she said.

Ellie walked in and closed the door behind her. She sat down in the little wooden chair in the corner. Erica noticed that she was wearing something new.

"That new?" she asked.

"Yeah." Ellie answered sheepishly. "How do you like school?"

"It's alright, I guess. Your's ok?" she asked without interest.

"Yeah, its fine."

"What's up with all the take out? Don't they cook?"

"She doesn't. Dad does. Sometimes. When he's here," Ellie said, shaking her head.

"When do we go get our stuff and when do we bury Mom?" Erica asked her.

"Dad is supposed to take us to go get all of our stuff but I don't know when."

"After an autopsy it is customary to bury the dead, you know," Erica said with disdain.

"I know," Ellie said.

"Well, when do we do it?" Erica asked irritably.

"I don't know!"

"Well, we'd better figure it. Soon!"

"I'm gonna go watch TV," Ellie said.

"Fine," Erica said coldly, shrugging.

Ellie walked out, leaving the door open. Erica was too tired to even get up to close it. She lay there for a while until she heard Karen and her dad arguing upstairs. She got up and poked her head out to listen.

"How long, Jack?" Karen was yelling. "Give me a date!"

"What am I supposed to do? Her mother is dead! What should I do, leave her out in the streets?!"

"I don't care but she can't stay here! One is enough!"

"Well, I don't know what I can do. She's only sixteen!" he yelled back.

"Can't she go live with friends?"

"Well, I'm working on that. It's not so simple," he said.

"Well you'd better figure it out!"

Erica went out to watch TV with Ellie, hoping to take her mind off of things. They watched a rerun of The Brady Bunch. What a bunch of crap that stupid show was! They would have been at each other's throats in real life.

That Saturday, her father drove them back to Plain to collect all of their things and lock up the trailer. They didn't talk much on the drive, just listened to the radio. The Police came on playing 'Don't Stand So Close' about a teacher in love with his young student. She thought of Mr. Peters again. She knew she'd never see him again.

Pulling up the driveway, there was no longer any snow. In fact, spring had sprung and it was quite warm. Alias' dog house was just where they'd left it, as was their mother's car, the trailer, the picnic table and the two little wooden chairs her mom had sat in the summer before. It made Erica think of the day she'd lost Alias that summer. Her mother and Ellie had been sitting there when Erica came back with him after riding in Mr. Peters' Jeep.

Her dad said they could go see Alias when they'd finished getting their belongings. Erica had called ahead so Katie was expecting them.

They finished loading the car, locked up the trailer and then went over to see Alias. He was so happy to see Erica. She hugged and petted him. She missed him so much and just couldn't imagine leaving him again but she had been forbidden to return with him "for now." Erica looked at her dog for a long time. She began thinking about how living in Plain had been and how it was living in Bellevue with her dad and Karen. She realized that, despite her troubles with Lacy and what had happened with Mr. Peters, she had been happy here. She liked being with Katie and she liked riding Jenna's horse. She wanted to stay in Plain with her dog and Katie.

"I want to stay here," Erica announced her epiphany.

"Well, we have to go. So say goodbye," her dad said.

"No, I want to stay here. For good," Erica said resolutely "I don't want to go back to Bellevue."

"You mean stay and live here with us, because…" Jillian stammered.

"No, I mean I would live in Mom's trailer. It'd be fine because Aunt Jillian lives close. I'd be fine," Erica said forming the idea as she spoke.

"I don't know. Are you old enough to live by yourself?" her father asked, not exactly saying no.

"Yes." Erica said solidly. No one spoke. "Yes!" Erica repeated. "I know Karen doesn't want me there and I'd rather be here anyway. I'm staying."

"How will you buy food and pay bills?" her father asked.

"Well I could get Katie to take me, or Jillian when she goes to the store."

Jillian shot Erica's father a look as if to say that she was not going to pay for Erica's groceries.

"And you could just give me enough money to cover groceries and other bills each month." Erica interjected.

"Like what bills?" her father asked.

"Like electricity, water, whatever. It doesn't cost much. It's a tiny little trailer. Plus, I can get a part-time job in town."

Katie looked shocked while Jillian seemed unsure, deliberately knitting her brow. It was obvious that she didn't want to be on the hook for anything. Erica's father, on the other hand, appeared to be favoring the idea while pretending to be skeptical.

"Well, I guess that could work. Jillian, would you mind keeping an eye on her?" Erica's father asked like he was asking her to grab him a beer or something.

"I don't know. What if something happened?" Jillian asked, clearly concerned.

"I'll go by once in a while and Erica could call every day to check in with us," Katie said hopefully. "Besides, I see her all the time anyways."

"Well, I guess that would be okay." her father repeated.

"Then it's settled. I'm staying here." Erica said brightly, kneeling down to pet her dog some more. "Hey Alias, we're staying here!"

Erica's father took her to the grocery store to stock up the trailer and then he and Ellie left for Bellevue. He left Erica with $100.00 in cash and a sideways hug. Ellie deigned to say goodbye and good luck as she got in to the car. Not much would change for her since she'd already been living with her father. Erica wondered if her sister would regret having left to move in with her father when she did. Erica remembered her mother had often said there's a reason for everything and everything happens for a reason. Erica had taken this to mean things happen for the best, but at this point in her life, she believed things happened for a reason because reason was the cause, not necessarily being for the best.

After they'd left, Erica went about sorting her things and putting away groceries. She fed Alias and took him for a walk. She felt liberated. She was sorry her mother was gone but she did like the idea of being free and independent.

Erica thought about Mr. Peters and she realized she *would* see him again. Would he be happy to see her? Why hadn't he ever tried to reach her? She wondered if he had been relieved to hear she'd moved away so he didn't have to deal with what had happened. What would he say when he saw her? What would she say? Would he still like her? She didn't know.

Erica walked back to her little trailer and called Katie. "Just checking in," she said jokingly.

"How does it feel to live by yourself?"

"Pretty good," Erica replied.

The next day Erica took the bus to school just as she had before her mother started work at the dental office. It had felt odd to leave the trailer without saying goodbye to anyone. Erica got on the bus and sat near the front as she had so often before. Before everything got so weird. Before

Lacy had stopped talking to her and before Jenna had so consumed her life. Before she lost her mother. Before she'd been forced to grow up and finally jump that fence she'd sat on for so long as a half child-half woman.

Erica's thoughts briefly went to Nick. He seemed so immature now, in retrospect. So arrogant and foolish. What did I see in him she wondered? She looked out the dusty window at the little houses along the way and remembered when they'd first moved there. She thought of the day when she'd lost Alias and met Mr. Peters for the first time. Now her sister was back in Bellevue and her mother was gone forever. Tears began to well up in her eyes but she fought them back successfully.

As the bus slowed for its next stop, Erica looked up to see Lacy standing at her bus stop, waiting among the throngs of younger children. She looked like she could be their nanny rather than their fellow school bus passenger. Lacy had always seemed dignified to Erica but she seemed especially so that day. That day she looked positively regal. Erica realized how much she'd missed her good friend.

Lacy lighted upon the bus like a butterfly, and seeing Erica, looked surprised. She smiled brightly, then sympathetically and immediately sat down next to her saying, "I thought you moved back to Bellevue. Sorry about your mom. How are you doing?"

"Ok, I guess," Erica said, fresh tears pooling in her lower lid like an infinity pool. She couldn't control them anymore and she burst into tears.

"Oh my God," Lacy said, her mouth agape. "I'm so sorry." She reached out to hug Erica. Erica sobbed for a while as Lacy kept her tiny arms around her like a mother after a skinned knee. She kept saying "It's okay. It's okay."

Eventually Erica felt composed enough to sit up straight and wipe her eyes. "Do you have a tissue or something?"

"No, I haven't. Hold on…" Lacy said as she stood up. She came back and handed Erica a tissue from the box the bus driver kept near her seat. Erica dabbed at her eyes not wanting to rub too hard and make them all red for school.

"So, are you staying with your aunt then?" Lacy asked.

"No," Erica said, shaking her head slowly, sheepishly. She smiled impishly.

"Where?"

"I'm living by myself in the trailer!" she blurted out.

"No way!" Lacy was taken aback.

"Yeah. I am. All by myself," Erica said proudly. "It's weird not having my mom there but I like feeling independent," she added, trying to fill the void created by Lacy's rare inability to speak.

"I'm…I…" she stammered.

"Can't believe it? I know!" Erica said, her voice thick from crying. "I just said to my father that I wanted to stay here and told him I didn't want to live with him and his wife. I knew his wife didn't want me there and that I could take care of myself here. Can you believe it?"

"Oh my God! My dad is going to be so worried about you. He's gonna call you all the time to make sure you're okay. Plus he'll stop by!"

"That's fine. I'm not like Jenna, you know," Erica said unthinkingly. Lacy looked at her hands in her lap and for a brief time, then she looked up at Erica, "I know that," she said quietly.

"Well, anyway, I'm here for the rest of this year and

299

probably the summer. We'll see after that," Erica said with both dogged determination and fear.

Erica wanted to tell Lacy about what had happened the day her mother died but she just couldn't bring herself to say it out loud. It was too soon, anyway. Maybe after they'd had a little more time together. Maybe then she could speak of it.

Erica and Lacy talked about school and what they'd like to do that summer and how their classes were. They talked all the way in to town, switching buses without even skipping a beat, just like old times. Familiarity and normalcy felt good to Erica. She'd missed it more than she had realized.

Arriving at the school the two friends got off the bus together and stopped on the sidewalk. "See you at lunch?" Lacy asked.

"See you at lunch," Erica said smiling. Then she turned and walked to class.

Susan Johnson graduated from the University of Washington in 1996 with an English degree. She resides in Medina, Washington with her husband, nine year old son and sixteen year old stepson.